Three Professional Ladies

G. F. NEWMAN

SPHERE BOOKS LIMITED
London and Sydney

First published in Great Britain by
New English Library Ltd 1973
Copyright © G. F. Newman 1973
First Sphere Books edition 1978
30–32 Gray's Inn Road, London WC1X 8JL
Reprinted 1979, 1983, 1985

TRADE
MARK

Set in Intertype Times

Printed and bound in Great Britain by
Cox & Wyman Ltd, Reading

CONTENTS

For the Lovely Lady
who wanted to
experience a day in the life of

Three Professional Ladies

Prologue
The Ponce

Every city and major town in every country in the world had its professional ladies, some were less professional than others; some were isolated in single apartments, while others were accommodated in entire areas that were given over to prostitution and all its subsidiaries. Prostitution was an industry in itself, high-geared and probably outpacing tourism, if the two could have been made separate and distinct, if only for the count; however, there was no Queen's Award! Its profits were vast -- and Harry earned more than his share; its language, like its appeal, was universal; a wet vagina offering a weeping penis some relief, in its most simple cloak.

Soho ought to be cleansed in some painful way, Harry thought, making his way briskly along Old Compton Street, more especially some of the soapy, disease-ridden habitués who promoted their diseases like devotees of Christianity on the Dark Continent.

9

Harry was feeling particularly irritated for having to trudge the streets of Soho looking for Jane. The bitch! They were supposed to have met in a club; he was late arriving; she had been in but had left. Like a bloody moth she was, attracted to brightness and noise; he guessed he would find her sooner or later, circling the brightest light. He wondered about Jane's prospects. He wanted her to go to work for him and didn't doubt he could persuade her, but questioned at times like these what sort of brass she would make, whether she wasn't a little too erratic, and how professional she might be.

Possibly she would prove no more professional than those kids spilling out over the pavement from the noisy, bright pinarcade, though she certainly had more class. Class was certainly something Jane had, something all the women who ever worked for him had had, at least in the beginning. That was what always attracted Harry. The dogs and pigs with lipstick could run themselves as far as he was concerned, their earnings did him no harm. He didn't really seriously imagine that those lacking both style and professionalism did him or the trade that much harm, but they irritated him for their shortcoming. Soapy whores!

Pushing his way through the kids hanging around on the pavement outside the arcade, Harry paused and stared into the neon haze; noise hung in the atmosphere there at a marginally more painful level than the cigarette smoke. The place was bright enough to attract Jane, but it wasn't likely to have done so.

At once the man became aware of someone by his side, and turning, saw a young spade chick. He guessed she was about nineteen, her face familiar as all spades' faces seemed to be to him. She had an unlit cigarette in her hand.

'Goda light, man?' she asked, her Brixton accent barely audible through the arcade noise.

Hearing wasn't necessary for the man to know he was being propositioned – the unlit cigarette was about the most trite ploy. Harry immediately felt indignation; then he

10

wanted to laugh. This fucking spade was trying to pick him up like he was some prick! He considered smacking her in the face, even having Old Bill giving her a pull, but instead gave her a frosty look.

'Fuck off!'

'Rasclaat,' the girl returned, and moved over to rejoin her friends.

Those kids tended to piss Harry off more than most, not just the spades, the white-dung babies too who hung around the cafés and arcades on the manor putting their diseased cunts on offer, often gratis. Most of them really did have a little touch of disease too, at worst syphilis, at best leucorrhoea. The very thought made Harry shudder, he was impatient to get off the manor and get somewhere and wash his hands. The prospect of going up one was definitely nauseating.

Skin 'em back and check that they aren't dosed – that was part of his constant advice to women going to work for him. It was a practice most of those kids never considered. How would they wind up? That was a constant puzzle to him. Also, where would they wind up? He knew their fairly immediate destination, that was up at the VD clinic in Charlotte Street when theirs became worse than enough and they had shared it out among more than enough pricks.

Harry resented Charlotte Street and all the clinics like it. He accepted that they were useful to a point, but generally they made a little touch of something nasty all too easy on all those concerned. Make the soapy bastards suffer, that was what Harry was in favour of. Give them all the umbrella-treatment. Having that shoved up and dragged down would make them all think twice. Penicillin, or one of the more refined antibiotics, was going far too easy on them, they were the permissive society's panacea. The whole question of the use and abuse of the clinics – paid for out of his taxes and rates – ought to be looked into, he thought, after all they made those women's lack of care and those guys' lack of discrimination all too plausible.

A prick was pulled by a spade inside the arcade. Harry watched as she led him out, wondering where she was going to accommodate him. Across the road in the car park on the bomb-site of old St Anne's at the bottom of Dean Street probably. He knew some of them earned pennies there on their backs on the gravel or against the crumbling age-blackened walls. What were the wollies doing? Lazy bastards! Some of the police were earning more than enough from him.

He would give all those soapy prats, and the guys who went with them, a big bell. They were worse than lepers.

Time was pushing on and Harry was feeling more annoyed with Jane. He even fleetingly considered writing her off as a bad investment, but he wouldn't yet. The man didn't get many of those; the odd one or two who were even bigger losers after he had finished beating them up.

The jazz club in Frith Street was a probable where Jane would have been drawn, Harry mused, as he moved on down the Street, he would look in anyway. He was known on the door, but the place wasn't his habit, it was a bit too noisy for him.

The club was quite busy, then it invariably was; by any standards they had good musicians there, though Harry wasn't a jazz buff.

After washing his hands, Harry had a drink in the bar downstairs. A face at the bar was familiar, a Malt who used to run a couple of brasses; he recognised Harry and tried to open on it, but Harry blanked him. The Malt was of no value.

Jane wasn't anywhere in the main area of the club that Harry could see. But he thought he saw a girl who used to work for him, only saw that it wasn't her on closer inspection. Anyway after he had had to sack her she would only have gone downwards. The girl in question was probably inside now – she had been a thief.

Don't rob pricks as it can get you a lot of police trouble – that was another piece of advice Harry gave novices. Even

short term the practice was rarely worth the few quid they
earned, it certainly did his reputation no good when girls
robbed clients he had recommended to them. He was the
only one permitted to rob the pricks – his way. Girls caught
at it were bang in trouble.

Having searched the main area of the club, Harry took
the trouble to look upstairs as Jane was possibly perverse
enough to pull a spade. However, she wasn't there either,
but after his effort Harry felt in need of a wash, and in fact
stopped off to wash his hands before leaving.

Why was he searching for her like he was? he questioned
as he came down the short perron from the jazz club. He
was merely going to introduce her round at Monty's place,
and he could do that practically any time. He had only
casually mentioned to Monty that he had a girl who he
thought would fit in perfectly into the Berkeley Square
set-up; then one only ever mentioned these sort of things
casually to Monty, as there was nothing blatant about either
the man or his club.

Fuck you, Jane, you bitch! The words careened angrily
around inside his head as he moved off down Frith Street.
The possibilities of where she might go were endless, and
there would be no problem for a good-looking girl like Jane
getting in anywhere, not with her winsome personality too.
He decided to quit the search and get a cab back to his place,
and let her turn up in her own sweet time. Her introduction
down at Monty's could be effected another day.

At the corner of Frith and Old Compton Street Harry
flagged a cab, but some bastard beat him for the driver's
attention. Harry searched around for another, adjusting his
camel hair coat after his arm-waving. There wasn't another
cab immediately, but two o'clock in Soho wasn't impossible.

As he waited, searching each of the three ways, Harry
noticed the old tom on the opposite corner of Old Compton
Street, and was about to peremptorily dismiss her with a
shudder of disgust, when he realised there was something
vaguely familiar about her. The man stared hard across the

road, searching his memory for a name to put to her broken, defeated face.

Jaset Nurse! That was it, he almost spoke her name. She had worked for him—how many years ago now? He couldn't remember. The woman hadn't started with him, he had got her from someone else; she had obviously been a good 'un in her time, but her time had been fast passing even then, and he had moved her on because her earning potential had shortly begun to drop. He supposed he could have put her in with one of the young girls as her maid, but maids could sometimes be more trouble than enough. There weren't many really good 'uns around nowadays, not like those days when the Messinas ran more than their share of brasses, and maids were put in as watchdogs.

The woman across the road disgusted Harry slightly, frightened him also. She should have been dead by now or working in Woolworths, not bashing, hawking her horrendous self, even on the streets of Soho. All he felt for her was disgust, no sense of compassion and certainly no sense of responsibility. She glanced towards him as though believing him a prospect. The man shuddered involuntarily and turned away, waving down a timely cab.

Part One
Jaset

"Large chest for sale, no drawers!"

1

For the moment the woman thought the man across the road was waving to her, but was a little relieved when she saw him step into a taxi that had stopped; when he hadn't acknowledged her on first recognising her it was fairly obvious that he wouldn't at all. What would she have said to him anyway? Hello, Harry, how are you? She thought not; that was why she hadn't been open in looking at him when first noticing him.

Harry Bleedew. He was still as handsome as ever, despite the passing years; what she called a fine figure of a man, square shoulders and a strong chin; a smooth purple scar ran up his left cheek and disappeared into his greying hairline at his temple. She wondered briefly about that scar now, no one had ever known how he had come by it, or no one she knew did. He had looked prosperous, and Jaset was mildly curious to know who he had working for him these days. One or two girls, there was no doubt.

17

The woman didn't feel particularly bitter about his sacking her as he had, nor even at the time; then she had been completely bemused. He had made excuses, said he couldn't use her any more, and had passed her on to a Cypriot – Jaset hadn't liked that man. She had suspected some of the other girls of putting the poison in to Harry about her, though why? and whatever had been said was lies anyway. There had been an influx of girls from France at the time also. However, then she had counted the loss Harry's rather than her own.

Watching the taxi draw away down Old Compton Street, she wondered if the man would look back. But he didn't, and Jaset turned away and walked down the short section of Frith Street between Romilly and Old Compton Street, trying to shut out that immediate reminder of the past. She walked back in a less abstracted fashion; that section of street wasn't much good for business.

The dingy looking entrance between the strip-club and the tailor's shop was a brothel, everyone knew that and the Lord Peters who ran things no longer even tried to disguise the fact. Old Bill made no moves to close it down; there was no pressure, and too many of them were earning anyway. Jaset glanced at the pretty young woman in the dimly lit doorway from where she attempted to lure the men in; she would like to have stopped and chatted, asked for a cigarette, but there was no affinity between them, despite themselves. She continued on up to the corner of Old Compton Street, that was the best street.

The familiar sound of a car as it crawled slowly along the road caused her to turn. She gazed somewhat forlornly at its approach. Perhaps it would stop, and perhaps the driver would invite her in; however, she knew there was little likelihood of that becoming fact. The driver looked at her but didn't stop. He was a crutch-hopper after the young birds who were prepared to open their legs around the nearest corner simply for the ride. The car continued along the Street and turned left into Dean Street. Perhaps it would be back, the woman mused, pulling her coat around herself and continuing without breaking her slow step. Another unlikely prospect; if the driver couldn't find a free-bird, if he grew desperate enough to pay a couple of quid for a short time, then perhaps.

It was a little after two, Jaset noticed by the delicatessen's clock. The Street was beginning to grow quieter now; the strip-clubs had closed, and the refuse collectors had passed, they being the last consistent noise in the City after midnight, with their machine churning up the garbage and empty bottles from the greasy restaurants as the handlers tipped it on to the back of the cart. Other noises were spasmodic, drunks who filtered through, vomiting as though their single object in coming to Soho was to get drunk and vomit on someone's doorstep; the last football-rowdies cheering or crying according to how their teams fared, left over from the early evening onslaught, and at loose ends until the first train out. Occasionally there was a few pounds to be earned from them, but all too frequently they had either spent all their money or moved in groups. Men in groups were courageous enough to run off, taking their money back once they had had their little bit of fun. What courage, she thought a little disgustedly. It hurt her deeply when the client ran off cheating her; she cheerfully endeavoured to fulfil her side of the arrangement; they paid their money and she opened her legs. She had always considered the exchange fair, there was no cause for either party to cheat, though some did.

As she progressed along the Street Jaset pulled her beige coat closer to herself again, through habit, the morning wasn't cold, in fact it was quite mild. It had been raining, but had stopped now. She liked to feel the coat close about herself, it afforded her a protective feeling, making her safe and secure on hopefully trudging the streets. Despite her basic vulnerability, Jaset felt no harm could befall her while wrapped in her threadbare coat; opened, it exposed her like a virgin at a deflowering.

An expensive maroon limousine cruised by. Jaset gave it a fleeting glance, not expectantly, or even half-hopefully; the driver was too well set-up to be interested in her and she knew it. At one time – she wasn't sure how long ago now – they all used to come after her. She hadn't been able to take the poodle she had kept in those days for a walk along the street without the most sumptuous vehicles drawing up, and drivers simpering for her attention. When was that? Last week? Last year? A lifetime ago? She watched the sleek maroon car go away, its brake lights glowing a fierce red at the junction of Wardour Street before turning, the driver obviously had one to meet out of a club. That prospect almost caused her to turn in for the night, perhaps even turn it in for good; most of the would-be clients had someone else to meet it seemed, and she wondered if her efforts could be considered worthwhile any more.

In seven nights she had earned a total of nine pounds; five clients, one of whom could only afford a pound. That barely paid the rent and fed her for a week, let alone made the business profitable.

A little over an hour she had been out now, and decided to make it two, which would at least show she was trying; for any less effort would hardly have been worth her putting her coat on. When seeing the rain earlier, Jaset had almost decided not to go out at all; necessity had dictated she did, but the rain had been a plausible excuse. There would be no prospective clients about in the rain, she had told herself, and her shoes let in anyway; it was wearying enough trudging the slow pace forwards and backwards along the streets, but worse for leaking shoes. The effort in stirring herself out of her room had become increasingly difficult as apathy and lassitude claimed more of her, yet her room was so depressing it was always a relief to get out of it for a couple of hours.

Now out and walking, she wasn't feeling particularly lucky and wished she was back in her room in the half-crumbling tenement. There wouldn't be anyone for her tonight. Where were those good old days with fifteen or twenty clients a day, every day, any day she chose to work? They were so far removed from the starkness of her present circumstances that it was almost impossible to imagine that they had actually existed. But they had. Days when clients were regular, faces familiar, real names known also. Now she was left to hawk for the occasional drunk, and lucky when finding one with two pounds. Jaset realised how utterly weary she was of drunks with their gross inabilities and vomit clouded breath.

A drunk, a swartzer, even a leper, she wouldn't have been too proud to take at that moment, provided he had the price. Anything, anyone to make her feel the effort was worthwhile.

Stopping at the junction of Dean Street, the woman searched all four ways. A car-client was needed tonight, otherwise it would have to be someone really drunk to tolerate the damp ground. She glanced up at the newish block of flats over the record shop on the corner; there were girls working up in those comfortable flats, earning good money, paying high rents, being looked after; girls who weren't entitled to such nice set-ups, who didn't know the difference between a hard and a broom-handle. Very few of the girls really knew what it was all about these days, Jaset considered, they didn't give the attention like their contemporaries of a few years ago, satisfaction was a thing of the past. Perhaps that was her mistake, giving clients too much satisfaction, too much value for money. She knew from bitter experience how things would be had she her time over again.

A car crawled slowly down Dean Street, causing Jaset to step briskly across the junction with purposeful strides. She had marked the car immediately – the occupants might well want to do business but not the sort that would pay her rent. It was a police car. Police in area cars didn't normally bother her unless they needed to make themselves particularly busy; however, she wasn't taking a chance on their capricious moods.

The car swung out on to Old Compton Street and paced

her for a few yards, she could feel one of the wolly's eyes on her but didn't glance round at him. The car finally pulled away and was gone. The woman sighed mentally. Things had been bad enough of late without going and drawing a fine for bashing, or worse a few months in stir; that would just about have finished her present struggle for survival.

Music, and the sharp pin-table bells flowed across the pavement at her from an arcade on her slow, uneventful return trip along the Street. The sounds hadn't reached her before. Jaset contemplated waiting half an hour or so in there until the place closed, and would have done had it still been raining, but putting coins into the Greek owner's machines would have been money she could ill afford.

She noticed the girls who were a regular feature of the arcades. They were little more than kids, hanging around waiting to be tapped, willing to give away all they had for the price of a cup of coffee; dragged-up slum-kids who were ruining the business. Some of them might have charged, have shown signs of professionalism, but they were never developed, there was no one to teach them; for the most part they went with men for kicks or a bit of pot or something, and wound up as sucking-whores at twenty-one, or drug addicts. Why didn't the authorities round them up, get them off the streets, and leave the professional ladies to look after the City?

Jaset sighed wearily and looked in, hopeful of a client – it was little more than wishful thinking. The lights of the arcade were too bright to favour her, and the manager there didn't allow drunks falling on to the machines and breaking the glass. One or two sunken, bloodshot eyes peered out at her before turning back to the tables. She passed on.

At the end of the street the woman paused; for a moment she was unable to move, and might have been on a precipice where any decision to move had to be the right one. Looking down the garishly lit street with its white neon drawing off life and coloured neon offering it when none existed, again she questioned the value of her effort. This was the world

22

through which she now moved, yet at that moment it seemed to have no connection with her at all, and standing looking in gave her a disquieting feeling. The harder she stared in order to reorientate herself, the more physically removed it all seemed. Jaset became momentarily alarmed and shut her eyes, attempting to shut out her fear. Giddiness touched her, so she opened her eyes immediately.

The woman considered making her way home; arrived at that decision, then hesitated. She wanted to go home, but instead found herself moving back down the street on the opposite side. Perhaps she should try one of the adjacent streets? – they provided far too many diversions for her to compete, and anyway one street was as good or bad as the next.

Two young women approached, they were merry and giggling, and had reason enough, Jaset considered, watching them draw nearer. They were in business, and had in tow two fairly prosperous looking men who had probably bought them out of one of the clubs – if the clip-joints they worked from could be called clubs; they were no more than dimly lit rooms with a few bottles under the makeshift bar. There men were enticed, then first striped through their drinks and finally the girl, paying a fee both to the club and girl to have her leave with them. The girls cheated too of course, invariably ditching the man as quickly as possible. Stopping at the all-night chemist's in Piccadilly and sending the man in for Durex had been a good ruse at one time, probably still worked; taxi and lady would be gone when the deluded guy emerged. No one wanted to give value nowadays, cheat anyone and everyone seemed to be the prevailing attitude.

The clubs she had known in the old days had given value, there had been no dissatisfied dodoes then. Jaset felt disgust, a sense of shame for those two would-be PLs as they drew nearer. She could mark the girls in business a mile off on a foggy night, in much the same way that crooks could mark the filth. The girls passed her, their chatter light, irrelevant, belonging to a world she wasn't attuned to any more. It was a long time since she had sat in a club while a client bought her champagne at five pounds a bottle – it was surely more nowadays. She watched after the girls as they moved on. One of the men raised his hand and a taxi drew up immediately for them.

Jaset turned away and continued along the street, growing vacant as her thoughts trailed through the cobwebs of the past; she would miss any client's possibly tentative approach in such a frame of mind, yet made no effort to snap out of it. Memories to a PL the wrong side of forty to still be bashing as a means of sustaining dear life were nothing more than a comfort sometimes, they wouldn't pay the rent or feed her. There was a good feeling to be found by wrapping herself in reflections, despite the tinges of bitterness over her mistakes. There had been silk underwear and expensive perfume in those days, even a fur coat, not mink, but a good skin none the less; clean bed linen, and a new dress whenever the fancy took her. How many clients? How many pounds had passed through her hands?

Thoughtlessly, unseeing, she stepped into a puddle. Water seeping through to her foot brought her sharply back to the reality of her present position, that of leaky shoes and a threadbare coat; of her urgent need to find a dodo with both the price lining his pockets and the need hanging in his pants.

A car went slowly by and stopped ten yards in front. Jaset checked around as she approached, making sure she was the prospect the driver had stopped for; there was no other unattached woman in the immediate vicinity! Pulling her stomach in and her coat tighter around herself, not that either move made any noticeable difference to the slightly excessive form on offer, Jaset continued purposefully forward.

The driver of the car leant over and rolled the nearside window down. The woman stooped to the door, trying the handle; had it not been locked she would have climbed in without awaiting an invite. Once in the car the battle was normally half over – there had been occasions when drivers had told her to get out after close inspection of the goods, though generally they were too embarrassed.

'Working . . . ?' the question stopped in the man's mouth. Without any, No thank you, Sorry or Goodnight, he wound up the window and let in the clutch, leaving Jaset on the kerb to make whatever of his departure.

The woman swore silently. She could have thrown up half a dozen reasons why the man hadn't pursued the proposition, and none of them because of herself; however, in truth knew the real reason, it didn't even hurt any more, her skin had grown thick with usage. Once upon a time the truth had hurt; then the prospect of no longer being particularly attractive to all men had been painful, the full realisation slow, the refusals biting. Finally necessity had dictated her accepting that painful reality, and eventually she came to terms with it. There were rarely tears or dramas as a result now. With her random business procedure the woman made on average about one in ten, and the insults even then were better than not eating or having to sleep rough, or the even greater humiliation of being processed for state charity by the Social Security people.

Her wet right foot was beginning to feel cold and uncomfortable; so she decided to walk the length of the street and back, then go home if nothing presented itself. Pausing at the junction of Greek Street, she searched hopefully for a car. With the same negative she found herself on the next junction; there were cars about, and with only one man who was looking for just one thing, but she didn't fit the bill. Again she waited at the junction of Dean Street. A hot dog vendor on the opposite corner seemed to be having an equally lean time – possibly people were becoming too discerning. Although the smell wafting across from the barrow wasn't at all appealing, it did serve as an added reminder to her that she hadn't eaten all night. She would have chanced her heartburn recurring and bought a hot dog if she could have spared the tenpence – the coin was more important for the gas-meter. While she stood there, the vendor paused from picking his nose and looked over at her through forlorn eyes, hoping she would buy his wares. The woman might have looked at him in the same way, but no move was made to further either proposition.

Finally the vendor switched off the light over the top of his barrow, he wasn't taking up the woman's unspoken offer, but simply quitting. Jaset ought to have followed his lead, but instead she watched him pull his barrow out into the street. As he passed the newish block of flats on the corner an egg hurtled down from a window – Jaset didn't see which window as it was promptly shut. The vendor screamed in his native tongue when the egg splattered over his shoulder. Jaset assumed that the words the man directed up at all and sundry in the block were abusive, and she smiled, glad that the misfortune was his, it could as easily have been hers. No one appeared at any of the windows, nor were any more missiles thrown. After attempting to wipe the egg off with his swamping-rag, the vendor moved on down the road muttering in his strange tongue.

Smiling again, Jaset trudged in the same direction – the egg incident seemed to make her effort a little easier and caused her dim prospects to recede slightly. She drew her coat around herself, wondering if the missile hurtler had a special grudge against hot dog vendors, or simply anyone who happened to be passing at the wrong moment.

At the T-junction with Wardour Street she waited hopefully for a couple of minutes, searching all three ways; then crossed the road to make her way slowly and wearily back along the Street. Passing wine shops she thought of drink, and food on passing the shuttered and barred restaurants. Thoughts of food remained hovering and dancing in the foreground of her consciousness, sharpening the awareness of her hunger. She cursed the pointless effort in coming out, for had she stayed at home she would probably have been asleep by this time, her hunger forgotten until the waking hours. Now she had to face that same prospect made more acute for her negative result. Cursing again, she pulled her coat tighter against herself. Just one client was all she wanted, one half-generous client, or one very drunk who would perhaps give her a jack's; that didn't seem like very much to expect. She wasn't craving the good-life she had once known, that was gone and couldn't be recaptured; reflections of that past era still nestled comfortably at the back of her mind, separated from the omnipresent priorities of existence. One client, one fucking dodo to help her eke out that stinking existence for a little while longer was all she asked.

The end of her return walk loomed again along with three o'clock. Two hours, and wet cold feet was all she had for her trouble. Perhaps she ought to walk the street just once more. Faint heart . . . once more might just prove lucky, a crutch-hopper weary of dragging along the kerb might have decided finally to spend a couple of pounds. But Jaset found herself moving away from Old Compton Street through the deserted night towards home.

A man lurched crazily from a gaping hole in the side of a derelict building off Covent Garden. The woman was startled, then thought fleetingly that he was a drunk who had popped in for a lag and who might have become a client. Drunk might have once described the man, she realised, watching him take a couple of steps in front of her before collapsing. She had nothing he wanted now. The man was a derry-dosser and rotten with red-B, Jaset could smell him as she drew nearer to where he lay in an untidy heap. There was a greenish slime down his left side where he had previously fallen over or lurched into a wall, but it might have been a fungus actually growing on him. Pausing and looking down at the body, Jaset recognised his smell as that of death, here was a living creature who was even worse off than herself, only the thought afforded her no sense of comfort, for her next stop might easily have been that or the graveyard. With an involuntary shiver she moved on past him.

Home for Jaset comprised one room with a small sink

and gas-ring; a bathroom and toilet in the building was shared by eight others in similar situations. Anyway, Jaset assumed the situation of the other tenants was similar to her own, but had never enquired or been invited to draw comparisons – no one surely existed on that level by choice.

The woman climbed the forty-two stairs to her room on the third floor wearily, and in the dark, despite only one of the communal light bulbs having burnt out. The noise from the creaking uncarpeted stairs seemed somehow contained by the darkness; the Armenian landlord didn't like noise in his building, especially not at night, and Jaset no longer had her arrangement with him. When business had permitted she had donated an extra five pounds a week to the landlord, and had been allowed to bring clients back to her room; then as the clients grew scarcer and money tighter the favour was abruptly discontinued along with the five pounds that never was entered in the rent book. That had simply been one more strike against her in the vicious, ever deteriorating circle of existence she struggled to maintain. There were a few dodoes she lost simply because she had no place to take them, and they either had no car, or wouldn't entertain the two-pound exercise in a car.

The second stair of the third flight creaked particularly violently, and usually she avoided it at that time of the morning. A child answered the creak with a single plaintive cry in the otherwise silent building. The woman stopped, but there were no ensuing cries, and so she continued on up. She knew there were children in the block, though rarely encountered them. Children were animals of daylight and sunshine, while she was a nocturnal creature; so their paths didn't cross naturally, which was as well. Children always upset her, they were Jaset's most bitter regret, not the ones aborted when she had slipped up and that had been necessary, but those she hadn't had. Back in the days when she had been at her peak she had always imagined herself with her children at this time of her life, their offering the contentment and security her life had been so empty of. She had

even selected names for them, Laurence, James and Sarah;
two boys and a girl, that was what she was always intending
to have. Children to love her when her life was slipping
away; however, not there, even if the chance came again she
wouldn't have wanted those beautiful children if it meant
having them there. That was no place for them, not her children, or anyone else's for that matter. She continued up the
stairs and let herself into her room.

Home. Jaset leant back against the door and looked slowly
round the room without switching the light on. Her home
was decidedly improved by the darkness. The harsh sodium
light of the street lamps caused shadows of leaves from a
nearby tree to dance across the ceiling and down one wall;
in winter after the leaves had fallen the branches became
fingers and arms dancing and prancing across the ceiling.
Sometimes when lying in bed Jaset was able to see her children up there, those happy laughing children she never had,
they became almost a reality, so real that on occasions she
could even hear them talking to her; they would ask her
questions, calling her mother the whole time, when finally
she would fall asleep sobbing gently and contemplating so
pointlessly all those fragments of a lifetime that had been
missed.

Her children were growing up now, she had seen five
winters out with them there, and didn't want to see a sixth
out with them in that room, though knew there was no
immediately better alternative; prison wasn't better, nor the
State reception centre.

One particularly bleak January she had considered the
icy embraces of the river, the New Year was just in and had
been celebrated by everyone but her; cold and hungry and
broke and depressed, she had seen no prospects for the
future and made her way wearily down to the river. Waterloo
Bridge had found her lacking the courage to clamber over
the parapet and drop. For an hour she had stood there looking down at the murky swirling water; no one had cared one
way or the other, no one had said don't do it, no one would

have missed her. Perhaps the Armenian landlord would have missed her, but only for the three weeks' rent she had owed. Even the policeman who had passed by, huddled in his greatcoat against the sharp winter air, had merely looked at her with indifference. Finally she had walked back to her room with a greater heaviness weighting her limbs for not having been able to take that course.

How long ago was that? Two winters? Three? It would have been done with by now anyway, and time passing would have had even less meaning than it did at present.

Standing off the door, her eyes travelled across the room and settled on the gas-ring; she had never seriously considered that way out, but had known a girl in business who had taken that route when things had got into a hopeless mess. It made Jaset shudder just thinking of it. Ending life in a sordid little room in a sordid tenement seemed somehow very wrong, an admission of the terrible loneliness, a total capitulation of the misery, which jumping off a bridge or under a bus never was. Gassing oneself or taking pills and expiring quietly in the loneliness of a little room displayed none of the defiance Jaset felt death ought to have. Death. Again she shuddered, then pushed the prospect from her mind. Tomorrow she would go out and find a dodo and life would suddenly be tolerable once more.

In her good moments with two or three clients on the spin the woman was optimistic, even enthusiastic about life. She would never reach her past peak, but there were the little peaks which could sustain her when they emerged in that intangible, cloudy region ahead called future.

Jaset hung her coat behind the door, but still made no attempt to put the light on. In the darkness she could contain her inexplicable yearning for yesterday, could grasp all her yesterdays and hold them as close as she held her children when they danced over the ceiling on winter nights. She turned on the gas-ring and struck a match to it. The orange flame from the stick partially lit the room in a strange unreal light, but Jaset refused to look until the gas had ignited and popped the match out. The gas-ring wasn't essential, she wasn't cold and her shoes would dry in time, but the blue hissing flame gave her some sense of well-being, it was a continuous noise which was created only by her coin in the slot, the noise belonged to her, it was solely for her benefit. She no longer owned a radio or tv, both having gone with her youth on the downhill slide, along with so many other things that she could no longer even afford to keep up the pawnbroker's interest charges on. Later on before her ten-pence worth of gas ran out she would heat some soup on the ring, if there was any soup. She was hungry, but the dilapidated armchair into which she had sunk was comfortable and the heat from the ring pleasant against her legs. Leaning back into the chair the woman closed her eyes, allowing her thoughts to drift to the past. There were some good times back there. Yes, really fine times and nice people, men who knew what a girl liked – Let me buy you some champagne! A smile wrinkled in her memory, lots of men had wanted to buy her champagne in those days.

She awoke cold and stiff with the fingers of dawn picking their way through the eastern sky. The gas-ring had gone out, and she imagined hearing her eldest son; Laurence had asked her reason for sitting up in the chair with the dawn breaking over her. The woman shook her mind free of the cobwebs and shivered convulsively and rose to her coat on the door for her only tenpenny piece, glad now that she hadn't squandered it on a hot dog.

The Armenian was a bastard, Jaset thought, pushing the coin into the meter and turning the handle, he doctored the meters in the building so that half the revenue went into his own pocket. Gas hissed freely, and the woman struck another match – there was no longer any point in not looking, the dawn was revealing the room's ugliness. Paper hung peeling from the exposed wall where the weather seeped through between the bricks whose mortar had fallen out like rotten teeth from an aged mouth. Once, in an age long since lost to the memory, the building had possibly been fashionable, even desirable. But now the ceiling paint, which had turned through the yellows to brown, was flaking and the floor-boards had shrunk and dropped; the window wouldn't open and the door sat out of plumb, needing weight and effort to close it into the jam. Five pounds a week was considered a very fair rent by the landlord; Jaset wasn't of the same opinion, but had no option other than to pay it. Five pounds was nothing when there were clients, even the additional five hadn't been begrudged then, but of late it was a struggle, and represented half her pitful earnings on a good week, and a seven-day working week at that. There was an additional charge for light and gas, and the bath which could be used as often as she could provide coins for that doctored meter. Invariably she couldn't spare the coins, and a weekly trip down to the public baths was cheaper, and certainly cleaner. Jaset wouldn't have been at all surprised what a body might have picked up in that communal bathroom in her apartment building, and generally she wasn't very particular anyway. There had been a time when she would bathe three times a day and certainly douche herself after each client; however, with the type of dodo she was attracting these days it didn't really seem so important; they weren't like her regulars, she owed them nothing more than their two-quid's-worth, then it was good night nurse! Perhaps she should have cared a little more, but pennies were so tight that even the coin for the public baths was difficult to find some weeks.

Despite the building, and especially the shortcomings of her room, Jaset knew the landlord would have no problem reletting with her out, and probably at a higher rent. She fully appreciated what the accommodation situation was like, quite desperate everywhere, which was why she intended clinging on to the little she had, even though it was ill afforded. The Armenian had whined bitterly on the occasions her rent had fallen in arrears, and had threatened to throw her out, while sounding off about the real value of the furnished apartment and what he could get elsewhere for it with some semblance of regularity. At that point the man had still lived in hope of the additional five pounds on the rent being resumed, so his threats had been idle; however, having since been completely disillusioned on that score, his tolerance wasn't something Jaset had any wish to test again.

There was a tin of soup among the odds and ends of food-stuff on the mantelpiece above where the gas-ring stood on the flat hearth to the blocked-off fireplace. Gratefully the woman opened the can and emptied the soup into a saucepan to heat. She didn't mind getting up in the afternoon and going the rest of the day and evening without eating, but going to bed hungry was something she didn't like at all. A gnawing empty stomach left her at the mercy of depression, she had noted it repeatedly; whenever her fortunes had taken a turn for the worse it was invariably because she was hungry, or so it appeared, though perhaps she was hungry because her fortunes were worsening, she had never really analysed it. The soup would settle her and then she would sleep right through the day until dusk started to enclose the City once more, when she would rise and make an effort again.

After her soup Jaset placed the saucepan and plate in the tiny sink to soak, then stepped out of her dress for bed. She removed her over-stretched girdle with some relief, and her excess of fat oozed, sagging in ribbons round her lower abdomen. She scratched uninhibitedly. Nowadays when out looking for business she didn't wear knickers, in fact hardly ever wore that garment any more, it only complicated the business which usually had to be conducted in awkward restricted places anyway, while the girdle was easily hoisted up with the dress. Knickers when worn had to go down and often be removed, unless of course they were crutchless panties, which she didn't much like. Somehow crutchless panties seemed perverse to her, and in the past she had been loath to buy them anyway because the assistants in the undies shops immediately knew what your trade was.

Jaset slept in her bra and petticoat. The bed was unmade, it had been like that for a fortnight. The original agreement when moving into the room was that the landlord supplied clean linen once a week, which practice had ceased when he had started taking the extra fiver a week from her, and it was never resumed, so the sheets were laundered when she could afford the laundrette. The woman could well remember the days when her apartment had had four dozen pairs of sheets. But those days were gone, she reminded herself, as she pulled the covers straight and climbed into bed. Reaching over, she dragged the single curtain across the window, blocking the dawn out. It didn't do the same for the dawn chorus which had started, though the birds rarely kept her from sleep.

Tomorrow – her tomorrow – she would make an extra effort, get started about eleven o'clock just as the pubs were turning out, maybe even find a dodo who would take her to an hotel. Then perhaps get another one immediately afterwards, possibly a car owner and oblige him in his car. There was no reason why three shouldn't be accommodated on her tour out tomorrow, she mused as sleep began seeping into her limbs. The clients were still around. She wasn't a chicken any more, but by the same token she wasn't a dog either, and still had what was needed to attract a certain class of clientèle. Some men actually preferred women who had a tendency towards heaviness, there were plenty for the finding.

The woman slid without effort into sleep, reassuring herself that she could still attract clients. More than enough to make existence worthwhile.

2

Arrows of sunlight pierced through the ill-fitting curtain which covered the window. It was daytime still, and there was some commotion going on in the street.

Jaset stirred and rolled around the bed for the best position to shut out both light and noise, but wasn't successful, both found and worried her. The daylight she could understand, but what was the noise? Hundreds of voices it sounded like, all shouting and crying in confusion, and bent on disturbing her. She pulled the pillow over her head, trying to keep the noise out, but immediately got the impression of suffocating.

It was no good, she had been disturbed now, and wanted a piss anyway. Rising up on the bed, Jaset yanked open the curtain and was immediately struck blind almost by the light on her raw eyes. Christ, what time could it be for the sun to still be so bright? She no longer had any form of time-piece – her Uncle was minding them. Around seven it started to get dark, so she knew it wasn't seven. Gradually the woman opened her eyes against the strange daylight. The noise was still going on somewhere below, only she couldn't see anything. Probably a car crash over in the next street was the cause, cars were always crashing there. Bloody nuisance. She knew getting back to sleep would be impossible. And she still wanted that pee.

Turning from the window, Jaset climbed off the bed, the thought of pulling the sheets up straight never entered her head.

The prospect of meeting some strange body on the stairs deterred her from trotting down to the toilet on the next floor. She didn't know the daylight people in the building and couldn't be bothered to dress – on such occasions the tiny sink in her room served her.

A thin film of congealed soup lay across the water hiding the submerged saucepan and plate. Jaset lifted both utensils dripping to the floor and pulled the plug, water gurgled away leaving soup round the basin for the woman to rinse away with urine as she raised her petticoat to the glazed earthenware. Jaset stooped for the utensils and returned them to the sink, for washing up later. Then she hunted round for a cigarette; that was a must on waking, and but for her routine being shattered today the fag would have been the first thing. Her handbag held no cigarettes, nor her coat; she foraged through the litter of packets on the table and mantelpiece, growing more agitated with each empty packet. There had to be at least one cigarette somewhere; she was finished before she began without a cigarette to start her off on her period of consciousness. There was no need for them when working, and she rarely bothered then unless the client was pushing; only on waking was there a need, which need was only second to her need of cigarettes when sitting staring blankly into the middle-distance in her depressing little room.

A snuffed end was all she could find, but it was enough to tear at and irritate her lungs on striking the match and

36

inhaling. She exhaled on raucous, staccato breaths. Despite the cough from lacerated lungs, Jaset persisted with the cigarette butt as though believing the cure lay at the end of it.

It was early and daylight, and Jaset felt a stranger in a familiar world, and didn't quite know what to do with herself. She no longer had any friends who she could go and visit, not even acquaintances, no one to meet for tea or to talk with. There had been friends in the old days, dozens of them, so many she couldn't keep track, to say nothing of all those who would smile at her, nod or wave, stop and pass the time of day. What had happened to all those people? They couldn't all be dead. Perhaps some of them were, like the girl who had gassed herself, some of them were bound to have died, but not all of them. Jaset so rarely encountered people from her past. She might have been a complete stranger in the city. But in fact it was the city that was the stranger, turning, living, breathing, constantly on the move, always progressing away from her, excluding her more and more of late from its secret circles and games. Things were going on these days which she no longer understood, where once she had understood everything; the city had become harsh and cold, when once she had been locked in its warm and generous embrace. Then there were the people, generations that had since grown up and moved away from her, so distant they seemed that they might have been from another planet. They were all strangers now. Apart from seeing Harry Bleedew on the corner of Frith Street last night, only once had she encountered a half-familiar face, a woman, and Jaset had been on the point of speaking when the woman had looked right through her as though she had been a ghost. Maybe she was a ghost, Jaset thought, sadly amused, she might just as well have been for all the business she did.

Tonight! she reminded herself. Tonight she was really going to make an effort – she remembered making that resolution before sleeping – and maybe find three dodoes on the spin. That wasn't impossible, the men were available still, men who didn't mind paying for slipping into an experienced woman. Most of the girls nowadays wouldn't know what to do with a hard-on, she consoled herself. Why, the silly little bitches, the way some of them performed they wouldn't have lasted five minutes in the old days, if they had tried it on then they would have been out on their ears and bloody quick. Jaset smiled thinly with that reflection. Yes, there were many men who liked the more experienced type of woman who was on the heavy side. Tonight she would sort a few of them out.

Continually Jaset shuffled around her room, picking up things and putting them down again. She could have used another cigarette, and tried to push the prospect from her mind. The woman was at a loose end, the early afternoon had for so long been unknown to her, usually she was still sleeping.

Early afternoon had been a stranger all her adult life, it seemed; even in the old days she had never been acquainted with that hour. Late mornings were known, then there had been time to scoot around a few shops and buy a few bits and pieces, say a few hellos, then get back to the apartment to start work between one and two, which was when the clients started arriving – some would have arrived before had she permitted them. All those familiar faces queuing at her door as if waiting for a doctor who performed miracles of medicine. There had never been any shortage of clients in those days, a bottomless well of dodoes whimpering and simpering for her. Where have you all gone, my lovelies? None of her lovelies answered as Jaset conjured their familiar faces into her mind's eye; just faces now, every one identical, faces as empty as her past.

Stepping into her girdle, Jaset forced her hand up across her suddenly constricted gut and released a tuft of pubic hair which had pulled against the elastic, then straightening her petticoat, she pulled into her dress. It was time she had a new dress, she observed, looking at the stains down the present garment as she smoothed it. If things didn't improve for her soon she would have to try hoisting a new winter outfit from one of the big stores, though she didn't particularly want to as stealing went against the grain. A thief stole because he was a thief, while she stole only to exist in the very lean times which, if reasonable justification, still didn't help the deed settle any easier. Anyway, winter wasn't here yet and anything could happen before then, she could even strike it lucky and get back on top again, perhaps even find a man who wanted to marry her, that was possible. In the old days men were always wanting to marry her. She had received at least one proposal a week, but had always refused them; she was a professional lady, and then a professional had been just that.

'Where are you now, you offers of marriage? You fathers of my children?' Jaset stopped abruptly and flushed with embarrassment, realising she had spoken her private thoughts, something she was doing more and more. She looked self-consciously around the room as though other people were within earshot.

The woman had had some direction when starting to dress, only now couldn't remember what; then she had had some purpose, now her mind was blank and the harder she groped at that idea the more out of reach it became. What with talking to herself about the fathers of the children she had never had, then the incident of her mind blanking off, Jaset wondered if she was going off her head.

'Baths!' the woman suddenly said out loud. It wasn't her usual day but she had decided to walk across to the public baths at Holborn for a bath as her day was so messed up anyway. Why should she have forgotten that? Jaset questioned. Insanity, probably your eyes are blank and glassy too, she told herself – a fractured piece of mirror was the best she had, but didn't fetch it to inspect her eyes.

Lack of money made ridiculous impossibilities; she would like to have taken the sheets to the laundrette; bought a packet of cigarettes; visited the hairdresser too, a girl couldn't really go places without a nice hair-do. There had been times when she had had a perm regularly and at least a set every month, and had even had the hairdresser come out to her, manicurist as well. Lately a brushing would be an occasion – some of her clients had enjoyed brushing her hair for her in those days. She didn't even own a brush any more, only a comb, which she forgot rather than was loath to employ. Hairs were blonde, split, broken; brown roots grew up from the scalp, soon the brownish colour would have reclaimed the lot unless given another going over with peroxide.

On leaving her room the woman carefully locked the door, not that there was anything to steal, but hippies might have got in. Jaset moved cautiously along the passage to the head of the stairs, her manner was furtive and she didn't know why, but assumed the strangeness of the hour was the cause, it certainly wasn't because the rent was owing, not yet. The passage and stairs were as bleak and ugly as she suspected they would be by daylight, for although the naked light bulbs at night did nothing to enhance, they didn't expose the scars and dirt of age as merciless as daylight. Odd noises pursued her down the stairs; in a room there was a radio playing music which she was out of touch with; somewhere, another child was crying, maybe it was the same child she had heard on her return that morning. Boards creaked without familiarity now.

On starting down the last flight of stairs a voice stopped her. 'Allo dare, lady' – the landlord had emerged from a room on the first floor. He came down the stairs to where Jaset was.

The man was short and thick, he had the look of a Chinese-Turk and sounded like a Welsh-Negro. The woman regarded him suspiciously, she would have addressed him only she couldn't remember his name, it was foreign and awkward to pronounce, she recalled.

'Ow tings go den for you, lady?' the man asked. He always called her lady, possibly he couldn't remember her name either.

Jaset shrugged. 'They could be worse, Mister, I s'pose' –
how much worse Jaset wasn't too sure. She couldn't readily
remember her luck being so consistently down.

Her reply was obviously misunderstood, the man's face
sagged as hope drained away. 'I was hope you will start the
extra paying some more, lady, you know? The room is
worth.'

'Soon I hope,' said Jaset, nodding vigorously. They continued to descend the stairs together. She hoped the man
wouldn't press her further.

'Yes, soon or 'ave to let for more, you know?' His greasy,
yellowish face crumpled in an apologetic smile, before he
moved away through the back of the house.

Watching him disappear, Jaset wondered just what chance
there was of her finding that extra fiver when even the
straight rent was going to be a struggle this week. A struggle
was an understatement, by all appearances it was going to
be a complete non-starter. Eviction, however effected, would
just about finish her. The professional lady wondered if she
might pay the Armenian in kind, but doubted it; he was far
too shrewd for that, and the rents were presumably his only
income.

There were some children sitting on the steps of the house,
seven Jaset counted. That was far too many for them all to
have belonged to her building, otherwise she would have
seen or heard them before. They were urchin looking United
Nations children, not quite ragged-arsed but very near. The
woman wished she had some sweets to give them, but it was
a long time since she had bought such non-essentials. The
small unwashed faces looked up questioningly at her, and
Jaset found their looks disturbing; they held a ream of unspoken questions, they were asking for things she couldn't
give them, and about things she couldn't tell them. All the
questions her own three children might have asked throughout their process of growing up were encompassed in those
looks.

Awkwardly, Jaset moved down the steps and away. She

didn't glance back, yet knew the children's eyes were following her. She could feel their accusing stares burning into her back, and quickened her pace. Why should their eyes accuse her? she questioned. Was it on account of all their unborn brothers wasted down thighs and over sheets? Could they know? Were children that perceptive? They knew, all children were that perceptive. Soon she would hear their feet on the pavement as they chased her, then their taunting voices; stones would follow, they would stone her in the street because of their dissipated brothers – didn't they understand that her own children were among those lost in the sacks of contraception? Panic welled inside the woman, she was alone, childless, lost of chance and taunted by the children of the world. Then hearing the bitter mocking voices behind as the children came after her, she began to run – why didn't they understand? To avoid their stones that she knew were hurtled in disgust, she fled across the road without any awareness of traffic; a car horn blared violently, causing the woman to stop abruptly on reaching the opposite kerb. Jaset turned, suddenly embarrassed, people were staring at her curiously, and whispering. She looked down the road and flushed, her skin prickling uncomfortably; the children hadn't moved from the steps, their interest being absorbed in their chatter and games; a broken-down whore meant nothing to them. She experienced some disappointment when finally turning away and continuing in the direction of the public baths.

Admission to the baths including a towel cost her fivepence. She could afford neither a piece of soap nor shampoo, nor any of the other toiletries sold in the kiosk; however, scraps of soap could normally be found on the floor of the bathhouse.

Waiting was necessary. The Negress attendant took her ticket and told her to have a seat, calling her Honey. Jaset thought the Negress's face was familiar, possibly she had seen her working the streets late at night, though couldn't swear to it; one darky looked much the same as another to her, and that held good for darky men too, it was just impossible to tell the difference between them. Recently she had been with one or two darkies. In the old days she had had no truck with them at all, the majority of them would have been too big for one thing, and for another they were nearly always off the boats and carrying all kinds of diseases. At that point in her career she had considered that entertaining them wouldn't have been fair to her regular clients, but now beggars couldn't be choosers, and size certainly made no appreciable difference.

'Next!' the Negress called out above the sound of rushing water.

There was no one waiting before or after Jaset, who rose and walked round the brick partition to the line of bath cubicles. The Negress indicated the cubicle, and Jaset stepped into the folds of steam, shutting and bolting the door after her. Immediately she wiped the mirror with her hand, but it proved a pointless exercise and so undressed without looking at herself.

Three layers of skin were scalded off, or so it felt like to Jaset as she lowered herself into the water. There were no inlet controls inside the cubicle and she didn't bother to shout for more cold water. Ten to fifteen minutes she soaked for, any longer would have brought the 'Hurryup!' from the attendant. Once upon a time her baths had never been less than a two hour exercise, soaking luxuriantly in perfumed water. Here she had managed to find a small piece of soap where it had caught on the drain grid over the gully, it was enough; however, there was no shampoo, not even a half-empty sachet along the top of the cubicle partition, then she didn't imagine other women often washed their hair in the bath. Jaset decided to do hers, with the soap, as her scalp had been itching lately. Bending her head forward, she soaked her hair before remembering that she hadn't brought her comb with her, but then it was too late to do anything about it.

Steam had run in long streaks down the walls and mirror

by the time Jaset finished drying herself, and after wiping the glass with the towel, she inspected her hair, it was a mess of rats tails on which her fingers employed as a comb made no impression before finally giving up trying. 'You look a bloody mess,' she said quietly to her naked reflection in the looking-glass, and the reflection concurred with a nod.

At forty-four the woman looked as though she should have qualified to have been drawing her pension for the last four years. Everything that was once firm and supple now sagged, even to Jaset's kindly eye; her chin; her breasts without a bra sagged like over-ripe melons that were a mystery of nature that they didn't fall off the vine; her stomach, too, sagged in familiar tiers. She weighed eleven and a half stone, but didn't really consider herself overweight – merely that tendency towards heaviness which so many men liked.

Who was she trying to fool? she questioned, as she stood staring at herself. If a man saw that naked by daylight he would probably turn queer. The woman almost smiled.

As she remained standing in front of the mirror her thoughts travelled back across old frontiers, when suddenly there staring out at her was the young woman she had always wanted to stay.

It wasn't at all surprising that she did such business and had so many regular clients having those trim neat limbs and firm rounded breasts which they all admired so. Also there was her little jewel-box, smooth and slightly pouting – their Pearl some called it. She liked that name. Who was it who had first called it his Pearl? Jaset tried to recall. A ghost of the past, a prominent ghost, she felt, one she shouldn't have forgotten.

The young woman staring out of the looking-glass was twenty-one and homeless; her father was a provincial shop-keeper whose world almost collapsed on discovering his daughter's pregnancy. The abortion hadn't been difficult for her to obtain, venal doctors having bred and prospered in the war just past. She had had enough money saved, but the whore's operation would have only increased her reputation at home; so she hadn't returned, but had gone instead to London where she had met Peter who had introduced her around and had taken care of her – Plater! He was that prominent ghost from the past.

Mr Plater, the chemistry teacher at school, had been the first ever to call her slit his Pearl. She had had a reputation even then; Mr Plater had heard the rumours, which was why he had kept her behind that evening.

'Jaset Nurse, you will remain behind,' Mr Plater said as the class began filing out. Immediately there were some sniggering. 'Stop that silliness or you'll all remain behind for extra work' – it was the last period of the day.

Eventually all the children had gone. Mr Plater avoided looking at Jaset where she had remained sitting at her desk in the silent classroom. While half-sensing what was about to take place, the girl could neither speak nor look at the man.

At fourteen her reputation was rampant around the school, more so in some sections than others; to hear some of the stories she had lain in the long grass with half the male contingent of the fourth year, the half who had attained puberty, when the truth was she had only ever let one boy do anything to her. How had the rumours started? At twelve she had been an innocent little girl who had played with other innocent little girls, to whom all boys were taboo; she had been neither pretty nor ugly and had been fairly inconspicuous as a result – a game in the school playground. Could her reputation have grown from there, when that boy had risen up off the ground and under her gym-slip, his head between her legs? The boy had stammered and blushed scarlet, she had been acutely embarrassed too, while other children had laughed, some jeered. Yes, that must have been the start. She remembered the taunting cries of children in the playground, the whispering and sniggering in the classroom, and suddenly she was endowed with a reputation.

Whenever boys needed proof of their virility, it was immediately asserted and made irrefutable simply by claiming to have shagged Jaset Nurse behind the cycle sheds, which was where Kenny had done her. She had felt sorry for Kenny, who was as unfortunate as herself, being taunted on occasions because of his clubfoot. Kenny was small for a boy, intelligent and terribly lonely, he wanted to be accepted, even by a girl. Jaset shared his feeling of isolation, understood his position and sympathised, she even liked him a little, but was finally betrayed by him.

The cycle sheds were out of bounds to those who didn't cycle to school, but regardless Jaset and Kenny Clubfoot waited there for the last cycle to be taken down from its rack and wheeled out; very few departures were delayed at going-home time unless for an ulterior motive. Jaset drew the boy down into the long grass that grew against the back of the cycle sheds, her own hands were trembling so she wasn't at all sure whether or not he was. They crouched looking at each other in silence for a few moments, then suddenly the boy grabbed at her small, slightly budding bosom; his hands were hot and awkward when they moved roughly inside her blouse, grabbing at the soft white flesh to tit her up. He withdrew, hesitated, then thrust his hands down and raised her gym-slip over her thighs. Jaset held the skirt at her waist while assisting the boy in removing her knickers. He stopped and shied away on the first confrontation, appearing un-certain as to how he should react. He touched her slit and withdrew, until at last he became bold enough to push his fingers into her, first one, then another.

'Do something to me, Kenny,' the girl whispered.

The boy seemed reluctant to undo his trousers. But Jaset encouraged him, and pulling his stained underpants down, his penis thrust out like a trembling finger, frightening her briefly, she hadn't expected it to be quite so violent. The boy pulled her legs wider and laid on top of her, he couldn't make it go in the opening, and finally the girl wiggled his cock in. Their timing was completely unco-ordinated as each raced the other, determined, it seemed, to make the best impression.

'D'you do it to yourself, Ken?' the girl asked as the boy

buffeted about on top of her.

'Yes, yes, sometimes – don't you?' – defensively, immediately reaching some form of climax before the girl spoke again. They both made raucous guttural sounds to convince each other of satisfaction.

After that Kenny Clubfoot was accepted as something of a demi-hero by other boys, while Jaset's reputation soared; she was the punch-line in every locker room joke, the reason for every snigger, every innuendo.

Mr Plater had certainly heard the rumours, and had at last decided to act when he told her to stay on after school. Jaset could hear the man's heavy breathing where he came and stood behind her at the desk. Seconds seemed to tick away with the weight of hammer blows, while neither spoke. Jaset wasn't even sure that she breathed. Mr Plater edged in closer to the girl and pressed himself against her. She closed her eyes, fighting the involuntary nausea she could feel welling inside her. Why didn't the man speak and give her some identity, some time and reference with which to label the channel her life was being forced along? She could feel a certain part of him pressed against her back, hard and throbbing, just as Kenny Clubfoot's had been, only rhythmically almost rather than wildly. Jaset tried to reject the man and his hard-on, tried to deny its existence, resist him by telling herself she was there for some other reason, but there was an inexplicable force impelling her now, and turning suddenly, she pressed her face into the man's stomach, trying at the same time to gulp in air and prevent her nausea.

Still the man neither spoke nor moved, but his breathing grew terrifying, and the girl wondered fleetingly whether he was having some kind of fit. Deciding he wasn't, she cautiously brought her hand round to touch the bulge in his trousers. The move activated her teacher, who instantly raised her off the stool and whisked her into the stockroom at the back of the classroom.

'I need you so much, so much,' he managed at last in a pained, hoarse whisper. 'Need you so much.'

After locking the stockroom door on the inside, Mr Plater quickly spread some spare window drapes on the floor; Jaset resisted momentarily as he pushed her down on to them, but when she saw his eyes and that terrified plea they held, she knew she would have to be kind to him.

With gently trembling hands he raised her skirt, exposing her young thighs, his fingers slid around the elastic top of her knickers where it had marked the skin and eased the garment down, almost as though he was uncertain of what he would find. 'Oh, Nurse, Nurse,' he sighed painfully and threw himself forward on to her. His chin was rough where he needed a shave, but the girl felt so sorry for him that she was unable to complain or cry out. 'Nurse, I need you so much . . . my Pearl – I need . . . ' He inserted his finger into her Pearl. His left hand ripped frantically at his fly buttons and suddenly his phallus erupted from his pants, quivering violently.

The girl leant forward and touched him. Hard as it was, the girl found it fascinatingly soft and knew it wanted to go inside her; that was where babies started.

Mr Plater carefully eased into his Pearl, but it hurt her and the girl winced.

'I'm sorry, sorry' – the teacher repeated himself several times, all the while trying to push further into the girl. 'My little Pearl is so tight – I'm sorry.'

Mr Plater, the chemistry teacher, worked and apologised; he apologised for hurting her, for having to do it to her, for being so weak and not being able to resist her. He whimpered and explained his need, then sharply digressing, told her how this was by way of an experiment above commonplace intercourse, explaining how the academic aspects of this exercise were of paramount importance. All the while Mr Plater was becoming more and more frenzied, his breathing running to a harsh rasp; veins bulged on his forehead and he clung to her more tightly.

Jaset could feel herself quickening to meet the man's frenzy, and was worried briefly that her loss of calm would ruin the exercise. But then something happened to make it unimportant, the man seemed to embrace death, as she imagined it, he convulsed violently and the girl was frightened and uncertain what had caused the paroxysm. Shortly she didn't really care, for she discovered a new experience that happened inside herself, its effect was debilitating and so nice, causing all of her to tingle. This experience was something she had never discovered by putting her fingers and things into herself.

The affair conducted in the stockroom with the chemistry master lasted two weeks, until the end of the summer term when Jaset left school for good. Affairs weren't conveniently continued between teacher and ex-pupil out of school; he had to take up his summer job in a canning factory, while she started work for her father in his grocery store.

The course of her life seemed marked out, predestined. She had been forced into a limited channel of existence where she could only go forward, accepting the values she found there, and could neither divagate nor turn; the path was as restricted in its own way as the route marked out for a convent nun would probably have been. There was nothing Jaset could do but accept however the carpet of her existence unfurled; she had had no designs on making sex a profession, if anything it was simply a hobby that got away from her along with her reputation.

There for the first time she realised she didn't even know his Christian name. Mr Plater almost certainly had one, but all the while he was conducting his experiments on the folded window drapes in the stockroom she had always addressed him as Sir or Mr Plater. While he had always called her by her surname.

'C'mon dare, Honey, others is waiting!'

The door was rapped by the Negress, and suddenly Jaset was transported back to the public bath house, the ghosts of the past vanishing, leaving her with that terrible feeling of loneliness again. She saw a broken, sagging old prostitute staring at her out of the mirror, one who had been crying, only now she wasn't sure whether the tears had been for the past or because of it.

Drying her eyes on the coarse towel, Jaset quickly dressed and fled the bath house without any sense of direction.

It was early still. Three o'clock was too early for anything, and she walked aimlessly, looking but not seeing, moving but not progressing, encountering people but not being able to reach out and touch them; they were unreal, eidolons forever beyond her grasp, while to try would have been like grabbing at the sky. The woman thought of going to the cinema only didn't have the price of admission even to the cartoon cinemas – a ten-bob wank there would have been welcome business today. Neither did she have the price to sit with a cup of tea in Joe Lyon's, and regretted bitterly having wasted fivepence on that bath, it wasn't so essential that she couldn't have gone without for another couple of days. She contemplated going back to her room to make a cup of tea, only the prospect didn't inspire her; back there she would be trapped again and maybe she wouldn't be able to get out this time, not even for work that night. The room was so overwhelmingly depressing, the aura of despair it created seeped through her bones to their very marrow. Getting out tonight was vital, then she was going to make a really positive start in improving her circumstances. Tonight she intended getting two or three dodoes – that would be positive! – and continue having two or three each evening, then things would soon improve and she would be back on top in no time.

The first thing to do would be to restraighten the Armenian; that extra five pounds would soon be no problem to her, and afterwards it would only be a short while before she was moving back into Soho and hanging her own sign at the door. Re-establishing herself wouldn't be too difficult at all. Finding a modest place that wasn't too expensive, but that was neither a cupboard nor a shit house, and well positioned in one of the side streets, then she would soon have them queuing again. An awful lot of men actually preferred the older, experienced type of woman, she assured herself once again. In fact a certain very nice class of clientèle nearly always preferred the older, more experienced woman! Oh yes, she would soon make the right start and get back on top there, it wouldn't take her long.

She almost convinced herself.

3

The park was situated behind the church of St Giles's Circus, and was maintained by the Church Commissioners on account of its formerly being a graveyard. There were one or two very old gravestones dotted around still. Jaset passed through the heavy cast-iron gates into the park, unable to recall ever having been there before even though it was only literally a stone's throw from her manor. She didn't particularly want to enter the park because of the children she saw playing there, they would stare at her with their large questioning eyes, watch her progress; but the park was somewhere for her to sit and rest, somewhere that didn't require money. She couldn't keep moving all her life, she had to stop somewhere. Anyway her feet needed resting in readiness for her onslaught tonight, and there was no profit in continually walking during the day.

Sinking to a bench set back off the footpath, the woman pulled her coat against herself, her eyes falling blankly into the middle-distance. After a little while she became aware of the action going on around her, mainly children playing. There were always children of late, no matter where she looked, not her children, though they might as easily have been. God might as easily have given those children to her, in fact He might as easily have made her one of those mothers she often saw with children; He was evidently annoyed with her for some reason. Why? What reason? – she had no idea, she had never knowingly done anything to upset Him.

Some minutes passed before Jaset realised a young woman was looking at her, and then wasn't absolutely certain. The young woman was along the path, just standing looking, and at first Jaset assumed she was looking across at her children or waiting for them to catch up. But when she turned and looked beyond her seat, there were no children there or any nearby. Shortly Jaset began to feel a little embarrassed by the young woman who remained looking at her, and wondered if she was lost or had lost something. Perhaps she should speak, or smile, but decided against either course in case the young woman thought she was a loony. Jaset didn't ever want anyone thinking she was a loony.

Finally the young woman smiled. 'Hello. How are you?' she enquired.

Again Jaset looked around to see if someone had approached silently on the grass. No one had. There was something wrong with the young woman, she decided instantly, there had to be, for perfect strangers didn't speak in such circumstances, not in the park or anywhere else. Jaset thought it best to ignore her, but the young woman came over to her.

'I trust you're well?' She smiled again. 'Isn't this a beautiful day. Such a perfect day. I always feel happy when the sun is shining. Perfectly happy in fact when the sun shines. So depressed when it rains. I think the rain is depressing. I don't think it'll rain today, they said it wouldn't. On the radio. Do you mind if I sit here with you on the bench?'

Jaset shifted uncomfortably, she pulled her coat tighter about herself, as if for protection, and as the young woman sat she eyed her obliquely, almost timidly, but didn't speak to her.

'Are you here with your children?' Nervousness caused her sentences to jerk out like quick knife thrusts. 'So many women come just to admire other women's children. I don't have my children with me today but I came here just the same. I don't think I've seen you in this park before. I would remember if I'd seen you here before, I always do. I've seen you somewhere before though. I'll remember shortly. I've an astounding memory for faces, they all say so. It'll come back.' Falling silent for a short while, the young woman seemed to grow agitated as if trying to physically wrest something from her mind's eye; then she smiled again and became still. 'You forgot to take your comb to the swimming bath with you. I'm always doing things like that. Would you care to borrow mine?'

Glancing apprehensively at her, Jaset considered rising and moving away, when the young woman, after briefly rummaging in her handbag, thrust the comb into her hands. Jaset hesitated without direction, her eyes searching and somewhat bemused.

'Go on, use it,' the young woman urged. 'It's perfectly clean. I know your hair is if you've just been to the baths.' She waited as Jaset hesitantly began pulling the long steel comb through her straggly, tangled hair. 'Would you like a mirror?' – she produced a compact mirror before the older woman could either decline or accept verbally. The little kindnesses she was able to bestow on this stranger seemed to give the young woman some intense pleasure. She watched Jaset with childlike delight, and when the hair was combed out, offered face powder, lipstick, mascara, suffering no refusal. Jaset was too frightened to refuse, even if she had had any real inclination.

It was surprising what a difference make-up made to her. She was almost glad now for coming into the park and meeting this young woman; she would have no trouble attracting one or two dodoes later on, transformed as she was.

'My name is Sarah,' the young woman said, returning the toiletries to her handbag and fetching out her cigarette case.

Despite the urgent need she had, Jaset didn't immediately see the cigarettes on offer; the young woman's name had stopped her dead, this might have been that daughter she had never had. Suddenly the young woman wasn't a loony encountered in the park, but was possibly her daughter; a little older than her daughter would have been, though not very much older, and as pretty, with white even teeth and a straight nose and clear hazel eyes. And the name, Sarah, refined, dignified, just like her daughter, just like the young woman who was sitting on the bench with her.

Taking a cigarette, Jaset cupped her hands against the lighter held by the young woman. Sarah had soft, white, unworked hands, and the older woman instinctively tried to hide her own hands.

'What is your name?'

'Jaset. Jaset Nurse.'

It was a long time since she had told anyone her right name. Occasionally her real name came out, such as when appearing in court, it had to then, as they had her fingerprints on record and checked them each time her collar was felt for soliciting. Sometimes when caught on the streets it was possible to give a wolly a wrong 'un, but never the Tom's Patrol – how she hated those policeman, especially their name; part of it referred directly to her and her kind and made her seem old and disgusting and something of an animal. She wasn't an old tom, but a professional lady, who, one day soon, would climb back to a position of near-respectability and safety.

'Jaset Nurse,' the young woman repeated. 'That's a nice name. I knew you'd have a nice name as soon as I saw you. Are you married, Jaset Nurse? How old are you, Jaset Nurse? Where do you live, Jaset Nurse . . . ?'

The young woman had a thousand questions to ask, it

seemed, questions which for some inexplicable reason Jaset felt compelled to answer, and answer truthfully.

'I know where I've seen you!' said Sarah, suddenly excited about remembering. 'On the streets of Soho, isn't it, Jaset Nurse? That's where I've seen you.'

Jaset looked at the young woman with a terrified, betrayed, disappointed, hurt expression, it was as though her daughter had discovered what she was, and she had never wanted her daughter to find out. Always planning to send the children away to school in order to protect them, her intention was to have retired to the country on her insurance pensions by the time their schooling was over. But now Sarah knew, and would surely tell her brothers Laurence and James.

'Yes.' Jaset nodded remorsefully. 'Yes, I'm sorry.' She lowered her eyes and nervously rolled the cigarette round in her fingers, never really having been ashamed of her occupation before that moment.

Sarah reached out and touched her hands. 'It doesn't matter. It really doesn't matter, Jaset, if you choose to be that – I'm sure its quite hard work.' There was a brief awkward silence. 'Is it very hard work?' Sarah asked at last.

The older woman stopped twisting the cigarette and nodded reflectively. 'Yes.'

The reply seemed to please Sarah, who smiled like a child once more. 'Yes, I thought it would be. I thought how tired you sometimes looked when I saw you walking the streets.'

'Did you see me often, Sarah?' – it was the first question Jaset had asked.

'Quite often. Sometimes I saw you even when you weren't there, whenever I looked for you I saw you. Can you understand that?'

'Yes,' lied Jaset, wanting to understand this strange young woman. It didn't really matter that she couldn't in fact. All that mattered was that she existed there, was someone from whom she could take a bearing in the daylight world.

'How did you come to be a prostitute?' The young

woman's enquiry, despite its lack of force, demanded a reply.

Jaset shrugged. 'I became pregnant in a small suburb; then got myself aborted, which made things worse.' She shrugged again. 'People were lost and at loose ends after the war, it was all too easy.' She trailed off vaguely, hoping the young woman wouldn't pursue the matter.

But Sarah had a thousand more searching questions, and wanted every minute detail that could be recalled from her past. There was some strange influence the young woman was having on her; Jaset didn't particularly want to go into details about her past, but couldn't stop herself replying. The same compulsion was present when Sarah invited her to tea at her apartment. Jaset went with her, knowing she was incapable of preventing herself, and not simply out of need for refreshment; poison could have been on offer and she would still have accepted.

They walked to Sarah's apartment. It wasn't that far from the park, yet Jaset had no clear impression of their route or where the apartment block was situated, only of walking and the young woman's questions as they walked. The hall-porter of the block called her Madam, and touched his forelock after calling the lift for them. Then she was aware that they were ascending in the lift, and she looked at her reflection a little timidly in the mirror panels.

The young woman smiled reassuringly. 'Don't you like lifts, Jaset? Some people can't abide them – here we are.'

The lift stopped and the gate slid back. They stepped out on to the carpet.

The apartment was large, light, modern. Jaset had never known such nice living accommodation, not even at her peak. To her it was all like something from a catalogue, something got up in a department store display window. She wanted to touch things to assure herself that they were real, yet was afraid to even move for fear of breaking something and showing herself up in this young woman's beautiful home.

'Don't just stand there, Jaset,' Sarah said. 'Do come in, the flat won't suffocate you. Let me take your coat.' She assisted the older woman, who was reluctant to part with her coat; her dress looked even more dirty in these opulent, spotless surroundings than it was in fact.

'After tea I'll show you around. I want to show you my things in the bedroom. Shall we have tea in the kitchen? I think its so much fun having it there, don't you? It's only fun in the sitting room when the maid fetches it to one.'

'I could fetch it to you, Sarah, if you wish,' Jaset offered quietly before she was able to prevent herself.

'Of course you could, but I won't hear of it. I invited you here as my guest – Mummy would be horrified if I allowed you to carry like a servant.' She moved towards the kitchen. 'Do come, Jaset, we can talk as I prepare our tea.'

Following the young woman through, Jaset found a kitchen that was straight from the pages of a glossy magazine, full of gay colours and sanded pine surfaces and ingenious labour-saving devices. What did her own kitchen amount to? – a gas-ring on the floor, odd packets of foodstuffs on the mantelpiece and a small sink in which to soak shoddy utensils, between its being used as a toilet. Immediately shutting the comparison from her mind, she drew up a stool to the bench as Sarah moved about preparing tea things.

'Do you live here with your mother?'

'Mummy? Oh no. Mummy doesn't live. Not here. Not any more. She had to go away to where it was quiet; she couldn't stand the city life.' Sarah's hands tensed nervously around the teapot, waiting for the water in the kettle to boil. 'I live here with my husband.'

'Your husband?' Jaset echoed vacantly.

'Of course, who else? And my children – Francis and David, only they're away at school at the moment. I wish my husband wouldn't send them, the vacations are always such a terribly long way off and I get very lonely at times. That's really why I spoke to you in the park,' she concluded apologetically, and continued to make the tea in silence, under Jaset's now sympathetic gaze.

Knowing the pain of loneliness herself, Jaset could readily sympathise with anyone who was lonely, even this young woman who seemingly had everything she could want.

Silence persisted at the kitchen bench as they drank tea and ate thinly sliced Madeira cake. Suddenly the younger woman said: 'Don't you sometimes get terribly afraid, Jaset?'

Curiosity set Jaset's expression for a moment. 'Afraid of anything especially?'

'No, just afraid . . . perhaps of dying or being on your own' – she shrugged and waited, hoping that the older woman would come up to expectations.

'Sometimes I'm afraid of growing old and dying without my children.'

'Oh, I didn't think you had any children . . . how many do you have?'

'Three. Laurence, James and Sarah . . . '

'My namesake! What's she like?' Sarah asked quietly, as though not to disturb a tranquil thought.

'Young. Pretty. Medium height, fair hair, hazel eyes,' Jaset replied abstractedly. 'Friendly, affectionate – thinks the world of her mother.'

Sarah realised the woman might have been describing herself, which pleased her, whether she was aware of the significance of her description was unimportant. She would do, Sarah reassured herself, having decided back in the park; Jaset would fit the bill nicely. She smiled warmly, and there was another short silence.

'Are you ever afraid at night, when you're walking on the streets at night working? Aren't you afraid then?' Sarah displayed some concern. 'Any man – I mean you don't know what he is, or what he might do to you. He might even murder you.'

'I don't know as that would be such a bad thing' – this with a wry smile.

The young woman made her move, she leant across the

bench and seized Jaset's hands intensely. 'That would be a terrible thing, Jaset, terrible! I don't ever want anything to happen to you. I don't want you to run the risk of encountering a homicidal maniac who would have his way with you and then strangle you. I don't want you to go on the streets any more.'

'There's nothing else I can do – it's quite safe really. You get to recognise the dodgy customers and know how they're likely to act. Don't worry about it.'

'But I will, Jaset. I will. I don't want you walking the streets.'

The young woman had become quite agitated, and Jaset grew a little uneasy as to her intentions. She considered whether she should leave, but had no will that would direct her up and out of the kitchen, out of the apartment back into the daylight world.

'It's my living,' she replied at last, 'I have to do it.'

'I don't care – I don't want you to continue being a prostitute and walking the streets. Too many nasty things happen to those sort of women. You can stay here. I'll speak to my husband about it as soon as he gets home – he's in oil, you know. I believe I told you, he travels around the world the whole time. He'll be delighted to have you here.' She nodded, settling the matter in her own mind, then calmly rose. 'Now when you're ready, Jaset, I'll show you around the flat – would you like some more tea first? no? Anything you want you need only say. Now where shall we start – the sitting-room?'

Jaset might have been a puppet, she rose without resistance to the young woman's jerk; then followed her about the flat like an obedient child to whom everything was carefully shown and explained. A peculiar feeling came over the older woman, she felt there was something very wrong about the whole set-up, something almost sinister, yet didn't know what. She wanted to protest, but simply couldn't summon the courage to do so; she wanted to leave, but couldn't wrench herself out of this strange young woman's circle of influence. Jaset had no idea what it was Sarah wanted with her, but she wanted something that was for sure; it was fairly obvious that she wouldn't offer her a home without seeking something in return. The prospect of that unknown, unexplained demand which she expected would either be made then or at sometime in the near future quite frightened her.

Sarah led and Jaset followed; Sarah talked and Jaset listened; Sarah questioned and Jaset answered – and still with such honesty. They were answers she would even have shrunk from the prospect of offering the social workers attached to the courts when they sought reasons or justifications for her way of life. Yet here she was imparting her innermost thoughts, closest kept reflections, wishes, hopes, secrets that had been guarded a lifetime, and to a relative stranger, a young woman who had abutted her life not two hours ago.

Alarm rose swiftly through Jaset, she so desperately wanted to run, to get away from this woman called Sarah, but couldn't; she was held there in a state of limbo, her feet not touching the ground, she was unable to progress in any direction. It was like running forward while looking the wrong way through a telescope. Then her entire life had been like that, Jaset realised, she had been travelling at quite a pace only had never achieved anything or arrived anywhere. That was the sum total of her entire life.

Scream; stop; shout; resist. Say you have to go, and leave. Jaset knew the words, they were going round and round in her head, only couldn't get them to come out. I have to go now, Sarah. Goodbye. Thank you for the lovely tea. Goodbye – there was no reaction from the young woman. Didn't Sarah hear her? Had she suddenly gone deaf? Why wouldn't her words come out? Goodbye. Goodbye. Goodbye!

As though sensing her anxiety, Sarah reached out and touched her, and almost at once Jaset felt herself grow calm. They had finished their tour and were in the large bathroom.

'I'm going to take my bath now. I always do after tea. You'll stay of course' – it wasn't a question.

Unable to make any reply, Jaset simply stood momentarily paralysed and watched the young woman undress, while the large orange bath filled from the central inlet. The professional lady could recall having had a similar bath herself in one of her apartments at her peak, it hadn't been sunken but had had all the fittings. She continued watching as Sarah stepped out of her dress, then rolled her tights down – they would have been even more of a problem to her than knickers were, and stockings always got laddered. Sarah had a nice body, quite slender, bulging slightly at the hips as one would expect after two children. Instinctively Jaset moved forward to assist her when she experienced difficulty with the fastener on her bra, just as any mother might have helped her daughter. The young woman thanked her, then finally removed her pants. Naked, she turned towards Jaset almost expectantly and stood as though waiting for her.

Hot prickles of embarrassment scored Jaset's skin. Never having been in quite this position before she didn't really know what to do or say, but was conscious to avoid letting her eyes settle on the young woman's private part, which left her the choice, it seemed, of either the breasts or looking away.

'You like my body, don't you?'

With great difficulty Jaset prevented herself simply answering in the affirmative. 'You're a lucky woman, you've kept your shape nicely.'

'Thank you, Jaset.' She stepped carefully down into the bath. 'Come and sit on the bath and talk to me – you can soap my back if you wish.'

The older woman had no particular wish to do that, but knew she probably would, as she obediently moved over and sat on the low ledge at the side of the bath.

'Why aren't you a successful prostitute any more, Jaset?' the woman lying in the bath asked in a sudden malicious tone. 'Why are you on the bottom, tramping the streets, pandering to the dregs of humankind?'

The snide attack came as a surprise, and Jaset didn't know how to answer. She wondered if her spiritual daughter was going to turn out to be a reforming, puritanical crank with less orthodox methods than the grey-haired, bespectacled dyke who had caught hold of her on the street one night, accompanied by her tall, bald, equally bespectacled crank male counterpart.

'Well?' persisted the younger woman. 'Why are you on the streets tramping for the dregs? – no, remain where you are,' she said forcefully as Jaset was about to rise.

'I was successful once,' the ageing prostitute replied meekly, 'some years ago now.'

'When – how many years to be precise?' snapped Sarah.

'Oh, I don't know, the years all seem to fuse into one long year, one year of a lifetime' – this a little wearily. 'Before the Street Act came in.'

'You blame the Street Offences Act for your sorrowful, degenerate position?'

Jaset shrugged – 'That, and the more permissive society contributed, I s'pose.'

'But surely any advancing promiscuity of society should make the cities a prostitute's paradise?' Sarah argued, curiously lighthearted now – 'more and more people to employ them.'

'Only if a girl has a place, and not necessarily then. How many men want to pay for their little bit of fun when they can pick up any young tart in a pub and do her for nothing?' Jaset sounded disgusted.

'Do you think you could get back on top if you had an apartment such as this?'

A sparkle glinted in Jaset's eyes, but vanished with the realisation that she would no longer be able to do enough business to justify such a place. Sarah reached her wet hand up out of the bath on to the woman's arm, and smiled comfortingly.

'You'll be all right, Jaset. I won't let you walk the streets any more. I'll see that you're comfortable.'

Fear caused Jaset slight nausea, only still she didn't really know what it was she was afraid of. A hot flush ran over her, and she wanted more than anything to pull away from the young woman's firm wet grip and depart, but couldn't. Instead she shortly responded to the younger woman and started gently soaping her back. Like a satisfied child Sarah made a low humming noise, and after a little while, said: 'Which incidents do you remember clearest, those with affectionate connotations or those that disgusted you?'

Jaset became still and pensive for a moment. 'There were some very nice times in my life, Sarah. Some very nice men at times.'

'I'm glad you've had some fun. We'll have a lot more together.' She squeezed Jaset's hand and smiled. 'Lots of fun, just as though I were your daughter Sarah.'

She drew the older woman's hand down into the water and stroked it across her lower abdomen and through her pubic hairs. Jaset was aware of what her hand was doing, what the younger woman was making her do; she was a little disgusted but couldn't stop herself, couldn't stop and pull her hand from the water. That weird force beyond her will continued to hold her in the young woman's control. Sarah opened her legs and inserted two of Jaset's fingers.

'Do your children ever visit you now, Jaset?' she asked conversationally – they might have been in a tea-shop.

Thoughts were running as a single track, and without concentration Jaset contradicted all she had stated before. 'I don't have any children,' she said vacantly, her fingers continuing against her wish.

Delight welled in the younger woman. 'Then my husband and I shall be your children. You'll like that. We'll be your James and Sarah.'

Her will effected greater control and the ageing prostitute's fingers massaged harder. Sarah's breathing grew heavier and faster and she closed her eyes at the tingle of excitement that quickly built up in her limbs. She tensed her lips. 'Oh Mummy, Mummy, you're making me, you're making me . . . '

Finally with a strangled, anguished cry, Jaset dragged her hand from the bath and regarded it with utter disgust. Then grabbing up a towel she rubbed it violently over her hand, trying to remove the skin along with the connotations, before fleeing the bathroom.

Still she was held in that limbo, running but not arriving anywhere; unconscious of purpose; unaware of direction; an existence of sorts suspended over a void. Perhaps eventually she would achieve positiveness, make progress and be able to walk away, to wherever she wished instead of wherever circumstances dictated.

On opening her eyes Jaset saw that she was lying across the white silk cover of Sarah's bed. The bed was large and luxuriant, and the woman's immediate reaction was that she might soil it in some way. Perhaps with her tears. She had been crying. How long she had been lying on the bed crying she didn't know, nor how she had arrived there, remembering only the bathroom incident and what somebody had been forcing her to do, and her revulsion – possibly bed had been the final submission, possibly she had given herself up completely to that other will. The prospect chilled her.

That sort of thing had gone on even in the days when she had been at the top. She had known of its existence right from the start, but had never had anything to do with those sort of carryings on. It wasn't natural, and she had always found it a little revolting. She had known quite a few girls who hadn't discriminated at all, but personally had only entertained men. No matter what women offered she wouldn't let them do it to her; she could surmount none of the barriers, not emotional, physical or spiritual. The act was unreal and immoral to her thinking.

Jaset stared vacantly across the bedroom at Sarah, who entered from the adjoining dressing room. She was wearing a dressing-gown, and moving slowly and awkwardly, Jaset noticed, but perhaps that was simply a distortion from her tear-blurred viewpoint. The older woman wanted desperately to rise off the bed and go, out of the flat and far away; only being in her presence again she couldn't move, her limbs were like lead, she was unable to raise them from the mattress. The young woman drew nearer, while fear took a firm hold on Jaset, causing her muscles to tense like rocks; she could offer no other form of resistance. She saw a bulge in the lower part of the young woman's dressing-gown and refused to believe that it was what she briefly imagined it might be.

'You've been crying, Mummy,' Sarah observed, sitting on the bed adjusting her dressing-gown. 'Tears of happiness, I hope. I don't ever want you upset.' She placed her hand on Jaset's large breast and gently caressed the nipple through her dress. 'You know what you made me do in the bath, Mummy. It was awfully nice – I'm going to do it back to you.'

Hearing her daughter's words, she was unable to reply. Words of protest, rebuke, resistance, disgust rattled around inside her head unable to find the audible outlet. She could feel the young woman's hands stroking her legs, moving on up her thighs, raising her dress, but still Jaset could make no move to prevent it happening.

'James will be so glad you're here, Mummy. We'll have such fun together.'

Sarah rolled up the older woman's girdle and sighed at the sight, then leant forward and kissed her there. Her fingers tripped over the tiers of crepey flesh around her groin like a child making delightful discoveries. She eased Jaset's legs apart, then smiled and said: 'I have something much nicer for you, Mummy – you're bound to like it.'

A plea, a prayer for the ability to move ran through the ageing prostitute's mind as Sarah opened her dressing-gown, the harness-dildo popped up like an instant erection. Jaset's prayer went unanswered, her dead limbs remained fast to the bed. She felt the contents of her stomach rise and fall as the young woman knelt between her legs.

'My husband gets so irritable at times – he'll be very relieved that I've found you' – inserting the rubber connection into Jaset, with the shorter tail-end into herself, she sighed momentously: 'Oh Mummy, Mummy,' and wept, 'that's nice,' and went to kiss the older woman's mouth in her excitement.

Recoiling fractionally by pulling her lips in, Jaset twisted her head; that was the beginning of resistance which was neatly lost in the overwhelming relief she felt.

'Mummy, don't do that,' Sarah said with alarm spreading through her.

'Fuck off! Get off – you're disgusting.'

'No! No!' – the young woman thrusted into the ageing prostitute. 'Don't resist me, Jaset, please – I want to love you, want you to stay with us!'

She poked harder now, like a stick in a rat hole, racing the older woman's growing resistance.

'Fuck off! It's dirty. Stop! – filthy, wrong!' She pushed at the young woman trying to get her off, when the dildo dislodged. Sarah clung desperately, dear life might have depended on it. 'Please don't, Jaset, please don't – I'm coming, I'm coming!' With a final thrust Jaset managed to heave her off of herself. She clambered up off the bed, wrenching her girdle and dress straight.

'Don't. Don't,' Sarah pleaded. 'You're just an old prostitute, you've got to. I'll pay you. My husband will pay you. Please. Please – he won't let me do it to him any more.'

Jaset wasn't listening, for at last she was breaking free, the young woman's will could no longer hold her. She was progressing away from this evil, immoral woman who had so devastatingly ensnared her in such a short time.

'You're a prostitute – that's why I picked you up. We'll pay you!' Desperately she chased out of the bedroom after the older woman, the artificial penis bouncing stiffly before her. 'Please, Jaset, we'll be very kind to you.' Sarah went on to her knees. 'My husband and I will be your children, you'll like that . . . '

'It's dirty and vile – you couldn't pay me enough to suffer that, you vile lesbo!' Jaset spat the words out, releasing her bile of disgust. Pulling violently into her coat, she fled the flat leaving the woman naked on her knees, whimpering.

Her flight was panic-stricken almost, blind where anger and loathing and fear raged in her; that had been a horrible experience and she would rather be dead than have to suffer it again. It made her feel dirty as she had never felt dirty before. She felt the need to wash, then open herself up and wash everything on the inside.

4

A shutter dropped through her mind and she was still at last. The horrors of the afternoon were severed from her consciousness, but lay at the back of her mind. It was doubtful whether she would ever shake free of them, but her distress was no longer so acute or immediate that she couldn't consider her situation again.

Darkness had fallen now that she had stopped running. She looked around for a clock in the street but couldn't see one and couldn't even guess at the time. There were a lot of people around, then there invariably were in Soho at most times of the day and night. The majority of them could either have been departing workers or incoming revellers, both moved with the same gait of purpose. Late evening, tennish, she guessed. Perhaps she could ask a policeman; that thought amused her. Time was rarely important, only the lack of it on occasions ever seemed so, then she supposed it was only lack of time that ever mattered anything to anyone.

Time was ceaseless, its passing sometimes tragic; life ever moving, always running out against the clock. Jaset remembered her purpose for that evening, her resolve through dire necessity; finding some male paying clients was essential or the possibility of being without a roof over her head next week was better than good. Her Armenian landlord was looking to realise more income from his property and there was no argument.

Jaset had been considering making her way back to her room to await that hour at which her kind of professional lady felt safest, but decided against it. If the Armenian wanted that extra fiver for the room anyway, she argued, then she might as well try and make full use of it immediately by finding someone at this early hour. There were several plausible places that she knew were worth trying for a client, only most of them required drinking money as the price of admission. Generally publicans didn't object to professional ladies provided they bought drinks and discreetly plied their wares. Unfortunately Jaset didn't have the coinage for the cheapest drink. There were a couple of cafés she knew, but the same terms applied, unless one had an arrangement with the proprietor. Scouring the streets for a coin wasn't really practical, there were too many already looking for that coin, and if her eyes were downcast she would miss that hesitant half-glance from a possible client in need of her spurring smile.

Her client appeared on one leg shorter than the other out of a pub doorway; another drunk, but at least it was male. Jaset apologised even though the man had lurched into her. 'I'm sorry – sorry.' There was nothing else to delay her, no light to request with no cigarette – the drunk wasn't very quick.

'I'm not,' the drunk said at last, 'not a bit sorry – madder'fact I enjoyed it.' He lurched into her again as though attempting an embrace but midway forgetting his intention.

Half-supporting him, Jaset started to walk away from the

pub; then they were simply a merry couple, and not a proposition, at which crudity people often stared.

'D'you wanna drink, darlin'?' the man slurred, doubtless imagining himself a lady's man. He had a razor-thin moustache, yellowing tombstone teeth, and he bore a marked resemblance to Tojo. 'Wanna go to the club? – fuckin' good night there.'

They continued their slightly lopsided course. Assuming the man had understood and accepted her proposition when she told him she was working, Jaset simply had to ascertain whether or not he could meet her price; if he didn't have two pounds plus cab fare then she would politely leave him against a lamp post.

'D'you wanna drink, darlin'?' Tojo asked. 'I know a fuckin' good club.'

'We'll go to my place if you have enough money.'

'I got money,' the man squawked in a sudden pocket of sobriety that was shortly lost again. 'How much d'you want, darlin'? Fifty? – a pound?'

He agreed two pounds, and Jaset hailed a cab. But the professional lady immediately began to have doubts about the man; whether she should take him to her place; whether he would be able to make the stairs, or the two-pound action. He was almost asleep in the cab. She regarded him anxiously as he slid from side to side with the vehicle's motion, and finally decided not to risk him at her place. She knew a quiet alley over the back of Charing Cross Road and redirected the driver.

Leaning against the cab, Tojo searched his pockets for change. He slid, and was bolstered by Jaset. Finding his change, he handed it to the woman. 'Think I wanna be sick,' Tojo said. 'The springs on that . . . keep having hot and cold sweats.'

The cab driver gazed almost pitifully at the ageing prostitute. 'You'll have fun with him, dear.' He took his fare and tip, then turned his cab in the narrow street and was gone.

The alley was a dead end, serving businesses only, a

couple of printers and a seamster's workshop, and was poorly lit. The light source was an archaic gas-lamp which was hemmed in on the wall by 'to-let' signs and name boards of trades past. Invariably there was waste corrugated paper from the printers' or scraps from the seamster's to serve Jaset and save her coat. She spread both paper and rags in the doorway tonight.

Getting Tojo on to the ground without his collapsing required effort on her part, and more hot and cold sweats on his. Once down he waited rather unsteadily on his knees while Jaset lay back and opened her coat, then hoisted her girdle and dress up together. The sight of naked white flesh, however blurred, was enough to stir Tojo, and he threw himself forward on to the woman, fairly knocking the wind from her, without thinking to open his flies. Jaset pushed her hand between them and unzipped his trousers. His penis cowered limply in his pants, and she extricated it from the tangle and gently pulled it to some semblance of life; a semi-stand was better than no stand at all. But no-stand was all she held in her hand again on trying to insert the member. Wearily Jaset heaved the man back up into a kneeling position; he groaned and started to fall, but she sat up and held him. At that point she considered telling him that it was all over and asking for the two pounds; it might as well have been all over for the difference the act would make to the drunk, but Jaset didn't like being cheated herself and so tried not to cheat. Do unto others as you would have them do unto you, that was the precept she tried to live by, and it pleased her whenever her existence passed on that level, however briefly.

Her efforts roused the man to almost splendid proportions, and she lay back in the doorway again, taking Tojo down with her. She felt round for him, and to her relief the phallus was still standing; she quickly inserted it, but immediately she started to work him it began to shrivel.

The man groaned. 'I can't hold it,' he muttered.

It happened to the best of men, and Jaset was a little touched by his apology – assuming his reference was to his receding part, only to discover otherwise much to her regret.

Tojo retched, and before the woman could push his weight off herself, he parted with the contents of his stomach in one fountain of vomit. Jaset felt its warmth and wetness as the fetid beer and hot dogs soaked through her dress and bra. She heaved the man off herself as he continued to retch. The smell on her dress made the woman feel quite ill.

She rose, holding her breath, and after straightening her dress and girdle, grabbed up a handful of rag ends and tried removing the sick; only the undigested sausage meat and onion was immediately removable, the rest was wet and sticky against her skin.

At that moment she considered the river was the only alternative and marginally better than the existence she was trying to cling to. What was the use? She was finished, nothing went right for her, luck had completely deserted her, why should she ever expect or hope it might change? She was still on that downhill slide and doubted she would ever stop herself, even temporarily. An ageing prostitute who had been sicked over by yet another drunk – Jaset realised how pathetic she was, how ridiculous her position was, and if it hadn't been so desperate, she might have laughed. Forty-four years old, and spent; finished, unwanted, unlucky. At her present rate she wondered what life would be like for her at fifty-four, and sixty-four. Quick and painless death was her only real hope. When? she questioned, how long did she have to suffer this pitiful existence? How many more drunks spewing over her? How many more encounters with loonies in parks? Or days without meals and mornings without cigarettes?

Pushing a handful of rags down the front of her dress to take off the surplus sick, Jaset found the smell was almost unbearable and started to retch herself. But she tensed her stomach muscles, holding down the tea and Madeira cake eaten earlier. Suddenly she wanted to cry; sicked over and didn't even have a change of clothes. One dress, one petticoat, one bra; that meant twenty-four hours without even trying for any business while she washed and dried them, as she didn't even have a coin to dry them quickly by the gas-ring. Her eyes glistened. She almost wished she had stayed with that depraved loony now.

The drunk groaned from his reclining position. He was something of a comical sight, spreadeagled, with vomit down his chest and his penis hanging from his trousers like a sick maggot. Only Jaset didn't laugh as she looked down at him, debating what to do. He should pay her the agreed two pounds, also pay her for her clothes to be cleaned, she thought, but hesitated at going through his pockets like a common thief. But she was definitely within her rights to help herself, she decided finally, and knelt down next to the man and started through his pockets.

'Wanna drink, darlin'?' Tojo slurred, startling the woman a little. 'Know a fuckin' good club.'

Jaset paused and waited for the drunk to slip back into his stupor. She found a few coins in one pocket which would contribute to cleaning her clothes, but her fee was required also. His weight was dead, pockets seemed like they were sewn, and he reeked foully. The whole scene put Jaset in mind of robbing the dead.

Suddenly a torch beam swept the alley and Jaset froze as it passed over her. The sound of familiar feet approached. Jaset turned, and looking into the beam of light, was momentarily blinded, unable to see the policeman behind it. The torch was clicked off and the constable was standing over her.

'What's going on here?' the young wolly asked in a slightly accusing tone.

Pulling her coat around herself, Jaset rose. 'Brought him down here to have a pee and he went and spewed all over me, then collapsed drunk,' she explained, more hopefully than plausibly – caught soliciting would be bad enough with her previous, but conducting her business in a public thoroughfare, that would truly cap things.

The policeman pushed his lamp on again and ran it over the man. He smiled at the white maggot glistening limply in the light.

'Sick, you say?' – he was doubtful until the woman opened her coat, offering him the sour smell. He stepped back, turning his head away. 'Make him decent. And make sure you're not here when I come by again, or I'll get the van down for you.' He would have called the van then but for making himself unpopular at the station by taking that smell in charge.

As the wolly moved away, Jaset turned back to the drunk. She zipped his member away and straightened him out a little, having decided against trying to find any more money on him. Possibly he had some somewhere, but she wasn't going to risk having her collar felt by an over-zealous young wolly on account of it. Tojo groaned again and muttered about going to a club for a drink, swearing to emphasise the good time to be had there, then fell silent. Jaset turned away, but stopped on the point of leaving, wondering if she should do anything about him; he might choke in his vomit or die of pneumonia – no, that young policeman would shortly return looking for a nicking. With that prospect looming, the ageing prostitute moved briskly out of the alley and away.

Now she had coins enough in her pocket to enter a bar or café in the hope of finding a client, but with the smell rising to her nostrils and causing her stomach to rise as if on a counter-weight, she had no inclination and made her way instead down to the public toilets at Leicester Square Underground station – a visit to try and clean herself up a little was the first priority, feeling sure people in the street were staring at her as she passed them.

The crone minding the toilets wrinkled her nose in disgust at Jaset's entrance. To her dismay Jaset remembered there was no washroom in the conveniences, only a washbasin and mirror by the exit, and the crone surely wouldn't allow a strip-wash and laundry to take place in that basin.

Jaset entered one of the cubicles under the crone's mistrusting gaze, and bolted the door. Flushing the toilet twice, she opened her dress between refills, baring her chest and shoulders; then soaking a wodge of toilet paper in the bowl, she cleaned herself and her clothes as best the facilities would allow. She made no note of passing time until hearing the shuffling outside the door, then a sharp, bony-knuckled rap on the panel.

'What're doing in there?' the crone rasped. 'I'm waiting to close.'

Suddenly? Jaset questioned, but didn't reply. Let the old bat wait, she had hours before sunrise and her return to the rafters. The thought amused Jaset, and even caused a thin smile as she straightened her dress. She felt better for the clean up, despite its fashion, but still she smelt. The sick was in her clothes, which she had wet but hadn't removed, even if she had removed them, there was then her skin, the vomit had seeped into her pores and would take a lot of removing. Rummaging in her handbag, she found a bottle of cheap scent and applied it generously, smothering the fetid beer and hot dog. Scent, however overpowering, was at least socially acceptable. Wrapping the whole in her coat, she drew back the door bolt.

The crone hovered like a hundred-and-fifty-year-old vulture. 'Waiting to close,' she whined. 'Some of us has homes to go to.'

The two women regarded each other; there was recognition in their eyes. They were years apart, and had never met, yet each instinctively knew the other, knew each had trodden the same streets and spoken the same words, had had the same encounters. Jaset was suddenly very sad at the prospect before her; the crone was the ageing prostitute's future incarnate. Was that what all professional ladies ended their days as, she questioned in an instant, public convenience attendants? She wanted to cry, and wanted to reach out to the glassy eyed crone, but instead fled up the steps and out of the toilets, into the night.

Running again. When was she going to stop running? she wondered. Why had she ever started? Her life had been a gentle, cushioned-walk at her peak; then suddenly the cushions were gone and she was running, forever running, trying to outpace the realities of her existence. They would surely be no more acute for walking, but somehow she no longer could.

The man's approach was quite unexpected – Jaset's thoughts were on another continent even though she was back moving through the noisy, restless nightlife of Soho – she hadn't seen the toff, and probably wouldn't have taken him for a prospect anyway, not in this age, pursuing her. A decade and a half ago and pandering after the woman she was then – fifteen years ago she had had toffs queuing with the worst of them. The man was young and elegant and educated, he might have been a ghost from her past, only his evening suit was up to the minute in fashion.

'Excuse me, Miss' – his voice was soft, almost apologetic, slightly embarrassed. 'Are you in business?' He seemed unsure of the question, perhaps the doubt was over the expression.

Seeing his nostrils twitch involuntarily at her perfume, Jaset knew immediately he was too much of a toff to withdraw or make any comment. She offered her affirmative smile, which even a blind man couldn't have mistaken.

'Do you have a car, dear?'

'Yes, parked round the corner.' He nodded over his shoulder, then turned. Jaset immediately followed.

The walked in silence, the young toff looking straight ahead. The woman experienced a brief bout of anxiety; perhaps he was simply walking away. She crushed the doubt, his acceptance was his nod towards the car. But perhaps she should decline on account of her sick-scented smell, make excuses and run; he would get the full draft when she opened her coat. That inclination was crushed also; he was a toff and would take her to an hotel where she could bathe first.

On turning the corner and seeing the young toff's Rolls-

Royce, the ageing prostitute was both surprised and complimented; Jaset had often imagined travelling in the Rolly
belonging to that rich client whom she would finally marry.
The chauffeur climbed out, performed his little half-bow
and opened the door for her.

Was that a sneer she detected on the flunkey's face? The
woman decided not, and climbed into the car, sinking low
into the petal-soft upholstery. She could have died there
without complaint as the car whispered out into Shaftesbury
Avenue and away through the night. The harshness and
meanness of the city might not have existed, it was outside
the car, safely at bay for those travelling within.

'What's your name?' the young toff asked, extending a
gold cigarette case.

'Jaset.' She accepted a cigarette and light. The cigarette
was foreign and the smoke strong; she was grateful for that,
it helped mask the scent smothered sick the car was quickly
souring with.

The young man switched on the air-conditioning and the
smells cleared instantly. 'The smoke is heavy,' he remarked,
'Turkish.'

They proceeded though the traffic in silence for a few
moments. This was a new peak of sorts for Jaset, and she
secretly believed at that moment in time that she had what
was needed to climb again. Not speaking of it and generally
being pessimistic was merely a game played with herself in
order to muddle Luck; it won't rain at five o'clock, she
would say when not wishing it to rain at four. She was climbing again all right, travelling in the best sort of car with a
young toff; chauffeur driven towards the very best part of
town, Mayfair, where all the toffs had once lived. Doubtless
they would be going to the very best hotel, probably the
Dorchester, where they would stay the night, and in the
morning she would have a champagne breakfast. The ageing
prostitute was suddenly feeling young and excited, and she
certainly hadn't felt like that since she didn't know when.
Making her comeback to the top flight of professional ladies

was what she was doing, being reborn almost. Yes, that was what this was, her rebirth. A rather discreet apartment in Mayfair, where she had been before, with an appointment book always full, but occasionally breaking off to take tea with friends somewhere. Sipping tea delicately from real bone-china and nibbling thinly sliced Madeira cake would be very nice, she decided.

The young toff had been saying something, but Jaset hadn't heard a word from the cloud she was floating on. 'Beg pardon?' she said, just stopping short of calling him Sir. She sucked on her Turkish cigarette.

'The question of fee, Jaset. I think we ought to settle it here.' He produced a neat hide wallet and opened it carefully. 'How much do you charge?'

Lack of money had always embarrassed her in various fashions, especially never asking for it when it fell due, but here with the situation completely reversed, if the man had asked for her services gratis, she would have agreed. 'Well,' she began through her embarrassment, 'I always say the client is always right.'

A blank expression dropped over the man's face. 'Always right? Oh, I see' – he smiled. 'Yes indeed. Fee on approval is an excellent arrangement. I'm sure your client will be most satisfied – my name is James,' he added conversationally.

Fear leapt through Jaset, locking her limbs. Visions of that loony lesbo from the park filled her inner eye; she had had a husband called James and they had lived in the better part of town, while this James had spoken of her client in the third person. On first trying to speak Jaset's lips simply trembled, and not even a stutter emerged. Finally she managed: 'Are you married, James?'

The young toff smiled deprecatingly. 'Naturally not.'

She believed him, but that wasn't really conclusive; the business arrangement wasn't after all what it had at first appeared. 'You said, my client – not yourself?'

'Goodness no, Jaset.' He took her hand and patted it

reassuringly. 'A young man who has just reached the age of consent. I want him to experience a . . . well, thorough ditching, we might say. An initiation by a real professional.' He smiled knowingly and patted her hand again. 'I hope you won't take exception to my little deceit, Jaset. I do assure you he's a thoroughly charming young man. Somewhat shy, that's all.'

Jaset was too relieved to take exception; fortunately her client was male, another toff. She was perfectly satisfied with James's explanation of the procedure. Lots of young men were shy when it was their first time. Briefly she remembered Kenny Clubfoot and his first time behind the cycle sheds. She would be gentle with the shy toff, she decided, ease him in carefully. Sometimes foreskins strangulated or dragged on that first time in and could put young men off altogether; she would be extra careful.

It wasn't the Dorchester or any of the other splendid hotels she was taken to – Jaset was only marginally disappointed. The car turned through Park Lane and finally drew up at a sumptuous apartment block in Curzon Street. The flunkey there who bounded forward from the lighted entrance to open the door was surely more obsequious than any flunkey even the best hotel sported. The lift swished them up to the penthouse flat in a trice and the toff whisked the ageing prostitute along the deep-pile carpeted corridor to the apartment.

The flat was warm, and filled with whispers and expensive perfumes and cigarette smoke, all of which she found difficult identifying through her own scent. For some reason there was total darkness, which made Jaset very curious. She was blinded and disorientated and clung tightly to the toff as he led her, as if by radar, first one way through the apartment then another, round and round until at last they stopped. A light was switched on and instantly attacked the woman's eyes, causing another kind of blindness.

'Will you get undressed here?' the toff said. 'Roger will be in shortly – when you're quite ready, that is, Jaset.'

When the woman's eyes had adjusted to the light sufficiently to enable her to see, James was gone, and to her amazement Jaset found herself in a completely magnolia bedroom; carpets, curtains, bed, walls. She was the only other colour in the room, and she was quite lacking colour in the fawn coat and cream dress. She smiled thoughtfully, somehow a white room seemed very appropriate for both her rebirth in the profession and the young man's initiation – at that juncture both were virgins of sorts, and would soon be virgins plus one.

After slipping out of her coat and carefully folding it on a chair, Jaset moved about the room, looking at things and into things, deciding on a bedroom similar to this when she took her new flat and practice. The whole place reeked of affluence and success, and everyone knew success bred success. The right situation for an experienced woman was practically a licence to print money. She could already sense herself ascending the ladder, and it was a very good feeling after having paddled around in the mire of misfortune for so long.

Fixed to the wall was a large mirror which she paused in front of, its effect was most strange and she had never seen a mirror quite like it before. It had a greyish opaqueness which gave an almost frightening realness to the two dimensional aspect. While standing there in front of the mirror, perception clouded and the ageing prostitute momentarily imagined she could step into the identically opposite world being reflected, that grey ghost-like world of reflected magnolia. Emerging from her reverie, Jaset remembered her purpose, she was there on business, the kind of business it was both a relief and pleasure to find after the past few days.

She reached round and unfastened her dress, which was still wet and had a large brownish stain from Tojo's vomit; it was a good feeling getting out of it along with her wet petticoat. A fine figure Jaset considered she cut in her bra and girdle; large thrusting breasts, nicely swelling hips, flat tummy, strong legs and arms; she would defy any man not to get a stand-on over her – drunks resembling Tojo being the exception! What a pity it all sagged on removing the support, she thought a little sadly, as she regarded what she had in the mirror. The cause was minor, once on top again she would take some correcting measures, get a nice massage and have her muscles toned up with some electric treatment, nothing would sag then.

On pulling her bra away, melon-like tits squelched and sagged wearily, Jaset sighed in the same fashion. Why wasn't the whole of the breast erectile rather than just the nipple? she considered a little dismayed. She raised the limp flesh and put her nose to it, the smell of sick remained in her skin beneath the scent. She would have liked to have gone to the bathroom and washed but didn't dare leave the room.

The ageing prostitute's sagging, rippling, uncontrollable flesh that spilled from the tatty clothes was an amusing, yet at the same time disturbing sight to the young toffs and their lovely ladies as they viewed her through the two-way mirror. There were twenty or so of them jostling quietly for the best view through the mirror, some silent, some giggling nervously. Generally they were revolted, even frightened, if only of what she represented, yet they couldn't not look, not with knowing that she now existed, knowing she was there in the next room waiting to perform her animal business with childlike naïvety. She resembled a sow awaiting a boar for the purpose of begetting more pigs, only hers wasn't the sludge filled sty, but James's beautiful magnolia room; and she was awaiting Roger, who looked quite magnificent in his togs and would give her quite a surprise. Tittering ran through their ranks when they saw Jaset roll her girdle down and step out of it. The tiers of fat quivered visibly through the mirror as she scratched her pubic hairs; they hooted as she pulled open her vagina and inspected the orifice, then inserted her finger and finally smelt it. Then James's appearance in the magnolia room swiftly brought an air of sobriety to the spectators.

Jaset turned a little startled by James, and modestly tried

to cover herself – no hands could have been large enough! She wished she had a dressing-gown, knowing the disadvantage she was at with him still dressed.

'Very nice,' the toff said, 'I'm sure Roger will be delighted. Are you ready now, Jaset? – did you want anything first, refreshment of some kind?'

The woman shook her head, finding herself somewhat tongue-tied.

'Well, just hop into bed then' – he folded back the bedclothes.

The sheets were silk, magnolia, warm, soft – the kind she hoped to be wrapped in when her number was thrown – and she purred mentally at their touch. What relief she saw with this new life at this rediscovered peak. She settled down in the bed which fitted her so well it might have been bespoke. Her hope was that young Roger wouldn't be too long appearing, lest she should slip into sleep in this euphoria where she re-experienced almost forgotten delights of comfort – at such sublime moments the truly deserving passed peacefully away.

'I'm going to put the light out, Jaset. You understand that Roger is very shy – and you will please be patient with him.'

The room fell into darkness and the toff vanished with the soft click of the door. Silence prevailed, while Jaset strained her ears for any sound of Shy Roger's approach. She thought she heard distant giggles, possibly a party way off in the night. There was no indication of her client drawing near. Her eyes were already growing heavy with staring into the darkness, she knew sleep would be so easy, but resisted.

Come on, Roger, hurry up! Her hand moved under the sheets to her vagina and she inserted her finger again, making sure she was sufficiently moist for penetration, nothing was worse for a young male virgin than dryness. Jaset knew all about love eggs. Some professional ladies inserted them to make themselves moist and a little tighter through their toning effect, some used them just for the nice feeling they supposedly gave. But she didn't really approve of love eggs and couldn't afford them anyway. Fortunately she was sufficiently moist tonight, but her finger worked up a little more lubricant just to be on the safe side.

As she lay there Jaset tried imagining what the young man would be like; tall and dark, short and fair, hairy chest, a small member – why should he be so shy? Perhaps he was deformed. One or two of the clients at her previous peak had been deformed, gimpy legs, humpy-backs and the like, some of them hadn't been able to get women on merits. No, Roger wouldn't be deformed, young toffs never were, they had to meet royalty and so any infants born deformed were instantly put down by the discreet family doctors.

Suddenly she saw shy Roger in her inner eye and her thoughts embraced him. He was young, nervous, honest, sincere; he would know loyalty, and respect her for the kindness she would show him. Jaset would be so kind, and would give the young man such gentle satisfaction that he would want to keep her, set her up in a flat, and keep her exclusively to himself.

Weariness gradually yielded more and more ground to sleep as she continued her vigil, conjuring further images of shy Roger in the darkness.

The ground between consciousness and unconsciousness had been reached by Jaset when the door opened and her client entered. Her mood then was beautiful, a delicate euphoric quality held her suspended, she was waiting to love and be loved; her purpose was no longer strictly business, but love with a capital L. Roger. She believed she spoke his name, and that he answered with hers – he was her knight, and had come for her. She was ready for him.

Suddenly her existence was seamless, she couldn't discern reality from non-reality, perhaps there was no dividing line, perhaps one stepped at will between the two. She didn't know then if Roger was a dream or reality when he pulled the bedclothes back and slid on to her. She felt him but couldn't see him in the darkness, she felt him awkwardly

position himself only couldn't hold him for his flesh had a
strange woolly touch to it. Roger, Roger, my love, her mind
screamed a thousand times, her breathing suddenly racing
his, her rhythm completely complementing his; that was
reality, she was caught in a vortex of passion, riding her new
wave of life. That was reality! Her Prince was between her
legs thrusting and withdrawing; her knight, the one she had
been waiting for all her life. Oh Jesus, Mary, she cried in
delight, surging and ebbing, surging and ebbing, giving him
the time of his life. Her Prince clung tighter, his embrace
almost crushing her, pushing and pulling from reality to
non-reality and back.

Daggers of light stabbed painfully in her eyes for the
second time that night; then she saw her lover for the first
time and tried to scream, but the power of speech had cruelly
deserted her. Suddenly it was a nightmare, the most horrible
nightmare; she had slipped permanently into hideous non-
reality. Her lover for all she could tell was a giant chimpanzee, its grip all powerful, paralysing; Jaset couldn't shift
him at all, it clung and continued to thrust into her. Why
couldn't she speak? How was this Roger? Lights started to
whirl in the magnolia room – who would decide if her lover
was satisfied? Voices were heard then, excited, drunk,
frightened, laughing, screeching; people were pushing
through the door into the room, young toffs and their lovely
ladies carrying bottles of champagne. Jaset's look pleaded
desperately with them for help, but they took no notice, they
continued screeching and laughing at the scene. The chimpanzee's endeavours were ceaseless, its passion implacable,
and its every thrust brought greater hoots of laughter from
the toffs. Jaset struggled more frantically to extricate herself,
but was firmly pinioned. She screamed and begged for help,
but the words flew around inside her head without emerging.
The toffs began exploding champagne corks, intermittently
showering the bed between swilling the wine and spilling it
down their beautiful clothes and over the beautiful carpet.
The wildness of the nightmare increased and spread like an

epidemic, more corks exploded and bottles flew about along with their contents. A lovely lady leapt on to the bed and started ripping her clothes off in her excitement, a young toff joined her and when he was naked also, they laid down and started fucking in a halting frenzy. The turmoil of noise and confusion around the bed assaulted the brain until at last it seemed that everyone was hysterical, when a champagne bottle was swung, catching the chimpanzee on the back of the head. Jaset screamed harder in muted terror, instantly believing her lover was dead, for it had stopped its seemingly irrepressible thrust, and for the first time she noticed that this wasn't a chimpanzee's plug face but the angelic face of a young man. The body in the ape skin was promptly pushed off her and one of the other toffs immediately mounted her thighs and continued, the interruption barely noticeable. Jaset noted that a lot of the toffs were naked now with their young ladies and clambering on the bed, doing and being done, partners changing rapidly and without order. Jaset was shunted around among the utter confusion until at last she was missed by her would-be pinion and broke free of the hysterical tangle. She started to run but was immediately tripped to the floor – it was Roger's body she had fallen over. She paused and raised his broken, bleeding head to her naked lap, his congealing blood spread through her pubes and on her thighs. Leaning forward, she kissed her beloved's lips before laying his head carefully on the floor. The professional lady rose up and fled the apartment, and down the building's eight flights of stairs; the flunkey held the main entrance door for her, touching his forelock as she fled through the sumptuous reception and out into the street.

Along one street and down another Jaset chased, she fled completely naked through the world, running, forever running from the world she was out of touch.

The Mayfair street she found herself on was known to her, and led her into the small market, where at her peak she had had an apartment. Harry Bleedew had managed her then. Her name had been on the blazing bell-push which was now displaying the name, Janet Orga. The ageing prostitute saw the youngish professional lady emerge on to the pavement in front of her, it might have been herself at her peak, poodle dog and all, she reflected, as she ran on past her.

She wouldn't stop now until she dropped or was arrested or knocked down.

Part Two
Janet

*"Beautiful butterfly,
rare specimen,
needs mounting."*

5

There were some strange people about, Janet thought as she watched the woman charge past her like the bastard of all time was after her, wanting to give her a taste. Generally she had the facility to disregard the cranks and freaks completely, but considered fleetingly what might have caused the woman to be in such a state. When there was no immediate answer, she disengaged the thought.

The early morning was pleasant, and ordinarily Janet might have enjoyed the walk around Berkeley Square – she rarely stepped out at two a.m. for obvious reasons. Even in Mayfair there were the lice-like crotch-hoppers who didn't know or follow the handbag rule; if a woman in business wasn't carrying a handbag then she didn't want tapping. That morning she had her departed temporary flat mate's poodle in tow. Reluctantly she had dressed, having finished work, to trot the dog out rather than having it mess in the flat; if it did that just once more it would go, she wouldn't wait for Masca to come back and collect it, the bastard thing would go out right through the window.

Janet hated animals, dogs and cats especially, poodles most particularly. Lots of prostitutes kept poodles, the breed being synonymous with the profession, and dating back to the early mademoiselles who first employed the little dogs as crotch-lickers. Probably the professional ladies who kept them today – her departed flat mate included – used them for the same purpose. Janet wondered what some of the pricks' reactions would be if they knew a dog had been down there first; that thought amused her. Following a dog in was very appropriate for the majority of the clients, and a mongrel dog at that.

The dog stopped for no purpose that Janet could see other than to waste time, so she dragged on its lead, having no intention of being caught loitering and indicted as a common prostitute. She made regular donations to detectives who rang her bell, besides what the Lord Peter claimed he donated on her behalf for her protection, but that didn't prevent some busy wolly springing her. The poodle tried digging its heels in and nearly got its neck broken when it was yanked along. Eventually it would learn that the woman was stronger.

Crossing the road with the poodle behind her, Janet saw a car creeping down towards the bottom of the Square and guessed what the pathetic driver was after. He would be a crotch-hopper belonging to that inadequate breed who drove super-sleek phallic symbols; if only they could have inserted those instead of their limp flags then their orgasms might achieve sublimity. Each had the same style, the car was always mentioned at least four times at the opening of any conversation, for they believed that any woman would happily slither out of her pants at the mere sight, and come at the prospect of a ride.

The car crawled along behind her, and she sensed rather than saw it. Janet maintained her course without so much as an oblique glance at the vehicle as it drew alongside. She knew the driver was ogling her, willing her to look, and she anticipated his unconscious thoughts: Look at me, look, look! I'm exposing myself to you.

'Excuse me, Miss, could you tell me where . . . ?'

That tack got him nowhere. He was completely ignored. The woman obviously couldn't have seen his expensive car properly. Without doubt he would make contact when he reached the next pool from the street lighting.

'Come for a ride?' – the words might be magic. Could he hear the young woman panting at the prospect? Or was it the dog?

Glancing at the driver for the first time, Janet sneered. The police whistle she pulled from her pocket had belonged to a policeman who she thought meant a lot to her once upon a time.

'You have three seconds to split, before I blow this,' she threatened, raising the whistle to her pursed lips.

Alarm spread rapidly through the crotch-hopper; the woman's refusal was inconceivable, but he didn't argue. Accelerating like the maniac driver on a wages-snatch, he caught the side of a stationary car, but didn't stop. Janet smiled at that, it almost made the nuisance of the dog worthwhile. She continued around the bottom of the Square towards home.

Two women were moving purposefully towards her, one fairly young, the other a good deal older. The older woman had a foreign look about her, Latin, Janet guessed, and smiled inwardly at marking the women. The younger woman was in the same business as herself, and Janet was sure she had seen her occasionally about the Market; she would have had a lock-up there, and was now obviously on her way home with her maid.

At one time Janet had employed a maid, or rather had had a woman forced on her by Harry. The real purpose of the woman hadn't been to keep the flat straight or act as a receptionist, but to keep tabs on her and report to Harry; then most maids were loyal to the Lord Peters. Finally she had made Janet paranoid, and when the big showdown had come, Harry had capitulated and removed the woman. Janet valued her privacy too much to tolerate another maid; however, she did call in regular housekeeping services from an agency, and when necessary her receptionist was the mute entryphone.

Janet's eyes measured the two women, and despite their affluent appearance and apparent high degree of professionalism, she knew where the young brass would finish up. The same place most of them did, as a maid to another or on the skids, where she had no intention of finishing herself after her own term of usefulness. There was brief searching acknowledgement from the chaperoned brass when her eyes met Janet's, but the latter cut her dead, silently cursing the dog which had so easily marked her. Janet wanted no contact with other professional ladies, not even those operating in her immediate vicinity of Shepherd Market, nor did she want any sense of belonging to their little society. She moved away out of the Square and up into Curzon Street.

Home was a neat four-roomed flat in Shepherd Market. Tucked away between Piccadilly, Park Lane and Curzon Street, the Market was the best part of town. There one frequently encountered lords and knights and movie stars, and could sit outside the little cafés in the summer and watch the entire range of the social structure ply by, from the young queen who was the current talk of the town on account of his whatever success, to the old dosser who collected cigarette butts and begged pennies.

Generally Janet was completely indifferent to the male population, rank notwithstanding; men were no longer anything more than currency to her, either they could afford her price or they couldn't, and when they couldn't she didn't allow them to waste her time. She was a receptacle to their passion, offering synthetic pleasure for a price. Her price was high, but even so if she could cheat and stint on what was exchanged for that rate then she would, and did regardless of client. While like the pathetic, masochistic cretins she always considered most of them to be, they came pandering back for the same treatment in smaller, more expensive quantities, and Janet laughed all the way to the bank.

Janet Orga. The name burned out in the darkened doorway where she had forgotten to switch the bellpush light out when finishing work; having the stupid dog to think about was the cause. There was a man waiting at the door, which wasn't surprising. With her light left on men would be pushing the bell all through the night; the lost, hungry, weary and in need, not that it would do them much good, as around two o'clock depending on how she felt, Janet usually disconnected the bell in her flat. Possibly that man could have been the filth, she couldn't see him very clearly, but as soon as he spoke she knew instantly that he wasn't a detective.

'I've been ringing the bell,' the prospect said, 'there's no reply.' He seemed puzzled.

'If you've been ringing my bell, then possibly it's because I'm down here. What d'you want?'

The man shuffled with embarrassment, making no reply as the woman opened her door and switched on the entrance light. A cretin, just as Janet suspected, as she considered she had done quite enough business for one day; so unless the trick had a particularly worthwhile price, double-time and inconvenience money at that hour. She stood in the entrance and held the door, the poodle started up the stairs on its own.

'Do you have thirty pounds?' she asked the still silent man.

'What for?' he managed through surprise. 'All right?' – the prospect of losing thirty was difficult to reconcile.

'Do you work all night, sweetheart?' she offered, purposely like a tart.

'Ten pounds?'

He immediately increased his offer to twelve when the woman shook her head, then fifteen. The man was desperate. He probably had an erection there at the door, and in the event the woman knew that on climbing the stairs she could bring him so close to orgasm to have it all over within a minute of allowing the prick to push up her, perhaps he wouldn't even make the sheaf.

'Twenty will get you a short time, lover,' she said spitefully, using the parlance of an epoch she had never known, really not wanting to make the effort. 'Then I'll be doing you a favour.'

The man breathed once more, and parted with his twenty pounds. Janet started work as she led him up to the flat, his five by five was standing proud, and when her hand stroked it, the man's intake of oxygen immediately increased.

Four minutes, five at the outside, and she was showing the slightly stunned man back down the stairs, his jollys off. Janet bolted the door after him. If inconvenienced, the fee was a handy little extra.

Wearily she climbed back up the stairs. She noticed the stair-carpet was bitty, and would have to remember to phone the agency tomorrow and have Duncan, her favourite resting actor, come round and clean for her. Locking the door at the head of the stairs and putting the light out, she went to her work room. Compared to the work rooms of a lot of professional ladies, Janet's was quite acceptable; it was simply a woman's bedroom which fortunately she didn't have to sleep in. Lots of girls had only the one room to live, work and sleep in, or else had lock-ups and lived off the manor, like chaperoned brass she had seen, which was almost as bad. The entire flat Janet had was very accommodating as a matter of fact, and not really too expensive at a hundred and ninety pounds a week; there were girls paying eighty and ninety for single rooms, without the area, facilities or trade that she had. The flat was safe, the landlord had been straightened; so she wasn't likely to be evicted, not by the landlord anyway. But her man would without doubt evict her the instant her earning power dwindled, Harry Bleedew was no philanthrope. When that day came Janet wouldn't mind one little bit, because by then she figured on having enough bread saved to enable her to retire comfortably, so all she would need was the word. Having seen the old drippers hopefully dragging their cunts along the street, she had no intention of joining them when her time arrived. Nor of joining the crank she had seen earlier.

The biggest part of her earnings was banked. The amount varied of course, but over the weeks she earned on average between six and seven hundred pounds. Believing three hundred to be the average, her Lord Peter took two-fifty, including rent, for looking after her, leaving Janet fifty to pay her living and running expenses. Cleverly she declared an average of twenty-eight pounds a week as a freelance film production secretary, and kept the tax man happy with her donations; she paid her correct insurance contributions also, wanting her full pension on retiring like any hard working woman! Janet's actual cost of living wasn't high, she could even have managed on that official twenty-eight pounds after all official deductions. She didn't smoke, and drink wasn't her comforter; there was no time for the movies, theatre or eating out at night, apart from during her period when she couldn't get fully booked with specials. She ate little more than one meal a day, and her snacks amounted to hardly anything. Unfortunately she could claim tax relief neither for the laundry of the fourteen pairs of sheets a week, nor the contraceptives she bought wholesale. Flat heating and cleaning cost money, though not such a great deal.

The woman had worked at the figures and had considered them many times. Expecting her present earning capacity to last until she was thirty-five, she then estimated to be holding something in the region of one hundred and fifty thousand, which wisely invested, as indeed a lot of it already was, would adequately keep her without too much hustle and trouble when she finally quit the business.

Another six years of spreading her legs and indulging pricks; that prospect didn't exactly delight her, but she suffered it with a wry smile every time she checked her bank balance. Everything to her was business, plain and simple, with nothing more involved, and fucking really meant nothing more to her than a swollen bank balance.

Lifting the used contraceptive off the carpet, Janet carried it through to the bathroom and flushed it down the toilet; one more arrow into the Pope's heart. If his God was so omnipotent the rubber would perish in saline water and its contents become children of the sea, then he would have no cause for complaint.

The sheath wasn't Janet's sole protection, she wasn't so naïve, but took the pill also. A pregnancy and costly abortion wasn't even on the bottom of her list! She was put out enough over her monthly bleed, and the money lost as a result – there were one or two special pricks who were gross enough and rich enough to help her out over those lean periods, but even so eating or a little buggery didn't earn the equivalent of twenty straights a day – she didn't use cotton wool or a diaphragm to enable her to continue with straight fucking during her periods.

After filling her bath, Janet stepped out of her négligé and into the water. She always took a bath after the day's long grind – cleanliness was the closest she ever got to godliness – to try and wash away the connotations of her often depraved clients. Christ, how they sickened her at times.

What manner of creatures were they, she frequently wondered, who would give a strange woman their presumably hard earned money to open her legs for them so that they could submerge their often inadequate, frightened, grotesque personalities into flesh that was softer and warmer, but had no more feeling for them than the ox hearts of their youth? What did they really want? Or truly hope to find there? On occasions they disgusted her to the marrow, when she felt the inclination to vomit; even then there were those who would have seen that as a new diversion and paid extra for it.

They were men, some with wives and families. But Janet sometimes questioned what sort of men they were away from where she met them, in their family homes, in their marriage beds; according to their terms of reference, did they long to divert and pervert the union, but simply lack the courage to broach the sordid form with their wives? Did they want to insert inanimates there? Rim their anuses? Be punished? Dress in their wives' underwear? Want their wives to jerk them off, fork themselves off, or urinate over them? What of the wives? They made Janet more curious. Some men spoke of their wives during waves of guilt, and she could often match-type a wife to a prick. It was the wives she sometimes felt sorry for; loyal, trusting, waiting while their bodies decayed. Frequently some of the men she had in were going to meet their wives somewhere in town for a meal or theatre immediately from having dallied with her. Janet would have betrayed those bastards to their wives had she known them; those women deserved better. Women always deserved better in her opinion. Men were loathsome pigs without exception, pigs deserving castration, her own living notwithstanding; that thought caused her to smile. A world full of castrated men might be pleasant at that.

Janet soaped herself meticulously, and carefully scoured her skin with a brush, that not only cleansed the last vestige of the day-long filth away, but also toned her skin and induced relaxation. She gently inserted the wedge of soap between the lips of her vagina, finding it warm and firm and comfortable there, and she laid back in the water. Janet eased the soap out and slid it in again, it was a decidedly nice way to wash that part; easing the soap out again, it was supplanted with her fingers to work a lather. Immediately she could feel her pulse quickening, the exercise never failed to cause that reaction when alone in her bath or bed – it was never the same in her work-bed with a man paying her to fork-off, then it was merely another form of prostitution and simulation. She knew she shouldn't masturbate really and to resist she crossed her legs to prevent herself. But it was so nice. Finally she resisted there, she would do it in bed. To drop off to sleep enfolded by that feeling of warmth and well-being which masturbation gave her was much nicer than suffering the anticlimax of stepping from the cooling bath afterwards.

Pulling the towelling bathrobe around herself, after finally rinsing herself beneath the shower, Janet raised her négligé off the floor for the linen basket, leaving the bath for the cleaner tomorrow. Négligés, like sheets, were an item in need of constant changing. The négligé was changed every day, and sometimes twice if unreasonably stained, while the sheets were changed twice a day, every day.

'You bastard dog!' Janet screamed on entering the kitchen and smelling its relief before seeing it on the floor. 'You bastard – what did I take you for a walk for?'

The dog cowered in the only clear corner of the kitchen, the pile of mess between itself and the woman. Frantically clawing at the air in a brief surge of irrational frustration, Janet wanted to throttle the dog; her second thought was to wipe up the shit with the animal before throwing it out the window. But finally she threw it into a cupboard and slammed the door on its yelping. It could suffocate for all she cared, her lodger should have taken the bloody thing with her on departing after her brief stay.

With half a box of tissues laid over the offending mess, Janet lifted it from the floor. It followed the semen skins, and finally the woman sprinkled disinfectant liberally.

The dog continued to yelp as Janet heated some milk to take up to bed with her, but the sounds were muffled and certainly wouldn't keep her awake, no more would stabs of conscience. If the dog suffocated that would be Masca's fault for not having taken it.

Her bedroom was special, it was situated in the front immediately above her workroom – there was a smaller bedroom and the sitting-room situated in the top part of the flat also. Janet liked her bedroom and enjoyed being there most of all. It was decorated in a pastel shade of green, and filled with curios and pieces she had collected, some taken from her previous life.

There hadn't been much she had wanted from the home

she had had in that previous existence, just one or two pieces; a statuette, a travel-clock, the framed photograph of him. No affection or sense of loss prompted her leaving her ex-husband on show, his picture was there as a reminder of what had been, and as a warning of what she never wanted involvement with again. Here she could reflect on that period without pain or bitterness, without any longing for revenge or to hurt back – perhaps she was paying all men in her way for what he had done to her. She could even smile at that period, though the thought of Juliet still piqued her a little. She hadn't been offered custody of her daughter, and preferred not to see her at all rather than once a fortnight; but for Juliet she could easily have dismissed the man completely. One day in the not too distant future she would make the acquaintance of her daughter once more and would offer her the world, then she would be able to afford the world for her.

It hadn't seemed such a bad life with Joe in the early stages. At the outset it had been quite pleasant – fun even, yes, they had had fun. She had just started her second year at Bristol University, and life had been the usual ball for students with exams a lifetime away and graduation at another age it seemed. Her part of the City had been dominated by the university, and the police station for obvious reasons.

Joe was a policeman, but not the kind that normally had many dealings with boisterous students. He was a detective; anonymous, insidious, ambitious; they were the words he had once used to describe himself – he hadn't stated that he was faithless, without feeling and cruel also.

She had been aware of him at the party, though hadn't been aware of his being a policeman; there were several present, their presence was social, not official. The CID had apparently supplied the blue-films – certainly the bluest Janet had ever seen; male and female homosexuals, school children, straight heterosexuals; plating and masturbating, **sexual diversions in every form, nothing seemed to have** been left out. But despite the carnal onslaught, in parts the films were surprisingly subtle and extremely erotic for that fact.

Drink, which invariably made men impotent and women randy, affected no one then it seemed, only the flickering two dimensional images of erotica had any effect. Some of the girls were touching themselves while others were coming straight; men were in difficulty too until someone suggested a daisy chain; the proposition was accepted instantly. Clothes were shed and people indulged in the increasingly necessary relief, the more inhibited finally being caught up and swept along with the uninhibited; suddenly men started grabbing women, while women grabbed men. Without doubt Janet knew it would be Joe who made a move for her, he had been watching her since she first arrived. The girlfriend she had been with was lost, forgotten as Joe raped her. The film flickered on as phalluses flashed with naked bodies, and in the tangle it became difficult to distinguish one kind from another.

Joe had been fun then, generous, thoughtful even, and quite gentle in his own brutal fashion. On occasions at first he was kind and considerate, but those qualities were shortly lost in the contempt of familiarity. He was a detective climbing and she was his girlfriend, when he had time. With her pregnancy she quit university and became Joe's wife, when Joe had time. Joe didn't often have time. Time was always in short supply when one was clawing for some perch at the top.

The pregnancy was regrettable, so was their marriage, but most regrettable Janet found was the child, the actual birth of their daughter. She wished Juliet had been aborted, or that she had gone away and given birth to her on her own without marrying the father. Increasingly it seemed to Janet that they were no more than an inconvenience to Joe and his career, a dalliance from his main purpose, a distraction he wasn't prepared to suffer generously. She wished her daughter didn't exist, yet grew more and more fond of her the more abstracted the relationship with Joe Detective became. .

People admired Juliet. She was a beautiful child, who took after her mother in looks; people admired Janet also and complimented her still, especially Ursula Ulick, one of her former lecturers at the university.

Ursula first called round on Janet in the police married quarters during one of her free afternoons, ostensibly to have a look at the baby. The woman was some ten years senior to her, and Janet had always liked her for the friendly independence she exuded; she was without fawning insincerity. Ursula was patient and tolerant, and people knew instinctively that they could talk intimately to her without fear of being chided or rebuffed, especially young women; she offered, it seemed, the qualities of priest, mother and benign aunt all at once, yet was rarely patronising.

On Ursula's second visit, Janet poured out her story on a flood of tears. The older woman comforted her where they sat on the sofa, taking Janet's head to her bosom in a half-embrace and gently stroking her hair. Sympathy prevailed, and the weeping subsided, and she eased Janet's head down on to her lap, where she continued to stroke her soft auburn hair. Every detail of her married life Janet imparted. Ursula understood the multifaceted problem, some of the causes and aggravations and she was able to justify on either or both sides, while she condemned others.

For the first time in a long while Janet felt at peace. She had never known such peace to juxtapose her marriage, and had never known a friend so evidently kind and generous, or a woman so warm and faithful. Ursula might suddenly have been her mother, and Janet wanted to climb back into the womb, to the permanent safety and comfort it would afford from the nerve-jagged irritation existence had been reduced to through her marriage. She snuggled her head in the centre of Ursula's lap; even the woman's perfume was pleasing, she found, in fact everything about her was.

Realising finally what was happening there, Janet became

a little afraid. Not afraid on her own account, because she was aware of herself reacting and the prospect was really quite exciting, she found. What scared her was the fact that she may have seriously misjudged Ursula, that the woman might not love her in the same way her own love was manifesting itself. Or if so, that that love might turn bitter, and their relationship deteriorate as hers had with Joe Detective. Relief was all that the man sought in their marriage, an act that was more acceptable to him than masturbating, while Janet infinitely preferred masturbation. He had emotionally debased the act, which with him was now an unpleasant effort at best, at worst an obscenity.

Then, as she lay on the couch with her head nestled so comfortably in Ursula's lap, Janet knew she wouldn't be able to indulge in the sexual act with her husband ever again and derive any enjoyment from it. He abused her, and all he could do would be to continue that abuse and force their relationship further apart. There was nothing left between them, only their daughter Juliet – that was the bitter regret.

Janet dug her fingers into the woman's thighs and pressed her face harder into her as if to be as physically close to the spirit of womanhood as possible. She wanted an indication from Ursula, desperately needed some positive gesture of acceptance. I love you, love you – the words ran through her mind and they terrified her – love me too. She was so afraid there would not even be tacit acceptance. The woman would be kind, and gentle, and very gently reject her.

'Janet.'

At first she didn't hear her name spoken or notice the woman's hand at the back of her neck. But when her name was spoken again she turned her head slightly and looked up. The older woman was gazing down at her, neither smiling nor scowling, but Janet knew in a pocket of clearness that everything would be all right between them.

Brushing the newly formed tears from Janet's eyes, Ursula leant forward and kissed her softly on the lips. There was nothing that needed saying; both women were motionless as they regarded one another, understanding intuitively, finding equanimity then.

Janet said quietly: 'I love you, Ursula, love you very dearly. I can't help myself any more.' Tentatively she reached up and placed her hand on Ursula's breast.

Ursula smiled affectionately. 'I know' – simply.

Rumours started as Ursula's visits grew more frequent, they were inevitable, for policemen's wives were no less gossips than other bored women, and they were surrounded by policemen's wives in the block of flats. However, rumours were no less malicious or hurtful for all their inevitability.

Eventually Joe Detective picked up the whispers, which was inevitable too, his reaction also. Janet wasn't at all surprised when the man, true to form, tried to verbally destroy Ursula; he achieved little but to further confirm how totally lacking sensibility he was. The third-degree he gave her got him nowhere.

Tenacity was the stuff detectives were made of, Joe being no exception, while cunning was what sustained them.

The man indulged rape as far as Janet was concerned; they were man and wife and in their marriage-bed, but that neither gave him licence nor justification now that mental and emotional compatibility no longer existed. Every sexual connection was without her consent, but she knew any argument as such would be futile, so didn't even bother – besides, to whom could she cry rape? The police? That was her husband, he was the law, official and otherwise.

Once again Janet suffered in silence when the man, after his late tour of duty, woke her up and pushed her legs open in the bed and positioned himself between them; knowing he would choose that moment, when her resistance was at its lowest ebb, to resume his third-degree over the extent of her relationship with Ursula.

A contemptuous smile might have passed her lips, but she could be almost as perfidious as her husband, and her smile then was simulated enjoyment. But as difficult as it was for her to sigh with satisfaction as pelvis jarred against pelvis, Janet made the effort, wondering if the detective believed in its conviction. He withdrew and thrusted again, his weight smashing down on her body; up and down he continued like an animal without finesse or gentleness. The motion knocked the wind from her lungs but brought about no other physiological change. He would never bring about any genuine emotional response from her all the while her thoughts rejected him. He couldn't reach her or make contact, his phallus was merely something inserted into her, something she couldn't feel, that wasn't touching her for all its size and effort.

'Is there any truth about you and her?' the detective asked, his physical purpose becoming secondary in spite of his approaching climax. 'Is there, Janet? D'you have her up here and fuck around together?' he demanded.

Janet offered nothing verbally. But her thoughts said: You're an animal, without sensitivity; brutal and crude; violent, ugly in love; hideous and repulsive, but most of all crude; I loathe you with every breath, your touch disgusts me! But she sighed effectively.

Perhaps in answer to her unspoken rebuke the detective thrashed harder, his body pounding her with the force of a hammer; down up, down up, down, he hit her again and again as his frenzied penis seized control of him.

'Isn't this better than having some dirty fucking lesbo pandering after you? – isn't it? isn't it?' he managed.

Another sigh parted the woman's lips, it might have been sublime agreement had she been conscious of the man's words; only she was running with her thoughts, miles from the detective, she was with her lover, her mind was embracing Ursula Ulick. The female lecturer had supplanted the detective on top of her. The orgasm she achieved was for Ursula, and was beautiful; that moment contained a world of infinite possibilities.

Joe Detective continued his diatribe: 'Wasn't that better than some crabby old lesbo?'

Emotions were fast receding, some answer became necessary.

'That was beautiful – so nice,' she replied, her thoughts still engaging Ursula.

Her apparent praise of that marital duty had been too high. Joe Detective had won her back all too easily from, as he considered, the vile clutches of female love. It might have been black magic or a no less odious practice than child sacrifice as far as he was concerned; however, peanut-throwing at freaks was all right. But in retrospect Janet realised that the detective had simply played the detective's game, had appeared convinced and awaited the opportunity to substantiate his hearsay evidence.

A bleak wet afternoon was made cheerful by Ursula's appearance. Joe Detective was on the two to ten o'clock relief, and was supposed to be away foraging for felons; so they were safe to go to the bedroom. The excuse was ostensibly to check on sleeping Juliet, not that they really needed excuses any more.

Janet recounted her recent unpleasant experiences with the detective to the older woman, and Ursula offered sympathy like a slave. She laid on the bed and beckoned her down. Janet slid down into her embrace and lay there still and silent, it was a nice feeling to be loved, very reassuring. How she regretted it not being Ursula's embrace she had succumbed to at that blue-film-party. She sighed almost forlornly.

Ursula craned her neck slightly. 'Why that sigh, Angel?'

'Thoughts' – her weary headshaking said the rest.

A small smile crossed the older woman's lips – 'I know how to make my little girl chase those away.' She reached down and moved her hand delicately up Janet's thigh, raising her skirt. Her fingers slid in at the side of her red pants, and she found her wet.

'You naughty girl,' Ursula scolded mockingly.

'You're so nice I can't control myself with you – plate me. Will you, please?'

Ursula worked down the bed and raised the young woman's skirt over her stomach, then stretched open one leg of her pants and did as she asked.

Frequently like that Janet lay paralysed as emotion washed over her, with each wave an orgasm, which put her completely at the older woman's mercy. First Ursula employed her tongue, then her fingers, then the vibrator which she had with her. The more the young woman came, the more excited Ursula grew until at last she wrenched her own skirt up and thrust herself on to Janet as a vortex of passion rocked them – breath didn't matter as lips pressed firmly to lips, each was welcome to the other's last breath.

How long Joe Detective had been observing them he didn't say.

Janet and Ursula were lying on their backs on the bed with their skirts raised and thighs exposed, each gently massaging the other's vagina. The detective pushed into the bedroom with two of his colleagues, exploding with unexpected volume and violence – Juliet awoke immediately and cried; that was one of the moments when Janet deeply regretted the child's existence. When she tried going to her baby she was prevented. The child was raised out of the cot by its father and given to one of his colleagues, who took it in with a neighbour and then returned.

Faint hope passed through Janet's mind, then a prayer that her husband's two colleagues would remain impassive, if somewhat biased, witnesses. But it was in vain, their presence was functional.

Abuse from Joe Detective was torrential, while the other two detectives were silent, leering, sneering. Janet was hurt on Ursula's account; the person she loved dearly was being reviled so obscenely and there wasn't anything she could do about it. For her own part she didn't mind the abuse and obscenities, in a fashion they were almost gratifying; that was her husband, the father of her child, in full odious bloom, confirming her every distressing description to her beloved.

Seizing his wife, Joe Detective punched her, first in the face then in the stomach, without seeming to break off his offensive oratory even for breath. Ursula screamed and tried to defend her young lover, but received the back of Joe's fist for her trouble and was sent sprawling across the bed. Joe Detective barked incomprehensible orders, and his two colleagues sprang to life. Before Janet fully realised what was happening, one detective had his trousers open and was laying over Ursula, whose protests were muted by the second detective. Janet shouted for them to stop, and as she did her husband hit her again.

The detective forced his way into the older woman and began pounding her thighs. Ursula's muted, terrified protests caused Janet to writhe mentally – seeing her beloved abused in this way was the cruellest punishment her husband could inflict on her, and when she turned away, unable to look, he wrenched her head back round and clawed her eyes open, forcing her to watch. The detective's pounding grew more violent, its design was solely to hurt, and Janet knew just how he must have hurt her. Ursula had never known a phallus, only the gentleness of fingers and a dildo, and her vagina was very small. The second detective momentarily lost his grip, the woman cried out, it was an agonised cry of despair – Janet hadn't even achieved such a painful cry in labour.

The ordeal was only half over when the first detective rose off the woman, but the fight had gone from Ursula. The second detective's blood engorged penis was larger for his excitement in watching, and his thrust was harder when he penetrated her thighs.

Janet felt she was going to vomit and there was the taste of blood in her mouth, but her thoughts were too occupied with Ursula's well-being to worry over her own. The second detective spent himself with animal frenzy no different from the previous detective's, nor that of her husband's –

she wondered fleetingly if all detectives were the same. When he withdrew, he wiped his disgusting, leaking penis over Ursula's belly and thighs, then rose adjusting his dress as though having done nothing more than used the toilet. Silent bitter tears were what Janet wept as she watched semen-mingled-blood trickle from Ursula's vagina and stain the bedspread. It was woman's eternal wound weeping at the bestiality of man.

'There, you filthy lesbos!' Joe Detective screamed. 'A good fucking, that's what you needed, that'll teach you. Play with her now, you prat, play with her now!' He ran his wife to the bed, where Ursula lay motionless save for convulsive sobs, and forced her face down between her legs. 'Plate her now and see how you enjoy it.' He seemed almost satisfied, appeased; then he released her.

Remaining with her head crooked in the vee of the older woman's legs, Janet wanted to kiss the wound better, kiss away the terrible hurt. Her husband lifted their implement off the bed and thrust it up into Janet from the rear. The final pitiless blow was the detective's raucous laughter.

'I want you out of this flat, and out of this city by tonight,' Joe Detective stated emphatically. 'You understand?' Janet understood. 'I'll crucify that fucking bitch under you if you stay here, and I mean it.'

The man stated the rest of his terms before departing with his two colleagues; the child was to go to his mother's and Janet wasn't to see her again. How she regretted the child, especially for the child's sake.

Janet complied with the terms. Ursula was hurt badly; physically she would heal, but mentally she would be horribly scarred. Things could never have been as they were between them, and she didn't want the woman she loved and was loved by to be hurt any more. After cleaning her up and helping her into a taxi, she shortly departed herself without seeing her again, and without seeing her daughter again. Joe Detective's threats would have held good, and no court would have given a practising lesbian the custody of her child when the father was a responsible policeman with a respectable family who could care for it. Haranguing in court would simply have meant further pain for Ursula Ulick, when Joe would have summoned up all the dirty linen. She afforded him no opportunity for further cruelty.

They were divorced finally on the grounds of her desertion, and Juliet was given officially into her father's custody with those visiting allotments which the mother never used.

6

An involuntary shiver ran through Janet where she sat pensively at her dressing-table; a ghost had passed right by her. She shivered a second time, but consciously.

At this stage it wasn't too difficult to smile at that regrettable period in her life, Janet found. Joe Detective was a blur in an age of growing up. He was a boor and without any hope, one of life's many unfortunates who was devoid of feelings, and who had never known love and never would. She presumed he had remarried. Pity the woman, whoever she was; he wasn't capable of offering her anything.

Raising the framed photograph of her ex, Janet smiled again, feeling no real bitterness, not even remorse. Complete indifference was all she felt, she realised, and replaced the photograph. One day she would throw it out.

Ceasing brushing her hair, Janet sat and looked at herself in the dressing-table mirror. In a matter of weeks she would be twenty-nine. Age usually crept on almost unnoticed

112

until in an instant of awareness it leapt forward, when one suddenly recognised one was old, a hag, undesirable, unwanted. Fortunately, Janet was still attractive, not the refreshingly lovely young woman who turned men's heads with admiration and women's with envy a decade ago, yet still appealing to many. Time hadn't abused her. But Janet wondered about the future and what it held. She would have money enough, assuming things worked out as anticipated, but was money the sole criterion? She wondered if there shouldn't be something more than a pile of money at the end of her most active period of life. Money wasn't really an end in itself, it survived nothing; all you could do with money was watch the elements of existence dissipate it, until the wind finally blew the dust of the last remnants away – what was there then? There should be more at the end of a lifetime, Janet decided, only couldn't decide what. Love? Fulfilment? Some reflection when you could honestly say, that was worthwhile. Achieving that would be extremely difficult, but such reflections were necessary to fill the void she saw looming in the future; money alone would only ever make the existence tolerable. Maybe Juliet was the solution.

At some point in the future Janet envisaged herself living in a large comfortable house, her daughter would be there, eternally young, crouched serenely on the floor at her feet in front of the fire on cold nights. They would be an island, not wanting or needing anyone; happy, comfortable, content, safe in their splendid isolation. She imagined that scene at both her fortieth and sixtieth birthday, and there was no perceptible difference. They weren't simple eidolons; mother and daughter.

The more she considered the prospect, the nearer Janet came to concluding that the thing she would most like to do would be to sit at home by the fire with her daughter. That was possible; it was her future.

Rising from the dressing-table, Janet reassured her reflection in the mirror that there was a secure, content future awaiting her.

The note Masca had left concerning the poodle's diet caught Janet's eye, and she lifted it from the dressing-table, but didn't read it again. Briefly wondering if the dog would be all right locked in the cupboard, and deciding it would, she discarded the note finally and moved over to her bed. A dead dog would surely be easier to dispose of than a live one anyway! Masca should have taken the thing with her, as she had simply moved into her own flat which their man had arranged. And having got rid of stupid Masca, Harry now wanted her to put up another young girl he had discovered in the sticks; she was going to work the clubs in Masca's place, so the man had explained.

Janet's flat was growing more and more like an hotel. She always seemed to be accommodating one of Harry Bleedew's protégés for brief periods. However, the guests didn't operate out of the flat, because as soon as more than one prostitute conducted business from one apartment the establishment could be busted as a brothel. The odd client was brought back late from a club, but Janet was never happy about it.

She hadn't met Jane, the Lord Peter's latest acquisition, but had only been warned of her imminent arrival. Jane was supposed to be something very special, so Janet was quite looking forward to their meeting. Possibly a friendship would strike up between herself and Jane, she considered, sliding beneath the sheets.

There was an acute shortage of friends in the metropolis as far as Janet was concerned. Doubtless someone, somewhere in London had friends, but all Janet had was business contacts and passing acquaintances like Masca, while she could have accepted none of the Mascas on any terms as friends; usually their different attitudes and levels of intelligence set them as far apart as psychiatrist and deteriorated schizophrenic. Masca's intelligence was only a little higher than her dog's, and sensibility certainly wasn't more marked. Masca was herself a contradiction in terms, opening her legs as she did with the thorough enjoyment of a nymphomaniac, yet maintaining fidelity to some equal retard whom she claimed she would marry on having saved enough. She would never save enough.

All too often Janet had seen that mentality in professional ladies, who at the conclusion of their careers were invariably broke and begging, bashing often syphilitic vaginas for pennies. Masca wouldn't escape that future, and as soon as she ceased earning enough in her new position, Harry would throw her away like a broken down shoe. A temporary repair was a place in a less favourable area, somewhere like Earls Court, which would merely be a stopping off point on the slide down, a place to pause a while. Probably there would be another parasite like Harry – if indeed Harry didn't sell her to him – reconciling his insect-life on that lower level, and Masca would think he cared, just as she believed in her pathetic way that Harry cared; until in turn the new ponce would throw her out for not earning sufficient.

That was the fate of the world's entire population which comprised the Mascas, and the prospect caused Janet to shudder. She was grateful for not ranking among those unfortunates who were subjugated by their emotions. For all those mothers of the world who wanted to give and give, and love their little men, theirs was the very worst profession to be in, both physically and emotionally, it bled those eternal mothers dry at a much faster rate than they could ever afford. Poor deluded women, Janet smiled sadly for them. The tragedy was that they believed the pricks appreciated them for their offerings, when in fact they could have died beneath them and their clients would have felt little; perhaps cheated or embarrassed as they withdrew their members from the cooling corpse and quickly departed.

Emotionally Janet gave nothing, she was in business and remained as detached as a pox-doctor throughout. The givers were losers, they always were and always would be. The woman knew how she wanted to retire, and when – there was no doubt in her mind.

Despite the dog being left in her charge, she was glad

Masca had quit the flat. The conversations she had had with the woman were at best acutely boring, at worst painfully embarrassing, while their brevity spared little suffering. The girl would push into Janet's room uninvited after work, perhaps three or four in the morning, offering vivid descriptions of the most magnificent prick she had yet encountered, or she would relate a customer's pet fetish or how he had reacted when plated. Once when Janet had gently stroked her hair and had invited the woman into her bed, she had been completely confounded; for money from a client the dyke-scene was acceptable, but not for real! Sincerity from a woman was about as welcome as VD. That had been something Masca hadn't the sensibility to appreciate as other than a saleable quirk, a kink, something dirty and automatically with a price attached. The unfortunate woman hadn't been able to grasp the fact that female love could be as beautiful and touching as any heterosexual love. At one time Janet could possibly have given her something approaching love, but now she was simply glad that the very limited woman had departed.

Lying in bed, she tried conjuring a picture of Jane in her mind's eye. Perhaps if nothing deeper they might at least be able to offer one another real friendship. Having a true friend in town would be very nice, thought Janet. The Lord Peter had intimated that Jane would interest her, and she puzzled over the suggestion. Perhaps she was intelligent as well as young, an erstwhile student even. It might be pleasant to engage a person of reasonably high intelligence in conversation once more; that was something she had missed since her separation from Ursula, and she had probably lost the habit of plausible conversation. There were educated clients of course, but the circumstances as she dictated rarely allowed conversation to blossom. Her hopes were with Jane. A short petite girl, not beautiful but extremely pretty, with dark soft hair, that was how Janet pictured her. A Jane who would delight in coming into her bedroom after work, to sit and talk, and delight in having her dark hair brushed out; a

Jane who would get frightened at times, scared of nothing in particular, yet afraid that everything in life was designed expressly to overwhelm and hurt her, and who, like a trembling child, would cling to Janet, seeking reassurance from her. They would climb into bed together and hold one another close, each seeking as much comfort as she was offering. Love would swiftly grow between them, and they would awake each morning with the sun slanting through the blinds and across their bodies, promoting it would seem eternal life, which in itself would embrace eternal love.

Thoughts warmed and excited Janet, while her arms enfolded her stomach and she tightly crossed her legs; however, that wasn't enough, nothing could contain the welling she felt inside, it would have to be given full vent until, like life itself, it expired. Suppression was harmful; release! Her emotions demanded it. Jane was in the forefront of her conscious thoughts, the image of the girl she had conjured up danced in her inner eye, soft and embraceable, beckoning, pleading for a sign of their future love. She would make a sign. Words of love floated through her mind, and Janet arranged them into sentences, then spoke them to Jane, some simply in answer to the girl's questions. Her hands moved down over her stomach and through the pubic hairs; two fingers gently massaged her clitoris, while her other hand kneaded the base of her abdomen. The swift rise of excitement as moisture from the Bartholin glands began flowing over her fingers caused images to change in her mind's eye, and Jane became tall and blonde, then was lost to her. Janet cried out mentally for her return, while her fingers worked harder. The second image returned; then a third was replaced by the first.

The path of love grew more precipitous for Janet, she was crashing headlong without restraint, her fingers thrusting and tearing as though trying to tear the matrix from her loins. The eidolons of Jane were washed away, and her mind screamed her would-be lover's name when the image in her inner eye became first Ursula Ulick, followed by women from other briefer love affairs. Janet sighed expansively, the relief she found there was beautiful; then she believed she had never known such exquisite orgasm and crossed her legs again, now trying to contain the delicious feeling and hold it within herself forever. Jane, my darling, I love you, love you – words jostled with the kaleidoscopic images she held, and she never wanted to stop coming, not until the physical manifestations of love had completely engulfed her, paralysing her body.

Sleep was easy, if unwelcome. Janet didn't want to lose her euphoric state to unconsciousness. But at last in sleep she lost Jane in those dark passages of the mind.

The morning hubbub of Shepherd Market usually reached the woman around ten o'clock, but for some reason it didn't awaken her until a little later this morning; then because a lorry trying to turn through the Market had caused a spate of impatient horns, which offensive gadgets might have had some magical powers for conveying vehicles through jams.

Rising, Janet drew back the curtains and immediately considered the morning better for the sunlight that bathed her. Sunlight always improved life, even the meanest form achieved a higher level for it. Janet loved the sunshine and could have regretted her profession simply for keeping her from it. Some girls had that regret, those who would have hawked theirs before the Street Offences Act, they complained of rarely getting any fresh air now, but just how serious they were Janet didn't really know; probably their conversation was synonymous with those straights whose sole conversational gambit was the weather.

Janet showered mornings, and that morning it was necessary to wash her vagina, which she did standing in the bath before turning the shower on. Janet was scrupulously clean to the point of being obsessional about the main tool of her profession, personal hygiene really couldn't be paid too much attention. She deemed it important in clients too. The area in which she existed, and the prices she charged largely dictated her clientèle, though Janet didn't for a moment imagine that wealth automatically indicated cleanliness, and had more than once turned pricks away after skinning them back – one who had stripped had utterly revolted her; sartorial elegance had left nothing to be desired, but his once white underwear had had the appearance of rotting on him. When she had told the man to dress again, that she didn't want his business, he had begged; she had made him shower, and had then charged him double.

There was no one quite so gullible as a prostitute's client, Janet always maintained; they had to be fools in the first instance to pay money for a fuck, for the transient joy offered at the apex of her legs, that briefest possible artificial pleasure. A drunk got far better value for his money. The woman guessed a smoker got even better value from a packet of cigarettes – fucking sometimes caused cancer too! With a little imagination she was sure that most of her clients could get as much pleasure and certainly more value from their hands; she was assuming that they had to employ some imagination even with her, that the physical aspect being the detached exercise it perforce was, wasn't enough. Love, or imagined love, was to her thinking the only way of deriving pleasure or fulfilment in the physical act of making love. Was it either fulfilment or pleasure that the pricks wanted for their money? she questioned. Or was it simply relief, having sperm drawn from throbbing penises like pus from throbbing boils? Either prospect made them equal fools. Having summoned the pluck to ring her bell, almost without exception they ceased to possess any kind of will, but became putty, and very few departed without having made some donation. Unfortunately for himself that breed of man could muster only so much courage, enough to beg but never enough to demand or protest at his dignity, his manhood outraged; generally he was an inadequate creature, which was obvious from his very presence, and once through her doorway he was trapped, as though on an escalator that he couldn't get off until let off. Janet could only judge those who came to her, while, perhaps those professional ladies in the lesser areas who possibly attracted baser forms of animal life had things a little different; however, not much different for she wouldn't accept there was any basic difference in any prostitute's client. Some would be a little more forceful, a fraction less gullible, have preferences for different fashions – nothing more dramatic. In the final analysis all were fools yielding to the prostitute's persuasion.

Much as she loathed and despised her clients, she was paradoxically grateful to them, they were donating to her pension fund and buying her that house in the country for her retirement. That fact, Janet never lost sight of, and it helped her check the hostility and contempt she would otherwise have openly displayed.

Pushing the shower off, she stepped from the bath and towelled herself briskly. Hairs spiked her legs in places, they weren't sufficiently bristly to worry her unduly, but she decided to shave. The electric razor whisked magically over her shins and calves; she remembered those frequently painful exercises wet shaving had entailed, and once when she had used a depilatory wax it had been even more painful. Janet only did from her knees down as the hair on her thighs was very sparse and fine. She ran the machine under each arm, then switched it off. Talcum powder on top of anti-perspirant was the finish of her toilet, apart from her lubricant. She squeezed out a line of the transparent jelly across two of her fingers and inserted them into her vagina, spreading the lemon-tasting lubricant around the inner and outer lips; she had no intention of wasting her own juices on tricks, and too much fucking in any vagina caused soreness and would soon have worn her out. Another shower or bath and fresh scent would be necessary about halfway through her working day – no client shied away from her because of sour body odour. The lubricant she used had to be replenished fairly frequently, about every hour, depending on how busy she was.

The woman dressed casually, her preference was for black; the opportunity for dressing up rarely presented itself.

Her bra and pants were black, silk and expensive. She wore black slacks, a close fitting jumper and black ballet shoes. She had decided to go out for a late breakfast.

The Market was growing busy with office workers rushing to cafés and sandwich bars for early lunches. The lunch period hadn't reached its peak yet and the cafés were still comfortable. Gino's establishment, literally a few doors away from her own, was the place Janet used most. After ordering her food inside, she carried her coffee outside, the table she moved to was in the shade as yet but would shortly be in full sunlight as the sun moved round. She settled with her paper – reading was a habit she had got out of, even reading newspapers – scanning fashion and the columnists, but avoiding hard news. At one time, before her marriage, she would devour most of the newspapers over breakfast, and had thought nothing of reading a book in a sitting. A lifetime ago, she thought, folding the paper in favour of watching the passers-by.

Fat ones, thin ones, short ones, and tall ones, round and oval shapes also, her eyes were discreetly pursuing the men, wondering how many were her clients. All of them potentially. Even you! her thoughts said to a man who had caught her eye and held contact as he moved down through the Market from Hertford Street. You arrogant bastard! – the man continued to look, and Janet refused to turn away, being quite capable of staring any man out. He was handsome, and he believed it, pretty rather, she decided, and he almost certainly imagined any woman would come just at the prospect of him on her thighs; he probably stood in front of the mirror and told himself as much as a thousand times a day. Janet turned and smiled. She knew the form with those pretties, they invariably practised coitus interruptus, having a withering fear of committing themselves to one woman – notwithstanding some being married – believing all women deserved a little taste of them. Invariably pretties were the most inadequate creatures of all. Janet knew the man would approach her before she departed from the café.

Probably he would take coffee and conversation, when she could take him back and let him be the first customer if she chose.

Moving down right past her, the pretty came round the Market Square again as Janet started her breakfast. He was so obvious he ought to have been arrested.

The distinction existing between male and female in the eyes of the law was in many ways iniquitous, not least the aspect of soliciting. Without fear of recrimination a man could approach a woman in the street and ask her to go with him for either an immoral purpose or simply to play marbles, but the woman trying the same could be cautioned, then on the second caution, arrested as a prostitute. Laws were gradually being reformed with some sense of equality, and perhaps when that particular one was, Pretty wouldn't be so confident in strutting about propositioning whoever he felt deserved him. What might the man's reaction have been had the Tom's Patrol suddenly sprung him, she wondered, and smiled quietly at her plate, missing the man's approach. When she looked he was standing at her table.

'Would you mind if I sat here?' Pretty asked. He hardly awaited for Janet's headshaking, when the chair was out and he was sitting, his hand up summoning the waiter. Few had the front! The waiter was a whimsical creature who much preferred any summoning to be done with the eyes; finally he came across to the table when Janet finished eating, and he raised her plate as the undaunted Pretty quickly rattled off his order. 'Would you care to join me with some coffee?' – he had turned to Janet.

The woman exchanged glances with the waiter, whose old watering eyes were smiling. On slack mornings they sometimes chatted, and he once said that he wished he had had the stamina for her. 'Black, strong,' said Janet. The waiter shuffled away.

'Are you slimming?' enquired Pretty.

'Do you think I need to?' The woman's manner was unfriendly. She resented clients trying to make her start work before her prescribed hour, and pretties who imagined they would be doing her a very pleasant favour she resented even more.

'I don't think you need to slim,' he apologised.

'Then why ask?'

'Conversation. A passing pleasantry.' He was growing more and more confused by her attitude.

'Oh,' Janet intoned, temporarily ending the conversation. They awaited their coffee in silence.

After the waiter had set the cups down and departed, Pretty spoke. 'Did you really not mind me forcing myself on you like this?'

Janet looked long and hard at the man until his discomfort was obvious. 'I would have said if I objected too much,' Janet offered. 'I watched you circle in the Market, so I wasn't really surprised when you stopped here.'

'I saw you watching me. Do you use this place very much?' He awaited the woman's reply, but she questioned with a look. 'Haven't seen you before,' he qualified.

'Perhaps you haven't had time spare to proposition women in the morning before.'

'Have you noticed me before then?' Pretty smiled in her blank silence. 'I would've made time if I'd noticed as an attractive woman as you. Do you live or work around here?'

'Both. I work in my flat just along the pavement there. I'm twenty-eight and unmarried; I have a high income and a high IQ. I like music, sunshine and eighteenth century porcelain.'

The man sat silently regarding her, trying to find some understanding of this woman and so anticipate her; he expected Janet to yield and smile at any moment, but she didn't. Silence prevailed and finally became a little embarrassing. Pretty fumbled with opening an expensive cigarette case, then proffered his cigarette. Janet declined.

'Do you mind if I smoke?'

'I find the habit singularly disgusting,' the woman said. The man returned the case to his pocket without lighting a cigarette. Janet considered him further as he played with his coffee spoon. He was a fool, yet worse, an arrogant fool, and she was enjoying treating him with contempt; probably he was used to silly simpering women who hung on his every word, and on his cock. A donation for a very short sexual interlude would do irreparable damage to his ego.

Janet's smile at the prospect wasn't reflected in her face. 'Are you a homosexual?' the woman asked evenly, finding difficulty in keeping a straight face, especially when the man nearly choked over his coffee.

'God no!' he protested, while the fashion suggested he may have been. 'Do I look as though I am then?' – confident that this affront to his manliness wouldn't be endorsed.

'Quite frankly you do,' Janet continued with a half-apologetic smile. 'You are rather pretty.'

'There's certainly no lack of candour in your manner.' The man stammered and flushed, possibly with suppressed anger, though probably embarrassment.

'Women have made similar remarks before?'

The man hesitated. 'Do you wish me to leave?'

Shrugging – 'Didn't beg you to join me – go or stay, I'm totally indifferent.' She watched the insult reach into him, laying his ego raw. The man was confounded, such treatment by a female was obviously a new experience.

His eyes searched the woman in one brief and final appeal, hoping she would smile and announce that her shabby treatment was a joke. But it wasn't, he realised at last, and flapped his arm limply for the waiter; he wanted his bill so he could depart and escape further insults. Had she been a man, his thoughts assuaged, she would have had a bloody nose by now . . .

'Would you like to screw me?' Janet asked conversationally.

The man was taken unawares, his flag-like arm sagged as though without wind to sustain it.

'That was at the back of your mind when you joined me, wasn't it?'

'Yes' – the word was awkward in his mouth, like a Roman Catholic confessing masturbation.

Another insult – 'I have some time to spare. We can go to my place.' She rose. The waiter joined them. Pretty paid for her breakfast.

It would be a very brief experience indeed for the man, Janet decided, brief and expensive; for him to have persisted after all that had gone before made him an utter fool. She began to work on him as they moved up the Market. 'Are you any good at sex?' If he wasn't then he wasn't admitting as much. 'Thought you looked like a man with some experience – d'you have an erection?' He had. She let him through the street door, rubbing his thigh as she followed him up the stairs.

The poodle! she suddenly remembered it. She hadn't heard it earlier. Perhaps it had suffocated. She went through to the kitchen. Pretty following her. The dog was subdued when let out of the cupboard, and cowered at first as Janet put her hand out, but desperate for any crumb of comfort, then warmed to her touch. When she stooped to give the poodle a bowl of milk, her jumper parted from her slacks revealing a band of naked flesh across her back.

The man made his move, and closing behind her, he placed his hands on her waist, pressing himself into her buttocks. Janet rose and turned, she began stroking the man now, the connotations being little different from stroking the dog. Pretty was ready, his thrashing pulse confirmed all that his erection stated. Zipping his fly down, the woman placed her hand inside his pants; he was fairly big and would probably have delighted a nymphomaniac, but did sweet-FA for her.

Time to talk terms. 'Do you have fifteen pounds?'

Initially Pretty was shocked. 'What?' he stammered but his tulip didn't wilt, nothing would slacken that blood-engorged organ save the vicious spitting relief described.

'Did you imagine I worked for love or something?' Janet offered indignantly, the words shredding the man.

'Y-you're a prostitute' – the admission was painful.

'Professional lady – you realised that at the café of course; none but the most unbelievable stupid and naïve could have failed to realise.'

Suddenly he was an all-perceiving man of the world – admitting his gross stupidity at this juncture would have completely annihilated him – he stepped on the escalator, and he would get off when Janet let him off.

A gullible cretin, Janet concluded, when she showed the man out and watched as he moved briskly away without glancing back, he deserved the shallow treatment he had received. She laughed silently and closed the door. Stupid, arrogant bastard, boast about that lost fifteen pounds! Fleetingly she wondered if Pretty would be obliged to explain or justify that fifteen pounds, perhaps to his wife. Janet hoped he would and that he got nagged for the loss as she hurried upstairs.

There were a number of things to do before she really started work and despite the fee, she regretted the waste of time through striping the pretty prick. It was her day for the bank; she went every other day and made her deposits; small amounts in her deposit account, which she emptied monthly through investments. The dog had to be fed and walked; she had to phone the agency for her cleaner. She called her agency first and the woman told her that one of their nice resting actors would be along to char for her within the hour. Usually it was the same one each time, Duncan, who often called during her worktime hours. He got on with his job with complete indifference to hers, the prospect did nothing for him.

Dressing again, Janet put on a skirt instead of her trousers, and she wore a jacket to match. She always made a conscious effort not to dress like a prostitute when going to the bank, even though it was only around the corner in Curzon Street. An embarrassing situation had arisen not long after she had opened the account there; she had been making donations regularly for about two months when one day after office hours the bank's chief cashier called in on her for a dipping. He hadn't recognised her naked, it seemed. But notwithstanding his loss of business aplomb in the rush between office and home, Janet had marked him. She had been reluctant to use the bank again, and couldn't guess the man's lunch break; however, she had finally put on a bold front and entered to make her deposits. At that point he had recognised her, frozen, then flushed scarlet, Janet had thought the man was going to suffer apoplexy. When at last he had calmed sufficiently for thought, he must have realised, as had Janet, that neither could expose the other without self-exposure – not that she had any intention of blowing the whistle on a customer, whatever view the bank may have taken of her custom if they had known the truth officially. Nothing of the incident was ever mentioned between them of course; she continued using the bank and he continued being civil, but he never paid her any more professional visits before his departure. On enquiring after him out of curiosity – never having known a client commit suicide at the prospect of discovery – she was told that he had transferred to another branch. No one even suspected her profession as far as she knew. Anyway she was convinced that banks didn't really give a shit provided there was money regularly going on deposit for them to invest, and current accounts weren't too overdrawn.

After going to the bank, Janet wandered around the Market, in and out of the shops, where she was known. There was nothing really she wanted, apart from food for the dog, but she enjoyed browsing in the shops, knowing the option to buy was entirely hers. There had been times in the past when she wouldn't have gone into a shop simply because she had no money; just to look and to touch but not own if she so wished, had given her no pleasure. And now, there was nothing she wished to buy, nothing import-ant. Food, clothes, of course, though they weren't so im-portant. She rather resented the artificial life she was living, it was temporary and had no foundation. Not until retiring from her profession did Janet see the foundation of her life being laid. She had a flat, which by some standards was very well appointed, but she simply existed there without belonging, without touching the surfaces, it wasn't the matrix in which her future was moulded. Simply remaining suspended in a void, watching life slip past, she was one of life's many observers, only she was making no notes for future direction. She couldn't collect the substances of life yet, the positive possessions which gave identity and a sense of belonging. All she could do was pass from shop to shop like some invisible, intangible body the shopkeepers couldn't see or hear, and therefore couldn't sell posessions to. Janet could only exercise the prerogative she felt she had and not buy, being afraid to clutter her artificial existence.

In an antique shop window there was a porcelain figurine of a young milkmaid, it fascinated Janet, and each day that she walked around the Market she paused at the window to look at this statuette, and each time she paused there so the milkmaid took on more identity. Her name was Rebecca, Janet had decided, she was seventeen and had never been beyond the Herefordshire village boundary where she lived with her widowed mother; Rebecca was a virgin and had never been kissed, although there were many men pursuing her, including the local squire; only she was saving herself for her Prince who existed in some nebulous ill-formed shape in Janet's mind. Janet loved the little milkmaid and wanted to own the figurine. She could easily have afforded to purchase it but was afraid to, afraid even to go into the shop and hold it, because she knew in the event she would have to buy it, which would mean taking little Rebecca into that unreal world of hers and once there she wouldn't be able to transfer her to the life she was planning afterwards in the country; the young virgin milkmaid would have no more meaning, the corruption and artificiality would have tarnished her. One day she would be gone, Janet realised as she stood staring in the window. Someone would come along and purchase her little Rebecca and take her away to a real existence and she wouldn't see the figurine again; she would arrive around the Market and the window would suddenly be empty. Janet felt a little sad at that prospect, but still couldn't bring herself to enter the shop and purchase it. Instead she turned back towards her flat.

7

There was a man in her doorway ringing her bell, Janet saw
on approaching. Silly bastard, she thought, he would get
about as much joy as that other wet sod last night had done
with her bell unconnected. She felt annoyed, assuming he
was another client; it certainly wasn't Duncan, her sweet
little male char.

The man was young, in his early twenties, and pathetic
because of it if he couldn't at that age get himself laid in
London for nothing. Anyone in London ought to have been
able to get himself laid for nothing.

He turned as she stepped in to the door recess with her
key.

'Miss Orga?' he enquired in that over-refined voice that
actors tended to have.

'She isn't working today, baby,' Janet responded, non-
committally.

'Mrs Pollishard sent me here for a job.'

130

'Oh, yes, the cleaning agency – where's Duncan then?' Janet opened the door.

'Taken poorly, his usual trouble,' he shrugged apologetically, as though the ambiguity was his fault. 'The lady seemed to think you'd understand.' Again he shrugged.

'You don't presumably? – shut the door.' She started away up the stairs, the young man after her.

'I rarely try,' he said, 'an intelligent nod usually gets me by.'

In the kitchen Janet threw the bag of dog's food on the table then skidded the dog across the floor with her foot when immediately it started yapping around her ankles. The young man waited at the doorway, and Janet invited him in with her hand. 'What can you do, feed dogs or make coffee?' The young man declared for the latter and was set to it after Janet had indicated where things were.

She mixed the food for the dog and placed it on the floor. 'D'you like dogs?'

'Can take them or leave them,' he replied with a watery smile as he poured coffee.

'You can take this bastard, after it's eaten – for a walk.' She indicated that he should sit with his coffee. He did, and sipped it black. Perhaps he always took it black like she did; only his expression suggested otherwise, but still he didn't ask for milk. Janet went to the fridge and fetched out the milk, then sat across the table from him. She smiled thinly, bored by the silence. 'What's your name?'

'Toby,' he replied, 'Toby Brace' – it might have been a disease.

'How come you're charing, baby? – you sound almost plausible. I'm sure you could bluff your way into something.'

He shrugged. 'What? – this feeds me between engagements.'

'You're an actor?' He was. 'Can't say I've heard of you. What have you been in, anything worthwhile?'

After rattling off a few things the woman had never heard

of, Toby finally admitted that he was simply a bit-actor and would probably achieve no greater height than a few lines on tv.

Concurring without sympathy, Janet added: 'Is the prize really worth the candle – all this sweat?'

'Don't really know,' replied Toby, 'I've never much considered it before.'

'What else? You equate effort with accumulative results; that pile you've got at the end.'

'But the price of labour isn't everything.'

'Shit, it's everything, baby' – with an air of finality. 'Especially when you're doing this sort of grind. There's sweet-FA ennobling in scrambling around shitty flats cleaning for people.'

'It's not what I wish to do in life, though.'

'How many ever get to do what they want in life?' Janet smiled reflectively. 'You're charing as a stopgap between acting engagements, it's not what you want but it's necessary to survive. On other levels people are offering the same excuses for their existence.'

The woman rose from the table, and the young man didn't further his argument, he watched her move across to the sink and rinse her coffee mug. Janet turned, catching the young out-of-work actor staring at her, he was momentarily flustered and averted his eyes; then glancing back at her, he said defiantly: 'What do you do to hold it all together?'

'You being amusing?' – she saw from his look that he wasn't. He was simply a rather naïve young man, and she regretted her tone a little. 'I'm an entertainer. Yes, I might as well be called that. I entertain as many men as possible in my bed – it certainly wasn't what I wanted to do . . . ' She trailed off dejectedly, and finally shrugged. 'Come on, I'll show you what I want doing.'

Without a word Toby rose and followed her about the flat, mentally noting the chores.

Back in the kitchen the woman said: 'Try not to frighten any of my clients away, some of the wet bastards are rather

132

timid.' An apron sometimes helped. She found one for him, told him to wear it, then left him.

The door buzzer, which acted as her dumb receptionist, was connected at the top of the stairs by means of an eye looped over a hook to make a positive contact with the bell-circuit. Whenever she had a client up, Janet simply lifted the eye off, disconnecting the buzzer, hooking it back on as she showed the trick out. After connecting her buzzer, Janet went downstairs and switched on the bell light; that was as necessary during the day as at night, it indicated that she was open for business, clients wouldn't push an unlit bell-push. She might have already done a twelve-hour stint judging by the way she felt on climbing the stairs, and she wasn't exactly looking forward to her day-long drudge.

The buzzer sounded before Janet reached the top stair. She wondered if the prospective client had been waiting on her doorstep for the bell to light up. But it was Thursday, she remembered, cheering a little. She turned a regular trick every Thursday. The man paid her twenty-five pounds for his particular diversion – an expensive ten minutes or so for him, she had once thought in an idle moment of compassion, but hadn't increased his time. He was usually her first customer on Thursday, and she released the lock and waited to welcome him at the top door.

It wasn't the regular she was expecting but a familiar prick all the same. Perhaps he had used her before – probably, for he knew and accepted the terms without argument. Or perhaps it was that all pricks were of a type, possessing no individual identifiable facet; sad-eyed, whimpering creatures from one mould, most of whom went limp immediately after their relief – not that Janet wanted them stiff and running again, clients in small doses were fine! The PL gave the man a synthetic smile as she accepted his ten pounds, she didn't charge extra for the rubber as most of the broken-down brasses in Soho did. She showed him into her work-room, closing the door after herself.

So that the clients couldn't get their money back, in the

event, Janet had two methods of putting it away – also she used the two places in case Harry paid an unexpected visit for a till-count and discovered just how much she really earned. One temporary bank was the top drawer of the chest, which was locked, access being via a small slot cut in the top with a mat over it; where it simply appeared she was placing the money received under the mat. The other stash was the walk-in cupboard, the arrangement was similar, better concealed, and unknown to Harry. Earnings alternated between the two. She slipped the money into the drawer slot.

The present client was going to get value, Janet had to undress, for which extra should have been paid as it did more for most pricks, but she decided not to pursue that extra payment. He was losing out on the sheets anyway, they were yesterday's; she would have Tony change them as soon as they were through. Janet pulled her jumper over her head, exposing her black bra. The client couldn't take his eyes off her, he would spend his ten pounds' worth in his pants before he even managed to get his own clothes off. She unfastened her skirt and stepped out of it. The sight of her black pants and bra was causing the man sitting on the bed to die by inches; he reached down to hold himself as the woman removed her bra with, as far as he was concerned, painfully slow movements. Her thumbs ran around the elastic in the top of her pants and when she rolled them down over her thighs, the sight of her pubic hair and the naked crotch finished the man, he yanked down his zip. Janet joined him at the bed with tissues, there her hand closed around his five by five and squeezed it until it spat venom; the client, blinded by passion as his life jerked from him into the tissue, buried his face in the woman's soft naked breasts and murmured love words which would probably have embarrassed him other than at that emotional juncture.

That was her money earned. The man doubtless felt a little cheated when he had calmed sufficiently to realise he hadn't had it in, but his weren't vociferous complaints. He paid another ten pounds and Janet obliged him. But he was spent, and pressure points needed working on to get him up again quickly; the sheath resisted going on Mr Softy and Janet might have been delayed; however, once inside she employed her time-proven tricks and the man came the second time fast enough, certainly faster than he believed he could come the second time around. He was dressed and shown the door.

Time? She didn't hold a clock to herself, but she knew she would be able to comfortably accommodate three more similarly within the hour. As she let that trick out, her next client entered, and still the sheets didn't get changed. She had pulled into a clean housecoat, a flimsy black nylon garment which seemed to excite the tricks as it flowed towards them when they followed her into the work-room.

The man was shortish and balding and incredibly nervous until money had changed hands; that gesture alone seemed to give him some confidence – money may have been his burden. When Janet reached down and stroked him he grew more confident. Janet unzipped him and reskinned it. She lay back on the bed, opened her nylon housecoat, exposed her gold mine, accepted the prospector between her legs and placed him at the centre of the dig. He lacked style, hacking and floundering like a spastic, perhaps because he was nervous; not that it mattered to Janet one way or the other.

Five customers were given their necessary relief in the first hour since opening. One who performed like a spastic; one who tried to talk a lot, but there was little time to waste talking; one who wanted it the french way and got it; one who wanted a trip around the world but couldn't afford it – Janet wanted fifty pounds to kiss and suck and lick round a client's prick and arse, because to do so she had to be sure he was scrupulously clean, which meant his having a bath there, and that ate into her time. Around the world was more a specialist trick anyway, and although Janet would try most things for money, she preferred straight fucking; that way she really felt she was getting the better of her clients, whereas other scenes seemed to give too much pleasure despite the price involved. The fifth prick spent himself in his pants only didn't need, or couldn't afford a second run. To the PL the five men may have been one; they were all walking, weak-kneed bank-notes.

The whirl of a vacuum cleaner started in the flat and the woman remembered the cleaner, until then she had almost forgotten about him swishing round with his duster and cleaning rag, rubbing and scrubbing and making the apartment shine. She pulled her housecoat loosely around herself and went to see how the young man was getting on. He was in the living room and switched the vacuum off when Janet spoke to him. He hadn't heard her. 'How's it going?' the woman repeated in the sudden silence.

'Oh, fine, fine. Be finished soon.' A silence, edged with embarrassment, fell over the room. The young man glanced down at her vagina and quickly averted his eyes; then repeated the performance.

Although rather amused at this display of coyness, Janet didn't smile. 'Are you a virgin, Toby?' – she doubted that he was, and knew he wouldn't admit as much anyway.

'Of course not; I'll soon be twenty-two,' adding as though for credence: 'I was in rep.' He blanched, realising how silly his reply was.

Neither his age nor the fact that he had been repertory theatre meant anything to Janet. But she didn't pursue the matter. 'When you've finished this room, take the dog for a walk? – get the keys from the kitchen. And make sure he does his business.' The out-of-work actor smiled. Janet smiled too, and went downstairs to answer the buzzer, wondering if his thoughts complimented her own; a rather attractive young man walking a poodle in that part of the world was more obvious than an out-of-touch-brass wearing an anklet. He would probably be propositioned half a dozen times around the Market.

Janet smiled again, and admitted her next client via the intercom. She waited at the top of the stairs and let him through that door. He was a man about her own age; smart

136

and intelligent looking, and something about him made her briefly curious. But she promptly dismissed curiosity to negotiate the service before ushering him into the work-room. He was there, present, in need, the why really wasn't important to her. At one time the whys and hows had been important, she hadn't been able to resist curiosity, and despite instructions to the contrary from her pimp, her questions had been numerous, the need to know about the clients compulsive – no longer. Familiarity bred contempt. She listened of course when the price made it expedient to do so.

The man tried to smile through the slight embarrassment he obviously felt as he removed his wallet. Janet allowed her housecoat to come open a little, letting the prospect see what was on offer was a good ploy, and she wasn't at all ashamed of her body. She smiled mechanically, her thoughts not with the man, but wondering what had happened to her twenty-five-pound trick. She was with the man instantly when he enquired the price.

'How much do you want?' He had the soft even voice that Janet liked in a man.

'Well, that really depends on what you require,' she replied. He didn't know, said he was embarrassed and felt rather foolish, so the woman striped him for fifteen pounds, having marked him as a weeper; he could now weep on her bosom for a few moments if he wished. And she considered that he might not even be able to bring himself to fucking her, she sometimes had instincts about such things. Janet led him into the work-room and across to the bed; there she had to show willing, and began going through the motions of undressing him.

Resisting, the trick said: 'Eh, no, Janet, not for the moment – that is your name, Janet?'

The woman nodded from the bed. 'Do you have some kind of physical problem?' she enquired, her voice ripe with sympathy. 'Or is it that you simply find me so unattractive?'

'No, no, not at all,' he insisted, drawing nearer. 'It's, it's possibly because you're too attractive' – he shook his head apologetically. 'It's not you, really it's not.' The man yielded a little and sank to the bed when the woman reached out to him. Immediately she began regretting her effort. He raised his head and looked at her bared front, then averted his eyes with a sense of alarm. 'It's a long time since I've tried anything like this,' the man said. 'A year, possibly two, I don't know, don't . . . ' Guilt crucified him – 'Not since my sister . . . '

Coolly Janet regarded the man, who nodded as though in reply to her unspoken question. She easily avoided the obvious reaction; usage was a good teacher. All kinds visited her work-room, making all manner of confessions. And she guessed, brothers confessing incest with their sisters wasn't nearly as bad as remorse-torn fathers admitting screwing their daughters; often PLs' work-rooms were as sought after as the confessionals, and the absolution was found there as easily. 'Don't you wish to go through with it?' Janet asked with an air of imperturbability.

'I'm apologising in advance in case I'm unable to.'

The woman gave an awkward shrug. 'Makes no difference to me if you can't do it. You needn't feel ashamed on my account . . . ' She was trying to be helpful.

'Ashamed?' he retorted, glaring fiercely at her. 'Ashamed on your account? It's my sister, my beautiful twin I'm ashamed for. She's my shame. I made love to her!' His face contorted through anguish, which was distressing even for the onlooker.

Briefly Janet allowed her thoughts to wander towards sympathy, and before she fully realised what was happening, the man had her legs held apart and had gone down on her – normally she charged more for oral-genital contact and now felt extremely annoyed with herself for allowing this conscience-striken prick to advance to such a position without her consent. Gently running her fingers through the man's hair as he nuzzled her, she sharply prised his head away. He was in tears and tried to hide his face against

Janet's thighs. 'I love you, Virginia, love you, love you,' he screamed over and over.

The woman felt a creeping sense of uneasiness but no real alarm, possibly Toby was still around, though probably he had already taken the dog out for a walk – that fucking dog was taking over her life!

Usually when pricks looked like getting out of hand she would simply intimate that the Lord Peter was in the next room and possible trouble would invariably disappear, but this type of trouble was different. The man was running towards hysteria, guilt forcing him higher and higher up the scale. Not being a psychiatrist Janet couldn't pretend to understand or know how to alleviate his problem, but assumed a major step for him would be taken if he could make a woman other than his sister; she had done all she intended by putting herself on offer, now all she wanted to do was calm him and get him out of the apartment. She raised his head again and hit him very hard across the face. The man's ranting stopped instantly, he stared inanely at the woman, then slowly shook his head.

'I've only ever made love to my sister,' he said, 'that's all, never anyone else . . . she never wanted anyone else to. I never wanted anyone else. I can't . . . can't' – he became calmer, apologetic, ashamed, embarrassed; he rose off the bed, avoiding the woman's searching eyes. 'I'm sorry,' he mumbled, then irrationally: 'Why couldn't you have been an old whore who I could've abused and ravaged . . . I'm sorry . . . ' His eyes were glistening with tears as he turned and hurried from the room.

Janet sprang up and followed him out, but the man was down the stairs and gone in an instant. Toby came from the kitchen with the poodle on its lead. He looked questioningly at the woman, who pulled her housecoat around herself.

'Everything all right?'

Janet smiled tightly. 'Problem client, one gets them occasionally – before I forget, the bathroom wants doing after you've taken that thing for its walk.'

139

'Where is the bathroom?'

'Through the office' – Janet indicated the work-room. She watched the young man go out with the dog. He would get her a bad name, she thought wryly; he looked much younger than twenty-two, about seventeen she would have guessed, had he not told her.

Closing the door at the top of the stairs, she moved back to the work-room, her life seemed suspended through the repetition of those few paces. The room smelt a little now. She was quite used to the smell, much as she imagined a pig-farmer grew used to the smell of his pigs; however, as with the pig-farmer, it didn't naturally follow that she had to like the smell which oozed in varying degrees from bodies. She sprayed an aerosol through the room and opened the window. Janet paused at the window which overlooked the Market. People using the late end of the lunch period milled around in the sunshine as though they owned life. At that moment she envied those people; they weren't free of course, perhaps one or two were, but the majority had jobs to mind or homes to keep and were only let out for set periods. She was freer in fact, yet still envied them their prescribed moments of freedom, because she was chained mentally by a hunger, by an urgent need of money with which to purchase her future, a perverse need affording her no licence or freedom for fear of missing a client. Those one or two who were missed would make no appreciable difference to the final balance, and Janet wasn't foolish enough to believe otherwise, yet that knowledge notwithstanding, the uncertainty of the possible loss remained; fear was there at the back of her mind, imprisoning her will, prevailing her joining those seemingly free persons milling around in the sunshine.

Thoughts became so abstracted as they engaged people and things beyond the window that she had no conscious awareness of her door buzzer. She could hear the buzzing, but believed it was something that had no connection with her existence, perhaps for the unknown woman next door.

The buzzer stopped and restarted. Then suddenly it reached her and was real and belonging to her world and her apartment, it announced her clients.

It was her Thursday regular at last. Janet received him at the top of the stairs. Mr Thursday was a man of around fifty, his appearance was sufficiently ordinary to be almost nondescript, a government official with a fairly high position of authority, though just what it was Janet didn't know, well qualified and obviously well paid. She didn't doubt the man's brain-power in normal circumstances, but when he fell under her sphere of influence he took on the general appearance of a mentally handicapped child, the simple smile he fashioned never left his face until he departed. His relief was something special, though only to him; it did nothing more for Janet than all the other boring exercises, it was merely different from the straight ejaculations into her comfortable receptacle. His pleasure was basically derived from underwear fetishism and very minor flag'. He wasn't strictly masochistic and didn't need whips, just a little chiding and slapping, that was enough for him.

Mr Thursday presented her with a bunch of flowers. There was always something on offer in addition to the envelope containing the twenty-five pounds he gave her. Last week it had been chocolates. Janet showed the man through. First the envelope was popped away, after its contents had been checked, then she disposed of the flowers before finally turning her attention to the man, who was slobbering through his childlike smile.

'Where the hell have you been?' – the woman attacked without warning. 'You're late, you bastard. I began to think you were trying to avoid seeing me today.'

'I'm very sorry, my dear, I was delayed at the office. I hope you won't punish me too much' – that prospect was arousing him.

'You bastard! You certainly need punishing.' She watched his eyes sparkle, his smile displayed an air of expectancy. Janet closed on him, her hand raised like a censuring school

141

teacher. The man quaked. Her hand sliced the air, cutting him across the face. 'I'm going to thrash you. But first I want all these clothes off.' That was a game she entered into with him, seeking some kind of justification for their scene; it would be wrong of him to simply take his clothes off and put her underwear on without evoking some reasonable ploy, and his clothes being removed for his chastisement seemed reasonable enough. Janet unscrewed his valuable pearl tie stud. Had she been a thief she could have stolen it anytime, and there were professional ladies who wouldn't have hesitated. But remembering Harry's early advice, she didn't try straight robbery with tricks; she wanted no trouble with the CID, and those scenes were designed exclusively for it. Slipping the stud into his pocket as usual, she removed his tie, then his jacket which she hung over a chair, along with his waistcoat, but his shirt and vest weren't hung. He had a weak, white body on which the fat had started to break and tier as on a badly used prostitute's body. Janet pinched the man's arms quite hard, then his rather large nipples. His delight moved higher, and she pinched him again on the tits, and slapped him hard as possible. In a pocket of irrational loathing she wanted to beat the man, smash her fists into him and really hurt him, release all her bile and anger. The feeling passed. The man remained un-moving on the bed; she knew what he was waiting for now. 'You rude thing!' the woman suddenly admonished, con-vinced at times like these that she should have been an actress. 'How dare you expose yourself in my bedroom?' Striding angrily across to the chest of drawers, she removed the red padded bra which she kept for the man and returned to him, she pulled the garment on to him roughly and fastened it.

The man was in his element when he sat on the edge of the bed holding the artificial excrescence on his chest. Janet watched him disinterestedly, only at approximately two pounds a minute this otherwise tedious procedure was made tolerable. His time varied of course, though normally he achieved everything he wanted within ten minutes. He was dressed and gone within fifteen. A couple of times she had given him tea afterwards, but didn't make a habit of it. He was married, he had once stated over tea, and quite happily. Janet hadn't asked whether he had ever indulged his quirk with his wife, but presumed not or he wouldn't be coming to her and paying. Not many women in straight, apparently content, social-constricted marriages would ever be able to accept, let alone satisfy their husband's often very necessary sexual diversions, which they themselves surely helped to develop; yet those women would still condemn out of hand those who offered such services, and in many instances preserved the appearance of the marriages as a result. Not that Janet took particular umbrage. She expected neither thanks nor condonement, not even the simple acknowledgement that she was necessary to present-day society as a valve, an outlet, a means of releasing the emotional tensions caused by the pressures of living in a modern, high-geared, sexually advanced, yet emotionally inhibited community. Janet equated her profession with the orgy which had been an essential release for the ancient Greeks, Romans and other early civilisations which suffered similarly from proportionate pressures – orgies were anything that provided emotional relief, from a gut-contorted fart to a drunken tit-shagging daisy chain. Most forms of sexual relief were on offer from professional ladies, all at various levels and prices. PLs were as necessary to society as alcohol, nicotine and the harder varieties of drugs. Janet never doubted that; however, she never imagined that the vice the professional ladies provided would ever achieve such a parity of respectability, where, like good wine, a prostitute could be laid at the best tables with the prescribed recommendation. She didn't especially believe it would be a good thing if such parity was ever attained, and the door opened, and she wasn't considering any financial loss she might suffer as a result – Janet knew she wouldn't lose, each day passing was the proof, for the more permissive society, the busier she became. The fact was that those sexual complexities of society which needed releasing through a twist with a prostitute were generally far more involved than those pressures which alcohol swamped. In part many of the former hang-ups evolved out of the need of secrecy, and by opening the door with total acceptance, society would be perpetuating the cause and offering far less effectual release. Her Mr Thursday enjoyed the secrecy almost as much as the final relief, if he had to go to a permitted street or licensed brothel his pleasure would probably have been so reduced that a new diversion would be necessary to start the cycle again. Guilt was one of society's inherent pressures which it found necessary to try and release; the process of self-perpetuating all the while the body didn't weaken beyond effort. Janet regarded the body on the bed and wondered how long before it was irrevocably spent – before her own retirement?

Unfastening Mr Thursday's trousers, she worked them off with his underpants, his shoes were pulled off with them, but not his socks. Janet scowled threateningly at the man before fetching her red frilled panties from the chest of drawers – she couldn't recall the last time she had worn the pants, they were laundered especially for him. He thanked her as she put the panties on him, he was nearing his time; his phallus rose to its miserable height when she ran her hand over the outside of the garment and pinched the soft flesh in his groin.

Janet stood away from him and opened her housecoat, exposing those parts which the clothes he was now wearing would normally cover; she caressed her own breasts and ran her fingers down her crotch. The man's moment arrived without him losing his smile; his hands ran over the outside of the red pants, but he didn't physically masturbate, the orgasm was achieved through visual-mental stimulation. Finally when he began to cool he clapped his hands over his eyes as if to hide his shame that was reflected there. He would sit like that unmoving for a few moments in the sticky panties.

The woman hadn't heard Toby return from walking the

dog, but assumed that was him she heard outside the door now; he had yet to do the bathroom, and probably wanted to brush on. She pulled open the work-room door. The young man in the reception area seemed embarrassed; the client didn't stir. 'Did he do his business?' – she could have been referring to either the dog or the man. Toby stammered the affirmative, his discomfort increasing. 'D'you want to get through and do the bathroom?' There was no reply as the temporary char's eyes flitted between the PL and her client. Janet smiled sourly. 'Come through – he won't mind you.'

The man on the bed squinted at Toby through the cracks in his fingers, and his eyes followed the young man into the bathroom, but he made no comment. It had been the same when Duncan, her usual char, had interrupted, only he had been rather turned on by the minor transvestite. But the client hadn't passed any remark, neither at the time nor since.

Soon he would lower his hands, rise, remove her underwear, clean himself up on some tissues, dress and depart with a few words of thanks. The same procedure was invariably followed on each occasion, presumably he was satisfied, but could just have been extremely courteous, Janet had no true means of telling. What was satisfaction anyway? There was no general yardstick, no one point that accommodated everybody, its assessment and value was entirely subjective, the woman decided, it had to be. She failed to appreciate how the scene just performed was worth twenty-five pounds to anyone, but then it did nothing for her, not sexually; while the man may have derived from the act some deep-seated pleasure which she couldn't possibly begin to understand. Janet didn't know if she really wanted to understand the quirks and satisfactions of those sectarians who paid her for such diversions.

After letting the man out, telling him how much she looked forward to next Thursday, Janet unhooked her buzzer and moved wearily through into the kitchen and plugged in the kettle to make some tea. Business had been brisk and the day had hardly begun – she wished it was just ending, one more day gone, one more deposit for her future. Wishing life away was wrong, she guessed, but there were moments when if wishes had been granted regrets would have been faced later; her immediate future was like a prison sentence, the term had been pronounced in judgement and had to be served; and as with most prisoners, the days were marked off the calendar, the hours counted off the clock, wishing they would only go just a little faster. There was no escape, she couldn't simply opt out, freedom could only be earned by serving the drudge in the prescribed manner; that was the only way Janet believed she could move on from this existence and on her terms.

It was some time before Toby, the emaciated actor-char, joined her in the kitchen; she imagined he was hiding, not wanting to encounter her client again – simply cleaning up the bathroom surely didn't take so long!

'Would you like some tea, Toby?' she asked when the young man finally appeared in the kitchen doorway. He came forward without speaking as Janet poured the tea.

At length he said: 'Was that normal?'

Janet suspected he had been shocked. 'Normal? What's normal these days? You mean usual?' The young man made no reply. 'A practice like mine attracts a fair proportion of the fetishes and kinks.' She paused momentarily to watch the young man's reaction, he wasn't accepting the education easily. Regardlessly – 'I don't s'pose it really matters very much how a man comes, through copulation, wearing my undies or being whipped. Certainly it doesn't matter to the clients like him, all he cares about is having his bit of fun, getting his off – they can pay for it, I can provide it. There's nothing more involved.'

'It's not really right, is it – I mean, doing it that way, wasn't how it was intended.'

The woman felt the inclination to smile, but had no particular wish to hurt the poor guy's feelings too much. 'That's rather a naïve outlook, Toby – I suppose you believe in love,

146

believe it's a positive emotion, or several emotions with the straight sexual union as the culmination.' She waited for him to respond, needing time herself to think out her route to save sounding like a bitter, spiteful lesbian.

Hesitantly the young man said: 'The two are closely intertwined, or should be. Yes, the sexual act is the physical manifestation of love, without love the act is nothing.'

He might have been earnest, or merely acting and quoting one of the less progressive playwrights, either way Janet wasn't sold on that product, nor would she ever be again. 'You might get lucky and be very happy with some woman looking at life that way through the telescope, but probably it'll simply prolong the process of disillusionment and make it that much more painful' – her tone was subdued. 'Love was prostituted a long time ago, and now its continued abuse is simply conditioning. Love and sex have nothing in common any more, they are two entirely separate commodities; living's a lot easier for recognising that, less hurtful if you accept that fact of life. They're no longer interdependent – they can be, but rarely are now, not as a matter of course, as a natural consequence . . . ' She might have been no more than thinking aloud. Suddenly she became aware of Toby's voice.

' . . . What about children then?' the young man argued, as though presenting irrefutable evidence in support of his case, 'people go on having them.'

'Only because they can't get aborted, not because of love, baby. Children are accidental, the result of the uncontrolled sexual act, they're not the fruits of love – quite the reverse is true. Invariably they're the bitter berries of a sour marriage.' Janet was silent as thoughts of her own child crowded into her mind. Juliet was one of those bitter berries. Love. Continually she reassured herself that she loved the child, but wondered if she wasn't simply keeping alive that feeling labelled love in order to use it in taking the child when the moment was right, and so finally hurting the father. Janet sensed the young man staring at her, as young men would, felt his eyes, knew his metabolism was rising, and she wondered if he had a hard-on then. 'Why did you begin masturbating when you reached puberty – curiosity?'

From behind his tea cup where he tried hiding his embarrassment the young man reluctantly concurred.

'And after curiosity?' Janet went on, 'habit, pleasure. You come to enjoy the exercise, continue it, then one day decide you must stop, and do stop, until tension mounts inside and demands release; your whole system craves the relief orgasm provides, and you either jerk off again or shift your affections to a woman, girl, an arse, and find your relief there' – she paused. 'At that transitional stage lots are deluded and imagine that what they've experienced is love, when in fact it's nothing more than a nice relief. Probably you argue for love because you were a bit disgusted by that old minor transvestite. The way he gets his off was further divergent from the socially accepted fashion, but that doesn't automatically mean the straight way, your way, screwing, is any closer to love, not in essence.'

Silence fell over the kitchen.

The young man might have been sold, he didn't comment further, but continued to regard the woman. Janet raised her shoulders, her smile might have been apologetic. 'Sorry if I sounded pedantic, I rarely get anyone who listens to me – I'm obliged to listen to stupid fucking men trying to tell me their stupid fucking problems.'

'Do you hate them very much?'

'Hatred; disgust; contempt, how easy they are.' Janet sighed and shook her head. 'I think I've progressed beyond all that now. There's nothing left. I no longer feel anything for the men who use me, they might just as well be paying a cabbage with a hole in it. That's about as insulting and contemptuous as I can be towards them without actual effort or expression. I suppose at times I'm a pretty good actress. There's no such thing as the kindly brass, or a whore with a heart of gold. I don't s'pose there ever was. Another myth shattered. . . . ' She laughed one harsh, scornful note. 'I'm sorry' – offered as though believing she might have robbed the young man of his most treasured illusion. She couldn't recall having been as apologetic for a very long while, or revealing so much of herself to a strange man. It was self-indulgence, and as much as she enjoyed it at that moment, she resisted the increasing urge she felt to reach out and make further contact with this out-of-work actor; that weakness she couldn't permit, for in order to remain invulnerable she knew she had to remain in her splendid isolation. Next she would be inviting the young man into her work-room for a freebee and calling it love!

Janet poured some more tea into her cup. Her eyes met his searching, questioning eyes – maybe it was merely lust she was mistaking for other qualities. 'Would you like some more tea?' Toby shook his head briefly, but his eyes returned to her. 'You're not like Duncan, are you?'

He appeared puzzled. 'How do you mean?'

A smile passed quickly over the woman's face. 'I can tell from the way you look at me when my housecoat falls open. You like my breasts and pubes.'

'You mean Duncan was queer?' – awkwardly.

'I believe you would even like to lay me.' She fastened her housecoat as though answering the young man's unspoken request to purchase the goods.

'I've finished now, I should be going.'

'Yes, your money is really better spent elsewhere.' Janet opened the drawer in the kitchen table and took out a wallet containing a few pounds and paid him for two hours' work. The out-of-work actor departed with alacrity, he seemed relieved to get away. Janet wondered if he had realised the truth, her truth, about the sex act being stimulated by relief rather than love – perhaps he was away to seek some relief in the nearest conveniences, or the most readily available girlfriend. She watched him from the work-room window as he went away down the Market, until at last he was out of sight. She didn't figure she would ever see him again.

8

It had been her intention to take a bath at the point, but after letting the young man out she had automatically connected her buzzer; when it sounded she let another client up instead. One more donation, the bath could wait.

Business continued with hardly a pause, as she let one trick out, the next was waiting to follow him in. There might have been an orderly queue at the door – Janet hoped there wasn't – the stream was endless it seemed; men in need of relief, with a need to ejaculate their tensions, a need to have the poisonous bile tapped from their bodies. No, not bodies, but rather body, for she had long ago decided that there was only one prick, whose shape and fashion varied, while his need of relief remained insatiable. Janet knew that that need would last forever, he would last forever, outlast her; that prick would outlast all the professional ladies of the world, he would never die or wilt, relax, tire or lose his desperate need. Paradoxically Janet found the prospect depressing. How many women had it taken before her to appease that prick, women lost, destroyed, wasted, ruined? – there were no records. How many women would it demand after her? Young women who would grow old and wither and die, while the prick itself continued thrusting and spitting its bitter seeds; the names of women would stretch backwards and forwards into eternity, their number countless. How many more times would her bell be rung? her bed creak? her legs be opened? How many more times would he climb the stairs?

Count was already lost, she had no idea what number of times she had performed the act, she had kept no score, not even in the beginning. The woman couldn't even remember the number today. She had been busy, had earned quite well, but whether the trick currently on top of her was the tenth or eleventh she didn't know, and as the prices varied, her receipts only gave a rough guide to the day's numbers.

The man on top of her was reaching his time now, his breathing was growing like a traction engine. Janet's dextrous fingers massaged the erogenous areas in his back with complete detachment. He had been on top of her for about three minutes, she guessed, but it seemed like three hours. He was heavy and awkward and had no sense of rhythm for her to control, which was why he was taking so long. He was like a fish floundering out of water, Janet mused, first this way then that way without making very much impression. Usually she could direct a man's rhythm and either sustain it, or draw him out to his conclusion in seconds, as though she were a machine. Yes, that's just what she was, she decided, a sexual relief machine; well oiled, well maintained, smoothly functioning; the analogue amused her, though she didn't smile, not that the prick would have noticed anyway. By all accounts the man believed the object of the exercise was to thrash at random inside her vagina while trying to stove in her rib cage. His floundering grew more uncontrolled, and at the right moment Janet eased her legs together on him, causing him a childlike quivering of excitement as

151

he spent himself. The woman felt his member go limp, and when she nipped the top of the contraceptive and eased him off herself, he seemed disappointed, rather like a child who had intended saving his chocolate to make it last, only to discover suddenly that he had eaten it all. Janet was careful and the sheath didn't slip inside her, and once limpy was clear she left the trick to remove and knot it himself. After the man had adjusted his dress and was seen off the premises, Janet collected a tissue and lifted the sheath in it from the work-room floor and walked it through to the bathroom to flush it away.

Now she really would take her bath, Janet decided, and opened the taps. The bath filled rapidly; the hot water was constant. But no sooner had the bath filled when her buzzer sounded. Still she had neglected to disconnect it, and she considered leaving it buzzing, or disconnecting it then, but knew the prospect of money walking away would destroy her. Money could walk away during the normal course of the bell being disconnected, but the difference was psychological, then it was clients and money she didn't know existed in the silence.

The buzzer sounded again, impatient, vociferous, offensive, like a loud fart; the prick whoever he was wasn't prepared to draw a blank, he would keep ringing until he gained entrance. Janet hesitated at the bathroom door and briefly considered the prospect, he would be a ten, a fifteen or maybe even a twenty spot. The bath could wait; it would be silly not entertaining this one, the woman told herself, as there might be a natural pause after him, when she could bathe and change the sheets and be ready for a fresh start. She didn't consider that there might be no let up as she moved through the reception area and admitted the persistent client.

The prick looked impatient, Janet thought as she regarded him, having passed him through the door at the top of the stairs, impatient enough for the shortest return, possibly horny enough to blow in his strides. Unlike so many before him he equated value to cost, he knew the terms but wanted a straight ten-pound run through the ditch for five; the woman wasn't interested in giving cut prices, she had had a busy time so far, and didn't even offer reductions to regulars. The man tried bluffing her and turned away to leave, but shortly realised Janet couldn't be bluffed. Finally he produced ten pounds.

How many professional ladies had he paid in his thirty-odd years of life? Janet wondered as she took him into the work-room. How many times had he been to her? There was no recognition, save the most superficial; each recognised their gestures of obligation, the admittance, the fee, acceptance, exposure.

Most of the tricks were like children, she found, obedient, lost, waiting to be told, instructed, done unto, even those experienced by frequent visits waited in a similar manner.

The client was soft-on and expected her magical touch. Janet sat on the bed near the man and took him firmly in hand, her other hand enfolding his testicles; his cock began to swell immediately. The woman reached into the night table unit for a condom; doubtless few enjoyed wearing the sheath, but even fewer complained about it. Very occasionally she made concessions and permitted an insertion without that rubber, but the circumstances had to be extenuating and her client scrupulously clean; the sheath was by no means an infallible safeguard against venereal disease, but it did afford some protection, and almost certainly made the contraction of non-specific urethritis non-existent. Personally she was always very careful and frequently douched herself with a mild solution of antiseptic. Most professional ladies harboured fears of VD, with some their fears were obsessional, and they suffered nightmares at the prospect of hardsores and vaginal discharges.

Janet rolled the sheath on to her client and he accepted it without complaint – sheaths worked for both parties as a superficial safeguard to health. The prick opened her house-coat and the woman rolled back on the bed. The man scrambled between her legs, his hand reached down and touched her cunt as though reassuring himself of its existence; Janet preferred that clients didn't touch her like that, and pushing his hand away, she had to take control of him as he worked forward on to her, for at the point of insertion, like most of them, he proved pretty inept. Making sure he was still wearing his sports jacket, Janet placed him.

He sighed voluminously, but seemed to imagine the expulsion of air was hers. 'D'you enjoy that?' he asked, quite certain he was affording her the greatest possible pleasure. 'You liked that, didn't you?' he persisted, beginning to sweat now.

'Nice, nice' – the woman was feeling generous, while her thoughts remained in opposition. Like those before him, and as surely those who would follow, the man was a negative for her.

The jelly she used always kept her moist and well lubricated, but most men considered that condition a feather in their cap; in fact it was never come, and rarely even the natural secretions from the Bartholin glands in the vagina. She never permitted herself to orgasm with clients, regardless of whether she had one a day or thirty, although often she simulated it for their benefit; they never knew the difference, their own climax was of prime importance to them anyway. With unfailing regularity she remained calm and uninvolved throughout, there was never even any involuntary release on her part, Janet would quit instantly if ever there was. She intended retiring long before her body degenerated to that state where she was no longer in complete control, or she reached that level at which the drippers existed – not all drippers were in fact old – those countless women who, ruined by the profession, could no longer control their emissions and leaked to a sort of climax with every client. Life dissipated there in the womb, to drip without control; those disgusting women, who were decaying and falling apart, frightened Janet, she had seen so many and loathed them and dreaded ever being like them.

'You like this, you like me fucking you!' The man's excitement was increasing. 'Verbal, love. Verbal, give me some verbal – say you love me getting stuck up you!'

There was no one more obliging than herself, Janet considered – 'Love it, love it; love you getting stuck right up me.' You conceited bastard, she thought, you stupid, insensible . . . suddenly she felt instant nausea on catching the full draught of the man's sour, halitosised breath. Feigning excitement, she wrenched her head away to avoid the next wave as he spoke.

'Verbal me, say you love me fucking you – say it, say it!'

'Ooohhh I love it, baby – come! Come now, I want you to blow with me now!' Janet was even more convinced of her acting ability. She might have been caught in the same paroxysm of emotional relief as the man obligingly achieved everything; however, she was calm and as detached as anyone participating in the act could possibly be. She possessed that faculty for complete detachment, that capacity for thought which permitted her to be anywhere she chose, embracing any subject on any level within her scope – she certainly wasn't engaging the halitosised cretin on any level other than a physical one, and even that wasn't strictly true because he wasn't touching her; here the man was copulating with a vegetable, a warm one, she would allow that, perhaps a hot potato. She laughed mentally.

The vegetable-lover was licking her breasts like a slobbering dog; that wasn't bargained for, he was now imposing. A bath was suddenly essential, even though Janet was quite certain halitosis couldn't be contracted externally by oral contact. She raised the slobbering dog's head and removed his limping phallus from between her legs.

'You enjoyed that, didn't you? You enjoyed that.'

'It was lovely – couldn't stop coming,' she assured him, and promptly turned her head away.

The man sat back on his laurels.

The bathwater hadn't cooled during those nine minutes – Janet made sure of disconnecting the entryphone after letting the trick out, and her bath was taken without interruption. It was cleansing and relaxing; normally she didn't relieve so many clients without taking one. After the bath she meticulously inspected herself; her cunt was cool now and comfortable and soothed, and she inserted another application of jelly ready for more punishment. Janet put on a clean housecoat, white nylon this time, it was sheer and soft to the touch, with yards of flowing material; then she fetched clean sheets and changed the work-bed – she would have to remember the laundry list tomorrow.

In the kitchen, when Janet went to make some coffee, the poodle yapped from the corner in which it was curled, and rose, but didn't approach her. The woman had forgotten about the dog, and wondered, as she filled the percolator, whether she ought to feed it again. But decided not to as feeding would mean walking the animal later and suffering the crutch-hoppers again. The dog yapped timidly, the threat of being put back in the cupboard looming. Janet relented and gave it a tiny amount of water in a dish; the dog would go out of the window instead of the cupboard if it pissed on the floor again. She threw a string of mental obscenities at the dog's absent mistress – had she known the flat in which Masca had been installed she would have put the dog in a taxi and sent it round to her.

Janet poured her coffee, it was strong and clear; she nibbled some biscuits and fed pieces to the dog as she sipped her coffee. He was a grateful little tyke and sat up begging for more after each piece. Possibly she could have grown quite attached to the creature but for the inconvenience of it, then probably that applied equally to clients, even men in general; she guessed she could have formed an attachment quite easily had she been foolish enough. An attachment of sorts existed with Harry Bleedew, but as far as she was concerned that was strictly business, and those occasions she opened her legs for him, nothing more than quality control on his part; perhaps the Lord Peter believed they were into something else then. Janet didn't know how many professional ladies the man had working in his various flats, she wasn't particularly interested and didn't make any social gatherings with them. Nevertheless she knew that a few of them formed other than business relationships for the pimp, opening their legs for him and yielding themselves up emotionally; they would shortly become drippers who he would then cast aside like old shoes – that was an apt analogy, Janet reflected – leaky old shoes which the man would have no further use for. Then she supposed their decline started the moment he recruited them, with them imagining they loved him, and that love was reciprocated, and that he would do anything for them; consequently they would do anything for him, then once they were on the firm and regularly earning money for him, the dawn hardly mattered when it finally broke. Most of the women hadn't the intelligence and the will to do anything other than continue working, hoping he still loved them. Some were as pathetic as their clients, and sufficiently stupid even to form attachments with the tricks, to call it love and run the full gamut of the climax with them, giving everything without reserve, believing they would eventually be married and live happily ever after – only in the movies did princes marry prostitutes, and even then the marriages didn't work! Yet there was no educating PLs with such aspirations, and Harry's occasional ominous words fell on stone ears too, including those words pertaining to the attachments with himself. Harry was the first to admit to being a louse and a bastard, when it was expedient to do so; he was a professional, if nothing else, and Janet knew he respected her for her own degree of professionalism. From the beginning they marked one another with their true colours. Janet hadn't been sold on a soft-sob, nor had she been infatuated, but had known what she had been getting into, and knew what she had wanted and the terms necessary to get it all. And her original attachment with the Lord Peter had never altered.

The woman glanced down at the dog, which sat up on its haunches, paws out, cringing for more biscuit. How like a whimpering, simpering man it was, she considered, tossing it another crumb. She would do as well forming an attachment with the dog as it was probably capable of being more faithful than any man. Was fidelity the essence of male-female relationship? she questioned, or the most essential factor of any relationship? She doubted that it was, or that it was even particularly important in the generally accepted physical sense, while lack of fidelity could only enter with perfidy. Faithlessness was never simply male seeds wasted over strange female thighs, or female thighs on offer, but the loss of understanding, of communication, it was the protraction of designed suffering, mental isolation. Betrayal through superficial physical contact wasn't really important provided the mind and will remained compatible with that person to whom loyalty was owed. However, Janet knew she wouldn't again be betrayed, certainly not in the immediate future; emotional interdependence of two personalities was necessary for that, and she foresaw none such, nor felt any particular need, and self-betrayal was unlikely. The ideal she strived continually to attain was seared into her inner eye, and she would never lose sight of it.

Perhaps some superficial relationship as she had tried with Masca, and which she had imagined with Jane, was necessary for her own relief, but she didn't feel she would crumble or crack up without such contacts. Janet fully appreciated how friendless she was in her existence, she was almost an island, but wanted it no other way; safe, insular, in no way dependent on a familiar personality, neither accountable to, nor for; interdependence would almost certainly mean eventual betrayal, and so Janet chose to give nothing, to yield nothing, to accept nothing other than the materialistic aspects of her profession.

The dog, finally realising there were no more pieces of biscuit on offer, slunk back to the corner of the kitchen and curled up, staring across at Janet. The woman stared back a few moments, then averted her eyes, where her viewpoint settled in the middle-distance and became vacant. Briefly she considered the future, wondering what it held without friendship, without contact or communication on a level higher than business. Also she wondered if she would still be capable of offering love at some point in the future after having smothered it for so long, after becoming so adept at keeping it locked within herself and not allowing the tiniest part to leak by. What might suppression do to the mental and emotional process of offering love? She grew momentarily anxious, fearing she would be dry, arid, empty of love in the future, incapable of offering anything of herself, unable to give warmth or affection, lacking even sincerity; for so long she had been cold and hard and professional that now the future was almost certain to find her the same.

Janet felt anxiety twisting a key inside her, and panic began to make its appearance. God! her mind started to cry in alarm – it was very rarely she consciously turned to Him for help. Her pulse rate increased and soon her hands began to tremble, she forced them down on the top of the table, trying to induce calm as in her mind's eye her future dissolved into a void, swirling with now worthless paper money which would buy her nothing of the commodity she most desired there in that life, affection. It was her recurring nightmare, only here she wasn't asleep, and couldn't wrest herself into the relative safety of consciousness. For a moment she believed she was going mad. She jumped up from the table and stabbed agitatedly at the buttons on the radio until noise was emitted. Yes, she was awake, and sane; her future was foreseeable and foreseeably comfortable, she reassured herself. The anxiety she was experiencing was nonsense, she wouldn't lose the ability to love, to offer warmth and affection and sincerity, all that was necessary was the right person. Juliet was the right person, and when they were together again in the future her daughter's affection and her own affection for Juliet would completely destroy the cynic inside herself.

Calm prevailed again, and Janet was able to smile at the panic forces that had emerged inside herself. She was sane,

intelligent, adult, self-willed, self-controlled; it was laughable
to think that she might deteriorate into an emotionally
barren stick who was incapable of offering anything of herself. Janet instantly decided to offer herself totally to her
next client, match him, run full-tilt with him and finally
capitulate with every fibre of emotion, regardless of what he
was like.

Her next client was a woman, and rather caught Janet off
guard. The woman was about the same age as herself, perhaps a little older, quite attractive with an intelligent face,
well-dressed and quietly spoken. Janet wondered briefly if
she was a detective, but decided not and wrapped her housecoat tightly about herself, growing almost embarrassed and
more puzzled by the woman's presence with each consecu-
tive thought that seemed to instantly flash through her mind.

'Do you take women . . . ?' the woman began, standing in
the reception area. 'That is, entertain them?' She appeared
even more uncertain than she sounded, and her eyes darted
nervously round at the door, then about the area at the top
of the stairs, as though afraid people were going to burst
forth and trample her, or worse, ravage her perhaps. Her
eyes were large and hazel, and sparkling, yet apprehensive,
eyes that had known pain in its most intangible form.

'It depends what you want. . . . ' Janet tried sounding as
kind as possible, not wanting to hurt or frighten the woman.
The situation wasn't new to the PL, yet somehow whenever
it occurred it always seemed to possess a uniqueness – pricks
were all more or less identical, but not women, they were
individual, and Janet accepted that no two were the same as
fact rather than simply as her personal bias. She smiled
encouragingly at the woman, wanting to embrace and reassure her, but first there were necessary preliminaries. 'I
don't have a man here,' she offered tentatively.

'No . . . no . . . ' The woman turned hesitantly, not knowing whether to follow the thought through or run. 'I
shouldn't have come up here . . . I'm sorry. . . . '

The first positive move was made by Janet, she placed her

hand on the woman's shoulder. She felt her tense instinctively, but shortly she relaxed slightly, then yielded a little more, before finally turning towards Janet, her inclination to run having abated. 'There's really no need to be sorry,' said Janet, confident the woman would decide to stay now that she had relaxed perceptibly. 'It's really quite difficult making contact, particularly for young women – even men have problems.' She smiled deprecatingly.

The woman regarded her curiously, relief danced momentarily in her eyes on recognising Janet's sympathies. 'You're not at all what I expected.'

Janet was amused. How often she had heard that, and for a variety of reasons. Some expected their mother or sister, their fiancée, lost wife, hag, queen, nymphette – some just couldn't cope with a straight, reasonably attractive woman of twenty-nine. 'What did you expect?'

The female prospect shrugged apologetically. 'An older woman, quite a bit older . . . I don't know. Certainly not as attractive.'

Perhaps she blushed, Janet wasn't sure. 'Would you like some coffee? – I've only just made some.'

The invitation was accepted.

Over coffee the two women talked, and Janet discovered that the woman's name was Sarah, that she was married, but in spite of having two children, it was a marriage of convenience rather than any spiritual, mental or satisfactory sexual union; they indulged sexual intercourse with little more than a sense of duty, and the prospect of pleasure there was quite unacceptable, something like saying cock-suck at the dinner table. The existence Sarah led was an unenviable one, the professional lady considered, on listening to the details; while vastly different from how her own marriage had been, it was paradoxically almost identical, and Janet soon found herself feeling sorry for the woman. She supposed the world was full of just such women as Sarah, women committed, wanting something better, only not knowing or too frightened to venture out and make contact; she felt sorry for them all.

They talked on, Janet imparting details of her own married existence – it was always easier talking to strangers, she found, as they rarely made demands. When conversation dragged into embarrassing pauses, the would-be client offered compliments on the kitchen which was functional and orderly; then the poodle received a mention, though no affection, for Sarah had little love of animals.

In another silence Janet debated whether she should make some move forward; her earlier fears about not being able to give anything of herself emotionally were perched on the edge of her consciousness. She could have offered more coffee, only had turned the pot off.

Silence prevailed. Neither woman offered anything. Somewhere a clock was ticking. Sarah smiled timidly, then immediately averted her eyes as though she was afraid they would reveal some sinister design. Somehow Janet knew she had to broach the matter that each had momentarily placed at the back of their minds, but didn't really know how without sounding crude; the volition had to be hers, it was business and the transfer from kitchen to work-room could be both awkward and hurtful now. Sarah had called hopefully, if somewhat naïvely, seeking something more than her husband's insensitivity, and logically expected something more now. Janet regretted this invite into her life; before it she would have been able to state the terms quite easily.

Sarah's hand moved along the edge of the kitchen table and cautiously closed over Janet's; there was no resistance and she grew bolder. Sarah raised the professional lady's hand and pressed it against her lips. Janet felt a little annoyed, not especially for that move, but for the fact that it was the would-be client who had made it when it should have been herself. Instinctively she rose with the woman and moved into her embrace, remaining there motionless as if completely spellbound, and quite how long she didn't really know. The woman placed her lips against her cheek, and

Janet could feel herself falling under her influence. She wondered if this woman wasn't in fact the answer to her unuttered prayer about all those fears for the future. Here she could test her emotions, prove to herself that she was still capable of giving. There was an immediate affinity with Sarah, she found, and for having her prayer answered, it was better that she offered herself to a female rather than a male; so she allowed herself to be drawn further and further by the woman. Sarah sighed with relief where she stood holding the PL in the kitchen.

'I'm so happy I've found you at last,' Sarah said. 'You can't imagine how much I've searched' – she led, while Janet fell into step.

Janet was thankful for having recently bathed and changed the sheets on her work-bed, and would have been distressed had the woman been offended by smells emanating from soiled sheets or from her body – the timing seemed just one more point confirming to her that their meeting was fated, a prick might otherwise have interposed to render her unfresh again. In the work-room Sarah opened the professional lady's housecoat and gently placed her lips to her breasts, and despite the woman's rising urgency, Janet remained unmoving herself. She was fully aware of the woman's lips, but wasn't at that moment ready to give herself over to emotion. She noted Sarah's move downwards until finally the potential client was on her knees, her lips making contact with the PL's crotch – Janet was doubly grateful for that bath! Strange guttural sounds of delight, somewhat muffled, were emitted from the kneeling woman, who suddenly locked her arms about Janet's thighs as her body heaved. Janet felt herself moist, but knew it wasn't from an emission and assumed it was saliva from where her pussy had been eaten. There was an emotional lull in the woman, and Janet knew that then was the moment to broach that possibly indelicate matter of money, before the woman had found all the relief she wanted. Janet took the woman by the shoulders and carefully raised her up. But Sarah immediately threw her arms about her in a firm embrace. 'That was very nice,' she said, gratefully. 'Thank you.' She lowered her head to Janet's bosom to start the process again.

Stopping the woman, Janet heard a voice inside, now, it urged, state the terms now.

'I hate having to bring this up,' she began . . . why was she faltering? – she never did with men, and it wasn't as if Sarah was her first female client. Perhaps it was because she was going to reach out to this woman and attempt to create an emotional equilibrium.

'Yes, of course, I'm sorry' – Sarah grasped the situation instantly. She hurriedly pulled ten pounds from her handbag on the chest of drawers. 'I'm sorry – sorry you had to ask, I should have given it to you directly.' She offered the bank note and watched the PL make it disappear.

Then they were together again.

Once the cause of her inhibitions was dispensed with, Janet felt able to offer herself to Sarah, and waited, expecting her to take the initiative again; only Sarah didn't, instead she stood regarding the PL with a slight look of distress. Janet considered fleetingly whether the woman had changed her mind, or suddenly didn't find her so attractive after all. But as though in reply to her unexpressed doubts, Sarah said: 'Oh, Janet, I want you so much, I can't control myself.'

The woman was losing control, and Janet knew where and understood her distress. Taking her to the bed, she removed her blouse and skirt, recalling herself as a very young woman who, when undressing a young man similarly, she had been able to mark her own excitement rising; however, now in a similar situation where she wanted to give as much, nothing was happening to her. She removed Sarah's bra, exposing her breasts which were white and soft and goose-pimpled around the nipples. Nothing at all stirred in her, not even when removing the woman's girdle to reveal her peach tinted pants; they were bright orange at the crotch where she had had an orgasm. Janet experienced anxiety when the woman's wet and pouting vagina was finally displayed, it did nothing for her; feeling would come soon, she tried reassuring herself, but the seeds of doubt weren't easily eradicated, especially when, having wiped the woman with tissues in readiness, there was still no stirring inside her. Sarah pulled Janet down on top of herself and their mouths met briefly, then more passionately; then rolling over with her, Sarah adopted the position of the male and her lips sought Janet's again, before moving down to her bosom, and on over her stomach until at last oral-genital contact was made once more.

Lips pulled and tore at her soft threshold, Janet was acutely aware of the physical contact, but still lacked any kind of mental stimulus, and without it nothing at all happened. Perhaps she was spent after all, emotionally bankrupt, incapable of giving anything, incapable of experiencing anything, not even orgasm, other than that induced with her fingers; nothing mutual, nothing shared with another person which evolved through respect or affection for that person, or just plain enjoyment. For the second time that evening, and for the very same reason, she felt anxiety escalate into panic, and writhed mentally, trying to hold herself in check.

So involved was she with her inability to feel anything that she failed to notice Sarah rise off her and collect something from her handbag. Immediately the client returned and Janet saw the canvas harness straps she knew what it was, and was a little relieved that the woman wanted to employ the dildo; that would fetch her on to emotional parity when she could run to a climax with her. Instantly she recognised a pocket of excitement as she sat up and helped Sarah to strap on the tool; the padded strap ran under her crotch and up to the triangle fastener, which adjusted the straps around her hips. Sarah carefully inserted her own piece, then assisted Janet to take the main shaft when she laid back. Sarah was coming before she had barely began working on top of her. 'I wanted you so much, Janet, so terribly much' – the words hissed out on Sarah's breath. At last she lulled, but it was simply a lull before the emotional storm. Her rhythm didn't miss, she continued working on top of the professional lady with an even strength.

Negative. Negative. Negative! Janet felt the woman's rhythm, but the implement penetrating deep inside her induced no sensation at all, certainly none pushing for delight. At that moment she wanted to weep, but was quite sure even that would prove impossible for her. She wanted to scream, only frustration had a vicelike grip which choked off sounds by crushing her vocal chords, expression remained locked in her chest, fighting for release. The woman's pace started to increase in anticipation of the approaching storm; Janet could sense that, and feel the artificial phallus hitting her harder now, but still nothing stirred for her part. She increased her intake of air, which merely simulated the race rather than sustained it – perhaps she was trying too hard. Relax, she told herself, relax and you'll be fine when the time's right. That seemed logical, only she couldn't relax, anxiety was a precipitous path which was causing frigidity to become self-perpetuating; finally she would have a classical sexual-block, preventing her from ever achieving another orgasm – the prospect terrified her. She tensed, and was sure the woman on top of her noticed. Soon Sarah would complain that she wasn't getting value for money – why had she taken money from her? that was the root of the trouble. Nonsense! she suddenly insisted, dismissing the thought.

She sucked in more breath and expelled it through clenched teeth in order to match her client, who was now sprinting full tilt into storm, her breathing racing her thrashing heart, which in turn seemed to be racing the thrashing spike. There was no involuntary, uncontrolled frenzy in the artificial member, however, it did all but ejaculate sperm into the cunt; its wearer was caught without control in her frenetic emotion, while the main recipient was like a log, experiencing nothing real.

Frigid. Even the word was offensive, Janet thought, while the actual fact of being frigid was intolerable.

After letting Sarah out of the flat, she moved back to the

work-room and laid on the bed to think things over. Sarah was attractive and intelligent and desperately in need of her, she reflected sadly, and she had wanted to offer her everything, including love if necessary; after all she was a woman, and Janet had often assured herself that she could only love another woman, and give herself to another woman like Ursula, while in fact Sarah had been just such a woman, and regrettably Janet hadn't been able to get going at all with her. Janet's eyes became glazed as she stared vacantly at the ceiling, and much as she would have liked to, she didn't cry; weeping would probably have helped relieve her pent-up frustration, but then she doubted that she could have conjured sufficient emotional current for tears.

What was frigidity? she questioned. Frigidity was invariably a mentally induced physical deficiency, an often simple state of mind, though definitely self-perpetuating, like impotency in men, if not put-down in its early stages. And a state of mind could only be cured by a mental process. She wasn't frigid, she told herself, and consequently wasn't; however, the act which had shortly gone before was proof to the contrary, and would remain at the back of her mind as that nebulous uncertainty until eradicated once and for all. Randomly she ploughed through a mire of thoughts, trying to grasp some logical process which might eradicate her doubts, knowing, while not consciously acknowledging, that through but one physical act counterpoise could be reestablished.

Vacantly she rose as the buzzer heralded another client; perhaps in her abstraction some had been missed. Maybe she should try for an orgasm with this prick, Janet mused, replacing the entryphone after admitting him; possibly her trying before was really all that had been wrong. If it was all allowed to happen, as it would, when it would, then there would be no anxiety and no problem.

Had she not been so rapt in thought Janet might possibly have marked the client as a detective when passing him through the door at the top of the stairs; however, in fairness to her usual perception in such things, the man, who was in his early thirties, didn't have the usual CID stamps marking him. He was smart and fairly good looking, and ordinarily she might have questioned the presence of just such a trick. It wasn't until she presented the proposition that the possibility of his profession began to dawn on her. The man smiled wryly at the price.

'Too high?' Janet enquired tentatively, wanting no CID problems. Harry Bleedew supposedly took care of the police on the manor, but even so she had visits from the occasional detective, who might either have been short of a few pounds, or wanting some relief, or both. Most PLs obliged the filth, even though the set-ups they generally existed in were fairly safe and would have given the police a difficult time bringing an indictment; it wasn't wise to rock the boat, in such an event the detective involved would in all probability have waited with a colleague for the professional lady to come out of her safe flat and then made his move, a fit-up was all too plausible. Janet knew the prospects, she had after all been married to a detective. She didn't rock the boat.

'What are you,' the CID asked, 'a brass?'

It was Janet's turn to smile wryly. But the CID liked the words, they usually wanted the words which committed people. The woman gave him the words, and he nodded deprecatingly. 'Yeah, you're definitely too dear, love.'

Without raising any objections Janet led the man through to the work-room, he would get his off gratis, and she didn't even mind very much. The fact that she had had a profitable day could have been a consideration, only wasn't; her thoughts were still engaging with the possibility of her frigidity. When she started working on the CID, he resisted.

'Who else is here with you?' His eyes flitted around expertly, as though expecting to find concealed cameras. Janet offered the truth about the flat's occupancy. However, the CID wasn't entirely satisfied. 'What about your Lord Peter?'

The man declined her offer to search the flat. He yielded a little and Janet began work. But the CID shortly stopped her again. 'Get your knickers down and let's see ya pisser.'

'I don't have any on,' Janet replied coolly, and opened her housecoat for inspection. The CID considered her thoughtfully. 'D'you want me to put some on for you?' she offered. The man shook his head, then like some insensitive medical officer, reached down and inspected her vagina with two fingers, which he finally smelt. Janet felt incensed at his attitude, but didn't say anything. The CID seemed satisfied and nodded grudgingly. The woman was obliged to undress the detective who would want full value even though he had made no donation. The man's cock was large and strong, with black hairs starting along from the base; he put her in mind of her ex-husband, and they were similar in other respects too. She wondered if all the CID sported such blooms. Janet reached for a sheath and broke it from the packet, only the man wasn't entertaining that, he wanted the skin job without membraneous interposition.

'How do you know I'm clean?' tried Janet. Her ruse to get the man into a sports jacket didn't work.

'I'll take a chance,' he replied, adding: 'I want you to plate me first anyway.'

That was a million. Janet had hoped he wouldn't demand being sucked, but it had been a slim hope indeed. The CID sank back on to the bed and the woman knelt forward to him, knowing any protest would be as futile as asking for payment. Her lips fitted him closely, and there was a slight saline taste immediately on her tongue; sweat she assumed, for it soon vanished. The CID was sensitive to Janet's efforts, he responded as her tongue worked delicately around his foreskin, brushing along the frenum at the back of the head. Her process here was to continually swallow and regurgitate, giving the bastard far better than he ever deserved. Janet's thoughts were suddenly very angry. She wanted to pull away and finish with this; she felt nauseated, not through the execution, she had blown too many for that, but rather the connotations of the detective's existence there. She wanted to spit, retch blood, and cleanse her mind along with her mouth, but continued to swallow and regurgitate. Her hand embraced his firm testicles, and her teeth drew along the skin nipping it lightly. A thought struck Janet as she continued sucking him, with just one firm bite she could ruin this bastard for life, in every conceivable way – she would of course ruin herself at the same time. How might the filth explain away his cock being bitten off? She paused from her work, increasing the pressure slightly with her teeth; a wicked smile wrinkled in her mind, but finally she swallowed to regurgitate once more. The man's hands moved down to her neck as his excitement increased – Janet knew instantly what that meant, the fucking bastard! The rhythm went and he started to throb – the woman wanted to pull off and let him blow in the bed, but he held her firmly in position. Then he came! It was a little sweeter than a woman's come, Janet remembered, as it burst on to her taste-buds. The CID still held her. She wanted to spit his come out, but instead swallowed once more, only didn't regurgitate this time.

The CID paused only briefly, just long enough to find his cool again and get his cock back up; it rose up like an olden railway signal. The CID mounted her thighs and slid into her without assistance. He performed well. There was no doubt of his strength as he jammed into her, withdrew and went in again, holding a steady rhythm, while the mass of animal poised delicately on her chest where his weight was taken on his elbows. His performance was admirable to a point, clean, controlled, detached. She looked myopically at the face suspended over hers; it had that utter detachment of an inquisitor. Ebb and thrust and ebb and thrust and ebb and thrust, like a machine, in and out, never missing. Whether it was the detachment with which she was being fucked, the consistent rhythm, the touch of skin to skin inside her, or the emotional allusions to a man she once had the misfortune to love, Janet didn't know, all she knew was that her metabolism was aligning with the CID's, and that annoyed her; for she didn't want it this way, she had wanted it her way with Sarah, or whoever she chose, not whoever chose her. Desperately she tried resisting, but it was no good; summoning every fibre of her resistance she still couldn't hold herself. It was as though she was being drawn through a smooth cylinder into a gigantic vacuum, when thrusting out her arms and legs did nothing to prevent her slipping in; the route was hopelessly precipitous, she was being caught in a vortex of passion along with the man. His phallus was enormous, and touched every part of her, heart and soul, opening doors on her emotions which hadn't been opened in years, permitting her very essence to flood out; nerve-endings tingled to the point of exhilaration while wave upon wave of sexual delight flowed in intangible form through her body as the man continued; his pace was her pace, she was running full tilt with him into emotional frenzy.

They arrived together when suddenly Janet felt what seemed to be her entire life fountain up out of her on a great paroxysm of the most beautiful pain she had ever experienced, pain made even more beautiful by its welcome significance. She wasn't frigid after all, but could ride with a lover to a climax; achieve a satisfactory orgasm; could come as well as any woman. The paroxysm continued to hold her, quivering, shaking convulsively with the man, uncontained.

But then in an instant pocket of thought she realised with some consternation, that at that moment, with that client, that bastard client, she hadn't wanted to achieve an orgasm; it was the very last thing she had wanted. Janet wept silently, secretly without a tear being shed – her emission continued as though it would never stop, nor would her non-paying client's member stop ejaculating sperm into her. She tried to shut out and deny the fact that she was deriving pleasure or anything resembling it from this act with the CID, but couldn't. She wanted to scream in protest, but couldn't. Nothing would stop her coming, nothing would stop him coming; her vagina couldn't contain the sperm, which would eventually spill out of her and fill the room until at last they both drowned in their intermingled come. Only then would their frenzied organs stop their loveless bleeding, Janet realised.

Part Three
Jane

"If I were but a whore I'd sell myself."

9

Harry had been pissed off with her, he had said she was totally unreliable and had been pissed off with chasing her all over town; finally he had told her to piss off, that he couldn't be wasting his time with her any more. However, when Jane had done just that he had soon chased after her. She guessed he must still like screwing her an awful lot. For his part Harry was pretty good; Jane had decided that the very first time the man had got into her. She had had some very good fucks in her time, but there was no doubt where Harry figured. The only thing that pissed her off with Harry was that he was always running, there was always some business to get together, he was never still for a moment. And she always had to meet him places, he never came to her pad to pick her up. A curt phone call, brief instructions, the name of the club, hotel, bar room, and the time.

The very best hotel, Janet mused leisurely from the back of a taxi, as it swung on to the forecourt; she liked these meeting places the best. If nothing else Harry had a certain desirable style, though nothing else wasn't her contention.

Harry Bleedew existed in a manner which was at the very least self-gratifying, something which Jane understood, and he had encountered Jane at one of her most vulnerable moments. Normally she wasn't as susceptible as she had been then, or so she told herself, but rather existed in a shell of indifference, which Harry had penetrated at the end of the fantastic love affair she had had. Now Jane was grateful – she had suspected Harry's scene at the outset, but he was a terrific fuck, so what the hell. In theory there was nothing she wouldn't do to oblige him, though in fact she knew herself capable of changing like the wind when things didn't happen her way.

The hotel soared into the clouds, its façade glittering with tiny spotlights; the entrance sparkled with polished plate-glass and flunkey's brass buttons. Wistfully Jane gazed out of the taxi at the building; this might easily have been part of a dream; only Jane rarely lost her hand-hold on reality. She had never been to this hotel, or any quite as splendid, yet knew instinctively how to behave; the more deprecatingly one regarded the flunkeys the more obsequious they became. Settling the cab fare, Jane permitted the porter to take her small overnight case, then strutted across the forecourt and paused to allow the flunkey to open the door for her.

A long time ago she had appreciated just how easy it was to get men to do things for her. At the drop of a hat the adorable creatures would pander round, even at the risk of reputation, marriage and career, and that was really one of the nicest compliments a girl could be paid, Jane had always considered. Her discovery of man's willingness and compliance, she recalled, seemed to coincide with her transition, along with swelling breasts, into womanhood, before which she had been a child, a nuisance, a thing shouted at or tolerantly smiled at, given a sweet and generally ignored, apart from by what was known as the dirty old man. Then suddenly to her delight she was attended and listened to, given drinks and invited out. A pupil in life still, but a very apt one who quickly learnt to trade with feminine guile for keys to whatever doors. Now at twenty-two she didn't know all the ways of the world, but at least had a good working knowledge; however, Jane didn't really know where she was going in life despite telling herself otherwise, she simply drifted from one love affair to another, a creature of whim and impulse. A reasonable marriage she supposed was what she was unpurposely seeking, and guessed that was what all young women were seeking. The right guy would happen on to the scene one day, perhaps not really Mr Right, but a man who would fit the bill at that moment, relieve whatever particular bout of boredom she would probably be going through, screw like a wet dream, and who out of gratitude she would probably marry. A comfortable marriage wouldn't be at all difficult for a beautiful young woman – she was quite beautiful, her beauty was worth much more than just a second look, and heads in foyers and restaurants invariably turned when she entered.

Jane was tall and angular, with slender hips and breasts that budded like soft peaches; long silky blonde hair floated in the most delicate breeze and bounced with her light springy step; her eyes were pale grey, wide, and sparkling; her mouth full and slightly pouting; intelligent, feminine, beautiful, self-willed, she was the kind of woman every man might create for himself as his ideal woman and then in all probability regret immediately. The prospect that anyone would ever possess Jane was unlikely, she was too wilful and headstrong, and needed to roam and flit from and to whatever was put on offer, and had the style to do so with impunity. Jane wasn't particularly insensitive, though was rarely hurt by life or its quirks, simply because she was a realist who, while frequently jumping in the deep-end, never did so without knowing just how far down the bottom was and what thrust would be required to propel her out; also while never losing sight of the fact that she could contract the bends if rising too fast from too great a depth. Jane Cream was acutely aware of what life had to offer, knew the paths and where the relatively easy route lay; she was a young woman who epitomised the progressiveness of her age, but were she to die shortly it was doubtful that anyone would truly miss her, for her best was superficial, which was the best she received. Tears were wasted on the dead anyway, and never brought them back to life – Jane would have it no other way. Perhaps Harry Bleedew would miss her for about five minutes, perhaps only five seconds.

Graceful, lynxlike movements carried the young woman across the predominantly gold hotel foyer; heads turned. Jane caught sight of them from the corners of her eyes and felt pleased. A faint smile brushed her mouth, the smile she employed when playing the game with men, titillating them with her eyes when they were in such places and positions where they couldn't hope to respond without ruinous consequences.

The reception clerk was stumbling, mentally fumbling, wishing and almost believing the young woman who arrived at the desk was within his reach, provided he made the right impression.

'Mr Harry Bleedew?' the young woman said, her tone endorsing their respective positions and shattering the clerk's hopes irrevocably.

'Ah yes, madam, your husband is in 418 – he told me to expect you.'

News of her marriage was accepted without surprise, though Jane was a little annoyed with Harry for not having warned her. As she moved round to the lifts she felt the reception clerk's lustful eyes on her, but didn't fancy him at all, nor the porter, who she relieved of her small case and stepped into the lift, leaving the man touching his forelock, untipped; Jane made no such donations. If female, young and attractive, tips weren't necessary, her presence was gratuity enough; she knew how men undressed women with their eyes, often making love to them in the same fashion. Jane knew a lot about men.

178

The lift rose with a gentle swoosh to the fourth floor. 418 was along the corridor, the lift operator directed her. Jane rewarded the man with a smile – his thoughts weren't original. The smell that hotel corridors were never without rose to her nostrils, dry, scented, rather like hospitals only more expensive and not so antiseptic.

The key to 418 was in the lock. Harry would have left it there for her, she decided, to save any embarrassment in case a flunkey had shown her up. Turning the key, Jane removed it and went inside, shutting the door. The suite, which overlooked the park, was delightful, Jane found; it was predominantly pink and broken with gold, colours she decided to have her own bedroom decorated in at the flat Harry was finding for them. Jane's eyes swept round, taking in everything. Harry was in the bathroom en suite, the door was slightly ajar and she heard water running. Harry's habit of washing his hands was obsessional, and often caused her to smile, but she was rather glad really, preferring men with clean neat hands, rather than calloused, dirty hands with broken nails; that was how she remembered her father's hands. He worked with his hands, and was proud of the dirt and callouses, believing they were ennobling, though Jane had always failed to see how; then she had never held any belief in the dignity of labour, not even the labour of childbirth, in the event she would have a caesarean section. But that was if and when, while for the present all contingencies were covered.

Opening her overnight case on the bed, Jane unpacked the few things she had with her, a shirt, some tights, some clean pants. The bulk of her stuff was at a friend's flat waiting to be collected as soon as Harry settled her permanently. She didn't imagine this stop would be permanent, and didn't know that she would want to live in an hotel for any length of time anyway. Her thoughts remained with labouring, pondering how long it might take one woman to clean every suite in the hotel; guessing twenty minutes a room and eight hours a day, a long time, she concluded, thankful for not

being that woman, or any like her. However, she had worked
at one time in an hotel, nothing comparable with this, but a
small place a few miles outside her home town. She had been
sixteen, and as a fifth-former had considered going on to art
school. Teddy Rooster had been the hotel proprietor's name.
Jane smiled reflectively, her employment during her vacations had been quite an education; Teddy Rooster had been
quite an education. About fortyish, he was what she had
then classed an old man, who promptly earned the prefix,
dirty. In her innocence his lecherous looks had meant
nothing more to her than the excuses he found for rubbing
against her – the dawn had finally broken one morning when
she was preparing a room. Teddy Rooster crept quietly up
behind her as she was leaning over the bed, and stood in
very close. She first became aware of him when his hard-on
had touched her bottom – she had had an inclination for it
the Greek way since. Jane remembered the hotel proprietor
with affection. She had continued in his employment but
never worked at the hotel again, instead flitted around being
nice to her employer, and his special customers, who in turn
were nice to her, and generous, Jane made sure of that.
Jewellery was a frequent present, and Jane soon got to
appreciate the value, and responded accordingly. However,
she had never understood Mrs Rooster's attitude when she
had suddenly exploded and called her all those unpleasant
names, whore and prostitute included. Jane hadn't considered that fair, she had never accepted money in exchange
for sexual intercourse; she fucked and sucked because she
liked it very much; men had of course given her money, but
that was simply on account of her plausible hard luck stories.
Mrs Rooster was a bitch. Jane had realised that from the
beginning, which was partly why she had fucked Teddy, as
much out of pity as curiosity or need.

The young woman smiled again. Generally she had fond
memories of that hotel and harboured no ill thoughts for
anyone there, not even Mrs Rooster.

From her case Jane took a few toilet articles that were

too large for her handbag and carried them over to the dressing-table, then glanced around at the bathroom door. The water had stopped running, but Harry wasn't forthcoming. Perhaps it wasn't Harry in the bathroom, but a business associate, this expected to be another of his so called public-relations scenes.

'Harry?' she said apprehensively and moved towards the bathroom, then stopped and called his name again. Still there was no reply. 'Harry,' she offered finally, 'did you know I was pregnant?' Jane edged cautiously forward, certain that if it was her man he would have emerged at that prospect.

Pushing the door carefully open, she caught the man's reflection through the mirror before actually seeing him. He was unmoving at the shell-shaped wash basin, his hands washed but not yet dried.

'You're not Harry,' the young woman said, rather stupidly she realised. The man shook his head as though just making the discovery himself. They stared at one another across the bathroom in an embarrassed silence.

The man was very tense, Jane observed, and guessed he had probably stood too frightened to move from the moment he had heard her enter. Perhaps he was a burglar? she instantly dismissed the idea, and wondered whether she ought to try another gambit or wait for him. Silence prevailed. The man was quite attractive, Jane mused, he was in his early fifties, distinguished, with iron-grey hair, a professional looking man; Harry seemed to make the acquaintance of dozens of such people; doctors, financiers, solicitors, even a judge once. Jane wondered if this man was a judge, but decided he wasn't; then considered what his reaction might have been had she just unzipped his fly and gone down on him. She quite fancied him.

Embarrassment had locked his muscles rigid; he wanted to speak, but was having difficulty breathing even, and felt an utter fool being caught like that. He had never even considered such a situation before. Ridiculous, he couldn't even relax sufficiently to dry his hands. How many times had he washed them since hearing the young woman enter? – what fatuous excuses he had sought for delaying himself and putting off the moment when they had to meet; he had never realised before what little there was in a bathroom to delay oneself, short of taking a bath. Fire was added to his embarrassment as he considered how he had allowed Harry Bleedew to talk him into this; the cost wasn't important, but the connotation distressed him here. The woman seemed equally put out – woman? Had she only been that, instead a girl, beautiful and so young. Certainly no older than his son Robert. What would he think of this? The boy cherished his mother's memory so. But was this conceivably abusing his wife's memory? he questioned. The young woman was incredibly lovely; however, she wasn't at all what he had expected.

'Why not dry your hands? – I'm sure they'll feel more comfortable.' She smiled reassuringly, and the man became animated. 'That's what towels are for.'

He tried to smile through his embarrassment as he raised the handtowel. The young woman watched him curiously; it wasn't usual for men of such apparent standing to be so tense – perhaps he was a protesting homosexual.

Finishing with the towel, the man returned Jane's look. There was silence again. At last he said, 'You're really very beautiful' – the words were managed without a falter despite tense vocal chords.

So many women were inept at accepting compliments, but Jane smiled appreciatively and simply said: 'I know,' then turned and moved away from the bathroom.

The man didn't follow, but stood watching her where she stopped by the bed, obviously expecting him to join her. He wondered if his legs would carry him; one foot fell cautiously in front of the other. The door was reached and he hesitated, but decided against swinging it shut after himself. In the bedroom he continued to silently watch the young woman, no less regretting his presence.

'Are you a friend of Harry's?' Jane asked, quickly adding:

'You're not a burglar or a member of the hotel staff?'

'No, neither.' He attempted a smile. 'I couldn't exactly call myself a friend . . . an acquaintance, I suppose. I know him.'

'Business associate?' the young woman offered helpfully. The man shook his head apologetically. 'I'm sorry, I shouldn't have come here. It's causing an awful lot of embarrassment. Obviously you had no knowledge of the arrangement.'

Adopting a bemused expression, Jane said: 'What arrangement?' She had realised what Harry had set up, but wasn't angry, or even put out particularly, she would simply have preferred him not to treat her like a child; if he really needed her to screw his acquaintances he had only to ask, and if he didn't realise that by now then he ought to!

'You were expecting to find Harry here?'

'This is Harry's suite – he is coming back . . . ?' When the man shook his head, she stopped, allowing him to see that she was becoming disturbed – having learned a long while ago that the ploy was worthless without it was seen.

'I'm most frightfully sorry. At this moment I feel about as proud as a wart' – he looked about that proud.

Nervous laughter parted Jane's lips, then ceased abruptly. She raised her delicate shoulders and tried to show willingness with a smile. 'Well, I suppose you want to make love to me or something like that?' – the prospect was making her feel quite horny.

'No.' He took two urgent steps forward, then one backwards as though afraid of frightening her in his earnestness. 'No, that's not what I want at all.'

'You're very kind, but it really doesn't matter. I guess it's inevitable.'

'It matters. It does matter.' The man came cautiously forward. 'It isn't right, not when the woman has no wish, or design to get involved – I'm sorry, my presence is hideously offensive.' The man hesitated, not knowing whether to go or stay; despite himself he wanted to stay and win the young woman's approval now that the truth was becoming eminently clear.

Slowly Jane sank to the edge of the bed; physical smallness was psychologically right, synonymous with humility. 'I don't imagine I'd be very good. . . . ' Perhaps a tear or two would complete the image. The man remained silent, uncomfortable. Jane looked up at him. 'You're presence isn't offensive. In fact you're really quite nice; decent about all this.'

'No, decency would never have permitted me to get into this in the first place, Jane – you see how involved, I even know your name.' His whole manner was subdued.

'I think you're nice anyway. What's your name?'

'Munny' – managing to make it sound like an apology. 'Gilbert Munny.'

'You called Gilbert or Gil by your friends?'

'I don't have many friends – most of my acquaintances call me Gilbert.'

Fleetingly Jane wondered if the man was emulating her style and trying for sympathy. 'I'll call you Gil if I may, Gilbert sounds too stuffy, and you don't seem stuffy.'

Gil smiled but didn't reply immediately. He searched the silence for something intelligent, or at least pertinent to say. Finally: 'Are you pregnant, Jane?'

'Pregnant?' the young woman echoed, puzzled.

'You said you where, when you believed Harry was in the bathroom.'

'Oh – no, I was afraid it wasn't him. I say that sort of thing when I'm afraid.'

'I'm pleased,' said Gil, 'very pleased that you're not.'

Jane's large grey eyes questioned.

'It's rarely pleasant for a young woman when she's unmarried, despite changing attitudes – I'm assuming you are unmarried?'

'Yes, and most decidedly unpregnant. You married, Gil?' she asked conversationally, and noticed what she believed to be dull pain cloud the man's eyes. Things were going wrong, she told herself, he should be offering her sympathy instead of her feeling any for him.

The man said quietly: 'My wife died three years ago.'

'Was that how? This?' Jane felt annoyed with herself for tempering her words; what the fuck did she care?

'I miss my wife, Jane, at times terribly; the libido didn't bring about this move. All that had become rather dormant, or so I thought, but all one seems to require in fact is opportunity.' He shook his head abstractedly. 'I don't know. I don't . . . yes, temporary loss of sanity, I think . . . I'm sorry, I didn't mean that quite as it sounded.'

Seizing her opportunity to reverse the positions again, Jane adopted a hurt expression and lowered her head slightly, while nervous hands fiddling in her lap completed the appearance and won the man's sympathy.

The man came closer, his tension returning. 'Really, Jane, I didn't mean to be so offensive. I'm sorry.'

'Doesn't matter. Anyone would be entitled to think the same, coming to this hotel.' She faltered on the verge of tears.

'You silly girl,' he said, taking her hands in a paternal fashion. 'No one has such an opinion of you. It's me, my clumsiness, my lack of tact. You seem to me a thoroughly charming, delightful young lady, and one I would be proud and honoured to know anywhere.' The man, having taken her hands in his, now had no idea what to do without giving further offence by simply withdrawing them. 'Oh God' – this with a note of despair. 'I find this situation hopeless. You're hardly what I expected. You're so beautiful and so young – I've a son about your age.'

Withdrawing his hands from hers, he moved away across the room to collect his hat. Jane watched him a little surprised. Her problem now was how to take him for bread without rekindling the image she had just put down. She didn't doubt that Harry had already taken the man for a donation, and saw no reason why she shouldn't also. On the whole she hadn't done very well so far. With the man offering so much sympathy, she realised how silly she was to have denied her pregnancy, regardless of images; with tears from her he would probably have produced a substantial sum for an abortion. The ploy now would be both foolish and obvious. The man returned to the bed and extended his hand. Jane didn't offer hers, or speak.

Embarrassment clogged Gil's throat, and he cleared it to speak: 'Are you going to stay here, Jane?'

'I don't know' – dolefully. 'I suppose so. Don't seem to have any choice. I'll have to wait until Harry shows up.'

'When will that be?' the man asked kindly; the girl might suddenly have become his responsibility.

Jane didn't know when Harry Bleedew would next appear and told Gil so; however, not that it would almost certainly be within the next twenty-four hours. 'I just don't know what to do.'

'Do you love him very much?' he asked, sitting on the bed.

'Love?' she questioned, having adopted her naïve attitude again. 'Never really thought about it. After my parents died, he sort of took me under his wing,' she lied smoothly; her parents were alive and well. Perception Jane never lacked, frequently being able to grasp the threads of a scene and instantly turn things her way. Perceptive-opportunist aptly described her. She saw what appeared to be a mental cloud lift from the man next to her. Why? Because he had believed her association with Harry was her own volition, and had now decided that she didn't in fact love him, but was only grateful to him? She decided to play according to that viewpoint; it mattered little provided she won, which she invariably did. 'I'm very grateful to him, he's been good to me.'

'This good to you?' – vaguely indicating the situation.

'I don't understand, Gil.' That bemused expression was back on her face. 'Isn't this good? It's awfully nice here' – she saw his anguish.

'You don't understand, Jane. Yes, this is all very nice, comfortable, grand. But the connotations aren't nice. Believe me, they're odious.'

'Harry wouldn't do anything to harm me. I'm sure.' She

wondered if she wasn't overkilling the ingénue, but decided not.

The man said: 'Not that you were likely to realise immediately. You know why you were told to come here? Why I was here? I'm not trying to excuse my part. Men such as me are essential to friend Harry. But don't you succumb to him, Jane, get caught up and become a willing party, as tempting or profitable as it all may seem. This hotel is enough to turn most young women's heads.'

Amusement was jostling for prominence, but Jane allowed it no freedom. The man sounded as though he cared what happened to her, and in spite of not particularly wanting him to care beyond a donation, she found the fact that he did rather pleasing. 'What else can I do?' – with a dismayed sigh. 'I don't want it to happen, but I suppose I always knew it would.'

'No, no! You mustn't allow that.'

'There's no alternative, I have to keep myself. Harry repeatedly says he's not going to keep me any longer. I have to eat, to live, even this suite, even this has to be paid for. You came here, it didn't matter that it was me, could've been any girl – and you offer me pious words, impractical and worthless.' Jane achieved a tearful climax, but noticed the man place three large bank notes on the unit beside the bed.

Gil seemed hurt as he offered her his handkerchief.

'I'm sorry,' the young woman said with sudden calm, 'I didn't mean to be unkind to you.'

'Honesty requires no apology.'

'It's not your fault, none of this is.'

Sighing wearily – 'But I feel culpable, Jane. I owe you something more, I feel. It's always easy to just pay. I would like to do something more for you. You're right, words are worthless; I want to be practical. But you must decide what it is you want.' He paused and regarded her awkwardly, then rose from the bed. 'Sixty pounds, Jane – not for your services or anything of that nature. I'm not forcing you into that situation.' Jane smiled thinly, showing encouragement. He continued, 'It will pay the hotel bill, buy you twenty-four hours in which to sit and think things over. I would very much like to help you, Jane, but you must say what help.' He gave her his visiting card. 'You can contact me there if you wish to; I would be pleased if you did.'

'Why?' she asked flatly. 'Why should you offer help?'

The man paused thoughtfully, 'Conscience perhaps. Guilt at allowing myself to come here. I think perhaps you're a person worth helping.'

Jane began to feel like she was hitting skid-row, and suddenly found the man's attitude irritating. 'I'm not a prostitute in need of reforming.' Her tone caused the man to become more apologetic.

'I didn't consider you were, Jane. Please believe that – anyway I'd doubt that sort of woman would either wish, or accept help.'

'Had I been like that what would your attitude have been then?'

'That would've been all too simple. Money's all they want, the only thing they understand. I would hope you seek something more – I think you do, which is why I hope you'll call and ask my help. Whatever, if I can do anything to help you I will.' That said like a well-meaning official, a silence fell between them.

Gil waited engulfed by uncertainty, he was on the point of departing only didn't know how to.

Given the right circumstances, Jane guessed that the man would moralise; such men bored her, especially those who did so having fucked her. With some it was guilt, others fear of making her pregnant, but each was as boring as the next – even the guys who thought that she was life itself sometimes bored her. However, she hoped she was wrong about Gil Munny, for feelings as varied as contempt and affection now floated through Jane – she instantly rose from the edge of the bed and kissed the man lightly on the lips. The gesture was impulsive, and despite herself she rarely trusted impulses. 'Thank you, Gil, for everything' – the words sounded too sincere for her liking. She turned abruptly away and threw herself on the bed; that was dramatic and conclusive, she felt, but Jane sensed his eyes on her, staring, awkward, embarrassed, probably they were lustful also. She wished he would either lift her dress and forcefully screw her or go now. Possibly some time in the future she would call on him for help, she would have to see what Harry had to say about that – Harry, the bastard, remembering she was still being cross with him for this set-up.

Long naked legs, without protruding veins or hairs, their shape leaving nothing to be desired, were just one of the perfect features of an adorable creature; Gil was almost tempted to ease her dress down over her legs, but feared the young woman might get the wrong idea. So instead he eased the pink bedspread up over her. She would weep, and the tears would help relieve the doubts confronting her, tears always helped. He turned and moved silently away to the door, glancing back once more at her still body where she lay.

Jane heard the gentle click of the door as the man shut himself safely on the outside. She lay unmoving, her tears having ceased. Crying to order was affected by means of a trick Jane had learned from a not very good actor, whose only asset had been his tears. Raising her head slowly, Jane glanced round to make quite sure her benefactor had gone – a simple precaution even though she believed him quite sincere. He was a donator, one of those men who were never happy unless they were giving, it really didn't matter what or to whom, a dinner party for twenty friends or a coin to a dosser, their need was compulsive, donating was their kick. They would give their right arm, then only be happy if the left one was demanded also. Jane had heard of the trait, and had encountered it even, only never in anyone she liked particularly or who had sufficient resources to give without being exhausted on the first excursion – having decided some time ago that she had had her fill of boyfriends who took her home on public transport after cheap seats at a movie, instead of to supper at the White Elephant. Her fondness for Harry derived from the fact that he didn't mind spending his money. To make the going plausible for Jane a man had to have a tolerable car also, preferably with a chauffeur.

The young woman pushed the bedcover back and sat round. The money on the night table caught her eye and she smiled. Gil was wealthy, the sixty pounds confirmed what his clothes and manners had only indicated; the money could have been saved, but it was doubtful that he would have parted from it with such alacrity; a poor man would have counted the going. Reaching out for the small white oblong card, Jane was surprised. Sir Gilbert Munny, she read. She had even heard of him, he was a financier, who was always flying off somewhere to some money conference. Jane was surprised and annoyed at not having associated the name with the face. But on considering the prospect, she decided that perhaps it was as well she hadn't recognised him or her reactions might have been different, and his less favourable. She wondered if Harry knew who the man was. Gil had called him an acquaintance – Harry had probably nodded in the Penthouse Club or somewhere and knew only Christian names. At that point Jane decided not to inform him; it was doubtful that anything further would come of their meeting but she could dream a little, and after all he had given her his card when he could simply have walked out. She read the neat gold scroll again and smiled to herself. Unwittingly Harry had promised her to a wealthy knight, and she found that amusing.

Both card and money she slid down between the lining in her handbag, as it was probable that Harry would go through her bag if the opportunity presented itself. The money was given to her and she had no intention of sharing it, as generous as the man was at times. Another man jumped into her mind! Lord Peter the Ponce, only he had been far less generous, and it had been very necessary to hide half the money she had earned or he would have taken it all. She remembered the hotel they had used then, seedy and generally distasteful, but very convenient; the proprietor had been very obliging.

If nothing else, Jane reflected, they had been amusing times round at that hotel, and often quite profitable. 'There's never anyone quite as gullible as a prostitute's clients' – the words belonged to Lord Peter the Ponce. 'But I'm not a prostitute,' Jane always argued, and if the man didn't capitulate, she would call him Lord Peter the Ponce, a title he detested, even though it nearer described him than ever prostitute described Jane. 'You're one in theory,' the man had rejoindered. In fact Jane had never opened her legs in bed for any john, though had often taken their money. The ploy was good. Either she would collect a would-be client from a pub, or Lord Peter the Ponce would effect the introduction, and Jane would take him to the hotel, where she always insisted on a bathroom en suite; the bathroom divided two bedrooms, one of which was designated, and this would be inspected by the young woman, the procedure assuring the would-be john that she was equally unfamiliar with the set-up. The man was asked for payment up front, having paid for the room in advance, and naturally offered neither suspicion nor resistance when the seemingly coy young woman, who had confessed not doing this before, suggested that he got undressed and into bed while she undressed in the bathroom. That never seemed such an unreasonable request from her lips, and such men were never more gullible; while they waited expectantly, their tepees pitched in the bed, Jane passed through the bathroom and out through the adjoining bedroom and away – few patrons ever complained according to the proprietor who was involved in the ramp.

That had been both an easy and amusing way of collecting the rent, Jane considered, while extra money for herself she had simply deducted from the fee and hidden in her coat or handbag before meeting up with Lord Peter afterwards. Jane wondered what he was doing now. She had heard he was busted with another girl and the hotelier for that ploy. Apparently the girl had picked up a rather treacherous detective who had managed to fuck her, then had arrested her. He obviously hadn't been quite so gullible!

Rising from the bed, Jane moved slowly, aimlessly about the room, pausing to look at furnishings; her purpose might have been to get value for money by treading every part of the carpet, absorbing the entire room. Drawing a vague comparison with that other hotel, she wondered if there was access through the bathroom to the adjoining suite, but hadn't noticed a connecting door.

Jane stopped at the window and stared out. Hyde Park opposite was dark and unmoving, like a massive blob of ink which had spread so far and was halted by Park Lane; everything was eventually halted by the road, paradoxically even the motor vehicle. The lighted dual carriageway, with its up and down confusion of chrome and reflected lights, was a pretty sight, she thought; then she had a certain fondness for cars, they were all phallic symbols, and the more sleek and proficient the better and harder for her to resist, along with their owners. One day she wanted to be fucked in a car while zipping along at about a hundred and fifty plus, completely caught up with the car's rhythm, though didn't imagine it would be the driver screwing her; they would have a discreet chauffeur, who in all probability would be a deaf-mute eunuch. Another ambition was to make it in an aeroplane; boats were commonplace, while just about everyone who travelled had screwed on trains between stations. Jane's aeroplane ambition wasn't very serious, but the car was all too plausible.

Thoughts turned towards food, she was hungry; she only ate twice a day, breakfast, then dinner some ten hours later, unless lunch became an occasion that couldn't conveniently be avoided. Now it was dinner time, and Jane couldn't decide whether to eat in her room with the tv or go to one of the hotel restaurants. She would decide by car-counting; if the tenth car up in the far-side lane was red she would use the restaurant, starting now; however, after counting seven, a bunch of cars came along masked by two large lorries in the middle lane, possibly the tenth car was red. She began counting again after the lorries had passed, but really wanted to go to a restaurant to eat regardless of what the system said. The hotel was expensive, the cost of eating there would be high, but that was Harry's problem, he had given her no instructions about not raising the bill.

The tenth car on the second count wasn't red, but then that wasn't the true count anyway, only a test run; the third go really counted, Jane assured herself, watching more cars go past. The tenth didn't appear to be red, though she accepted that it probably was, deciding that night-lights and colour blindness called it wrong. She would eat in one of the restaurants! Her only indecision then was whether or not to invite a friend – if Harry questioned the bill she could simply say it was Gil who had dined with her. Jane didn't particularly enjoy eating alone, especially not in restaurants.

Raising the phone, Jane gave the switchboard a number from her address book. Dominic Browne was queer, but the young woman never held that against him as he was usually very amusing company. The phone seemed to ring for an age and the man down the line sounded annoyed when he finally picked it up. Dominic had been washing his hair, he explained on identifying the caller. 'I would've loved to have had dinner with the Town's most gorgeous woman, at the Town's most gorgeous hotel, but unfortunately I have someone to meet, my darling' – he didn't qualify that. They gossiped for a while; someone had a new car; someone had contracted a nasty; someone had married someone.

Jane gave the switchboard two more numbers to try but both rang unanswered. Finally she decided to eat alone.

10

Dinner was excellent. Doubtless some could have faulted it, and Jane guessed in a moment of extreme bloodymindedness she could have, but there was no need.

Over her bombe au chocolate she allowed her eyes to wander across the restaurant to the lone diner whom she had noticed on entering. His near-entranced stare had been countered with demure disapproval as she had started dinner, but the man hadn't been discouraged; throughout the meal he had given her his attention, and Jane had expected an approach before now. But perhaps such a move would have been rather forward, and all this was one of the respectable hotels. When their eyes met again she allowed a smile, fine, barely perceptible and had the man suffered defective vision he might have missed it. The waiter carried the invitation with utmost discretion, refusal here couldn't cause embarrassment; the gentleman wished to know if Jane would care to join him for coffee. As if seeing him for the

194

first time, Jane inspected the man indicated by the waiter, then smiled, deciding to accept. If nothing else the man would certainly pick up the bill for her dinner, but looked attractive enough to screw.

'My name is Turlough,' the man said. 'Most people call me Thor, it's much easier.'

Suppressing a derisive smile, Jane instantly decided that Thor would simply pick up her bill for dinner. Her eyes were obviously failing, for close to she saw the man was rather unfortunate. Thor wasn't indicative of strength, perhaps conceit, as he was coming apart at the seams. His hairline was too sharp to be anything but false, likewise his teeth were too white; his eyes sparkled too much – she doubted they were false – he probably put in eye drops; his stomach was extremely flat, she had noticed when he rose as she joined him, a feat for a man in his middle-forties and living well, he almost certainly wore a corset, and build-up shoes; probably carried a dildo to help him out in that department too. As far as sexual gratification was a prospect, Jane guessed Thor would be about as much use to her as a melted candle. They talked through coffee, mainly about him, while Jane considered her ploy for parting company while having him pay her bill. It wouldn't be difficult, for the conceited generally defeated themselves and she would simply allow him to think he was into her knickers.

'Do you often stay at this hotel?' the crumbling man asked.

Rolling the brandy balloon in her hand, Jane replied casually: 'If I can't get in next door.'

'There isn't much to choose between them – you're a movie actress?'

A smile brushed the young woman's lips. 'You're terribly kind, Thor. But I'm not a film actress, or any other kind.'

'Well, you ought to be, Jane, you ought to be.' He swallowed some coffee then gazed across the table at her, his eyes penetrating, unblinking, his expression pensive, as

though awaiting a reply or qualification to something unspoken.

Shortly Jane began to feel a little uncomfortable, wondering whether she had underestimated the man, if in fact he
hadn't realised her game. Perhaps his suggesting she ought
to be an actress was the put down. No, she decided, it was
simply the cliché proposition; next he would probably offer
to get her into movies. In order to make quite sure of the
man, Jane adopted a perplexed expression: 'How do you
mean, Thor?'

'Simply that you ought to be in movies. That may sound
rather corny, but I'm serious, you'd be an absolute wow,
Jane. You'd immediately captivate the entire male population' – his voice was low, slightly embarrassed.

'You are kind!' She smiled, wondering when he would
offer to get her into movies. 'Such compliments will make
me high without wine.'

Ego ruled the patched-up man completely, and Jane felt
a little piqued when it caused him to pass up the opportunity
in order to expound his conception of himself; he stated that
he could have been in movies, only Jane wasn't interested
why he went instead into his father's business, but she just
knew he would tell her. With people such as Thor, in who
she had no intrinsic interest, she had developed a technique
which permitted her to shut out their words and allow her
own thoughts to take an entirely separate tack whilst offering intelligent nods; the advantage was hers of course, as
such conceit would never admit that there could be no
interest.

Watching the man attentively, Jane interjected his oral
noise with nods, and considered how she would like to raise
his toupee and read his mind to see what method he employed inside her pants, which was doubtless where he
already saw himself.

What? – the word suddenly raced through her mind, she
had missed something; the glue and elastic man having
made his proposition sat silently regarding her, awaiting a

reply. Her technique wasn't infallible! She swore at herself – he surely hadn't the front to suggest getting into her at this juncture? That proposal was in the pipeline, but could he consider himself so desirable? she questioned, beginning to feel indignant. 'I'm sorry, Thor, the brandy's clouding my head' – she hoped that wasn't too much of a ridiculous return.

'I simply wondered if you might care to have a drink in the bar with me.'

'I'm sure that'll be delightful.' She looked round intently for her waiter. 'First I must settle my bill ...'

'Please, I'd very much like you to be my guest.'

Thor the Bore was improving – but Jane was seen to protest: 'No, I wouldn't dream of it. I feel I'm imposing as it is.' She wondered if her refusal wasn't too emphatic as the waiter started towards them, but fortunately Thor was insistent, so Jane backed down, and he signed both bills, then they departed for the bar.

Sixty pounds on the same terms as from Gil was a possibility, the young woman considered, sitting in the bar with Thor waiting for the waiter to fetch their drinks. She wouldn't mind suffering his company in her suite long enough for a tearful ruse and a handout. Possibly he could be persuaded to lay out more than sixty if she handled him right, but she definitely had no intention of fucking him. Seeds for the possible ramp quickly germinated in Jane's fertile mind, and shutting out the man's words, she began to develop the prospect until it shattered when the bore signed for their drinks, mentioning conversationally that he had had no need to carry money on him for years. Jane felt suddenly frustrated; she could have taken a cheque, but wouldn't any more, as once, after a clever scene, a would-be benefactor had given her a cheque for ninety pounds which he had then stopped at the bank; his foolish move simply proved inconvenient for Jane, for after a little blackmail the cheque was exchanged for the amount in cash, plus expenses. But still Jane adhered to the rule, no cheques or credits, not even when bank guarantee cards were offered.

If nothing else she was taking value from the male repair job in drinks. He signed for their fourth cocktail, then edged a little closer to her, and launched into the fifth volume of his verbal autobiography! Boredom persisted, and Jane decided it was time to say goodnight. She shunned the direct method; then considered conveniently seeing her husband and rushing off, but feared the bore had had enough to drink to get uptight; so simply rose and excused herself to go to the ladies' room.

Alcohol-softened eyes embraced her, she sensed, as she moved across the bar, and not only Thor's.

Passing through the ladies' door from the bar, she continued straight on through the second exit to the reception area, and round to the lifts. Fortunately she hadn't offered Thor the Bore her suite number, not that it would have been difficult for him to discover, only Jane doubted that he would try, after all she hadn't promised him anything, but had merely wearied of his company. None the less she glanced cautiously over her shoulder as she moved along the corridor on the fourth floor.

For some reason she thought Harry would be in the suite, but he wasn't there and she wasn't really disappointed. A light, carefree mood had enveloped her, and she didn't really want to engage anyone or anything at that moment, but simply wanted to float, like a feather dancing in the gentlest breeze. Kicking off her shoes, she danced gaily across the carpet, then around the room wherever there was a clear space, and running out of space, she sprang on to the bed and bounced there; her hair floated up like magic strands with the movement of her body, like the dream-sequence movie directors shot in slow-motion, only Jane had no power to slow the motion. Leaping from the bed, she stabbed the radio on, electric music jangled out shredding her mood, and suddenly the whole atmosphere vanished.

Selecting another channel on the radio, words gushed forth, gibberish as far as she was concerned. Her finger found another button, more electric music, which was finally silenced. Her will was despotic. She flicked on the tv, and colours pushed through the spectrum, forming into images. Playing was a cowboy movie she had seen a lifetime ago, the sandstone in the foreground of shot was as familiar as the action; the plot reworked a thousand times and good for another thousand. She hovered attentively for a few moments. The Good cowboy was one of her mother's favourites – with his bulging biceps instead of bulging balls he was all mothers' favourite. Breaking the spell, Jane pulled away from the tv, and leaving it with bullets ricochetting across the screen, she decided to take a bath.

Perhaps a shower instead, she considered on inspecting the unit in the bathroom. But no, a bath, there she could float and relax and dream a little. Opening the water inlets, Jane moved back to the bedroom to undress, taking about a minute to remove her only two garments, hanging her dress in the wardrobe; the doors revealed mirrors, and those she found hard to resist any time. Jane stood and considered just how beautiful she was and how nice her body was; she smoothed her hands over her small, firm breasts, then down across her delicate rib cage and over her flat stomach into her crotch, where they covered her like flesh coloured pants. Jane stroked a finger down the outer lips of her vagina; there was nothing quite as nice as touching herself there, she reflected, unless it was having a guy she really turned on to touching her there. Her fingers stroked the small spread of pubic hairs; despite her colouring being fair her pubes were dark brown, which had made her curious ever since they started turning colour from that silky blonde at around the age of twelve. Why did they grow? she wondered, they weren't necessary or had no purpose she could recognise. On the unclean they encouraged crabs, then perhaps that was the whole point. But what about those who were clean? On men they were necessary, or at least attractive; somehow dark, coarse hair surrounding a man's genitals and spreading up his stomach seemed right, manly even. There was nothing feminine about body hair, though there could be, she guessed, if styled; then smiled at the thought of pubic hair stylists' saloons springing up all over the place. Jane decided to style her own pubes, she sometimes cropped them, so why not shape them?

There was something amiss in the bathroom, she sensed on entering it again, and paused thoughtfully, but couldn't grasp what it was. The bath was almost full and she shut off the inlets, then spun round in the sudden silence as though expecting to find someone behind her. There was no one behind her. Steam! Of course, there wasn't any. All the bathrooms she had known had filled with steam, but this one had an efficient extractor.

The nail scissors from her bag, and a wet-razor the hotel was either very considerate or negligent leaving in the cabinet, were her only styling implements. Thought was needed over the shape. A diamond was discarded in favour of a heart, and if that shape didn't work out she could go back to the diamond. The exercise proved quite awkward – pubic hair stylists probably would be necessary. First she squatted on the stool and used the scissors, then shortly found standing easier; it shaped well, but had her hairs been thicker or spread wider she could have shaped an arrow through them. Inspecting the effort frequently through the mirror, Jane decided she had gone as far as possible with the scissors; the razor wasn't particularly sharp nor the lather from the hotel soap particularly efficient, and she hoped she wouldn't get a shaving rash.

Blotting the surplus water finally from her lower abdomen, she combed the hairs out then danced through into the bedroom to consider the effect in that mirror. The heart was delightful and she smoothed it with her hands, covered it, then wrenched her hands away to get the sudden effect. Jane was pleased with it, but sad that it had to be covered with her pants, as she would like to have worn her pubic heart in public.

Occasionally her hand crept under the silky green bathwater to reassure herself of the heart's presence as she lay submerged; it was there, and wouldn't go away. That was another thing for her to play with and take delight in; Jane wanted everything in life to have a hedonistic quality, and if there wasn't intrinsic fun in whatever, then it wasn't really worth much; things were rarely tolerated for their own sake. Even a bath was made fun by what was brought to it. Rarely was she so dirty as to warrant a bath, being one of those girls who could play in a coal-yard and still remain clean. Suddenly she remembered Micky, he was good fun in the bath, even that little bath in the flat she had shared with a thousand other girls.

Jane had been stretched as far as was possible in that bath when Micky had come into the bathroom looking like a C and G – he had shared a flat at the top of the building with a thousand other guys. 'Do you mind if I clean my teeth in here?' Micky had asked with casual disregard to her nudity. 'Our water's off.'

Jane's grey eyes had measured the young man. 'Provided you don't use my tooth brush.'

'Which is yours?' he had asked, sorting through the brushes in the pot above the basin. Assuming he had been joking, Jane stated the blue one and watched him use one of the others. That had been amusing and had decidedly brightened lying in cooling water. 'Would you do me a kindness now? Put a coin in the meter and turn on the hot tap.'

'I can be kinder than that. I could get into that little bath and warm you up.'

Jane had smiled. 'Only if you get in with your clothes on.' She had believed all the young men in that flat queer. Promptly Micky had kicked off his boots, explaining they were his only pair, had stepped into the bath and lowered himself. Jane had accepted him with as much dignity as she could. Then it was a fun bath; the young man adequately replaced plastic ducks, rubber balls and such nonsense.

Pensively the young woman considered Micky now, she had been quite fond of him and regretted his departure at his father's death. They had half-promised to write to each other, both knowing neither would; when was there ever time to stop the process of life to communicate with death or a spirit that could never be recaptured? She wondered what he was doing now, probably he was married with at least two children, he had always had a thing about children, kept wanting her to have one, had even wanted to experience childbirth himself. Poor Micky, he was more than likely mad; the closest he would get to childbirth, she guessed, was a wife he loved too much and who loved him the same way, perhaps then he would share the experience of her labour, though Jane doubted that Micky was capable of such deep love, and had recognised that she wasn't capable herself of such love for him, which was partly why she hadn't wanted his baby.

Once she had been unlucky enough to fall pregnant, not Micky's effort, but another guy who she had been only fond of. Jane had been rather naïve and silly then, and contraception had been harder to say than abortion. Fortunately the guy had access to finance, and a skilful Harley Street abortionist could be afforded; her twenty-four hours at the clinic had been an education, and contraception became a much easier word to live with.

A shiver ran through Jane, despite the bath-water remaining warm. Her past wasn't particularly sinister or frightening, in fact hers was quite reasonable, yet for some reason it always made her shiver; the past was dead and generally quite worthless, and its sharp points should slip into a soft void, then she wouldn't shiver in a hot bath.

Rising from the water, Jane wrapped herself in the pink bath-sheet, which she opened slightly to inspect her pubic heart again, before moving back into the bedroom. There her mother's favourite cowboy was still persisting, notwithstanding bullets, arrows, stampeding cattle and apocalyptic rock-slides. Squatting on the edge of the bed, Jane watched the flickering tv colours – finally the hero kissed the heroine behind the rolling credits, swept her on to his horse and rode away into the sunset, leaving the familiar sandstone for the next movie.

The telephone buzzing finally distracted her. After screwing down the tv volume, she demurred at the buzzing phone; it might have been Thor the Bore looking for a return on his dinner, then again it could have been Harry – but would he have phoned? she questioned. Yes, after what he had arranged at the hotel for her, of course he would ring first.

She raised the phone and the hotel switchboard enquired if she was Mrs Bleedew. Deciding it was Harry, she replied in the affirmative. But the voice through the handset wasn't Harry's, and took her a moment to identify Sir Gilbert Munny. Quietly spoken and hesitant still, he managed to enquire how she felt; stated how glad he was that she was feeling better; reiterated his earlier offer of help, and shortly rang off. With the dead telephone handset against her cheek, Jane paused thoughtfully; having Sir Gilbert Munny, not three hours out of her company, pandering back, enquiring after her well-being, she found rather comforting. Maybe she should have fucked him after all. The switchboard cut in, and Jane thanked the woman and dropped the phone back in its rest.

Standing off the bed, Jane strutted arrogantly around as though modelling the bath-sheet – she could have been a model, but that life didn't appeal. Passing the open mirror, she turned gracefully – 'Here we have Jane wearing the latest in Pucci bath towelling, the pink huckaback perfectly complementing the delicate white Caucasian skin.' And sweeping the sheet open – 'With this garment the pubic hair is worn in the shape of a heart. Though shape is a matter of personal taste – perhaps a butterfly, or a diamond for those less ambitious.' She strutted around some more and finally discarded the sheet.

The tv news was as depressing silent as it was with sound, so Jane lay on the bed jumping the set through the channels; then did the same with the sound, making words hop from one mouth to another, from a newscaster to a politician to a private eye. But soon she wearied of that particular sport. She was very horny and began wishing Harry was there; then she almost wished she had stayed with Thor the Bore, at least he could have been blamed for her boredom.

Finally Jane phoned down for coffee, deciding to have some sport with the waiter. Throwing the door catch, Jane moved back to the bed to watch silent tv; however, she felt deflated when the ninety-year-old waiter, who was presumably blind, entered with the tray, placed it down, poured some coffee and departed as if she didn't exist.

Sleep was difficult coming and had she any tablets she would have taken some. She turned first one way, then another, and back again, it couldn't be the strange bed as she had the urchinlike ability to sleep anywhere. It was Harry who was preventing her sleeping, also Sir Gilbert Munny, they were opposing forces dancing around in her thoughts; the problem was that she probably wanted both of them, while knowing both weren't obtainable at one and the same time. The young woman saw Gil as some kind of father-figure in her life, possibly incestuous – that would depend on how much she could influence him and how good at screwing he was; however, in the event of becoming such a figure, Gil surely wouldn't approve of her continuing relationship with Harry, or even condone friendship with him. And Harry certainly wouldn't approve of Gil's likely sphere of influence.

Sir Gilbert and Lady Munny. Jane conjured images of herself at the distinguished Sir Gilbert's side. Lady Munny, was it remotely possible? It was possible, she told herself, stepping surefootedly over the threshold into her fantasy world. The man wanted to possess her, and would accept any terms she imposed, marriage would obviously mean so much to him – it would probably be an unconventional marriage, without them fucking, which Gil wouldn't want, he would simply want to be near her innate warmth. He would be generous enough to understand that her sexual appetite would want satisfying, and would therefore permit her Harry. But Harry wouldn't understand, he would be incapable of perceiving Gil's need to give with little return; everybody wanted something more than they gave, that was Harry's philosophy.

Of course she was intending to cheat Harry by withholding Sir Gilbert Munny's identity; that thought was underlying her fantasies. Possibly Harry already knew who Gil was. Jane considered the situation between herself and Harry. She had a kind of love for Harry, not pure or all-consuming, but respectful enough, a love that would out of gratitude have been returned however he chose to ask for its return. But he hadn't been and wasn't being honest with her, he tried to take her for granted by simply sending her to the hotel for a scene with a strange man. She would give him no return that way, for if she was ever going to be some kind of prostitute she would be her own kind, she wouldn't allow Harry to state the terms and take her for granted.

Finally Jane considered she had found justification for not telling her man about Gil. Yet in spite of herself, part of her thoughts projected towards Harry, embracing him in apology, while the remainder leant towards Sir Gilbert's protecting embrace. And in that confused frame of mind she slipped unsmoothly into sleep, falling without warning into dream pockets; the murder they said she had committed derived from the old cowboy movie on tv. It was ridiculous, she knew she hadn't shot anyone and that she couldn't be hung, yet they were fixing the gallows – she ran without moving through an endless restaurant, chased by a man without definition, who was gaining on her. Seizing hold of her, he started to shake her. The sheriff then grasped her left breast, it was time for the hanging, she had to rise out of her pit. Jane protested, her arms flayed trying to knock the man away. The pressure increased on her naked body as she was shaken – why was she naked in a sheriff's jail? Her confused mind groped for the answers and she forced herself across the barrier into consciousness; only the reality, if it was reality, seemed equally confused.

The sheriff was there in the bed still shaking her, softly speaking her name. She desperately wanted to escape, wanting to slip back into a warm untroubled sleep. It was Harry, she realised dully, though that in itself didn't signify reality, he could have been no more than an eidolon of sleep. His hand reached out and immediately light flooded across the bed, striking Jane's eyes; that was reality. 'Put it out,' she said, and the light was cut. 'What time is it?'

'About three o'clock.' It might have been three in the afternoon. Harry settled down in bed on his back.

'How did you get in here?' Jane suddenly felt vulnerable.

'I'm your husband, remember? You left the door unlocked – expecting someone else, Mrs Bleedew?' His tone was mocking.

The young woman rolled away from him in bed. 'What do you want, Harry? You woke me up?'

The man moved in close behind her, he was naked also. 'You're glad really, aren't you?'

He had an enormous hard-on which Jane felt, and she was quietly pleased that this expensive hotel suite might have some point after all. But she had no intention of yielding to him at a word. Harry achieved his will too often, and Jane was detemined to dominate this scene. She was a little uncertain about whether to scream at Harry immediately over what he had had in mind for her earlier this evening, or wait and play things out and see how he shaped; however, if he saw she had no axe to grind, then possibly he would assume she was happy in the rôle in which he had cast her and would take her for granted again and again.

The man's elegant hand reached down across her bottom to delicately explore for an opening into her. Keeping her legs tight together, Jane edged away. 'Don't you want me, baby?' Harry asked.

'You don't want me. I don't want you.'

'What do you think this is, a joke?' – he prodded her in the buttocks with his cock.

'Don't do that' – resistance wasn't easy. 'I'm tired, you shouldn't have woken me.'

'Should've just climbed onto you like succubus.' He rolled away from her on to his back. 'Sorry I even breathed, baby' – he wasn't apologising.

Jane lay unmoving, listening to the man's heavy breathing; he wanted her but was incapable of compromise. She wanted him to beg, while knowing he wouldn't; independence and casual indifference impinging on contempt, they were facets that attracted women to him. But Jane grew more determined.

Stillness prevailed in the suite, and at last the man's breathing relaxed. An occasional heavy laden lorry strained by, piercing the sound-proofing, no other sounds were heard, not of rape or love. The only things stirring were her thoughts which raced and jumped in a turmoil. Sir Gilbert Munny was there again battling with Harry.

Just what had gone on between them? Harry had obviously arranged a sale, it couldn't have been any other way, so why hadn't he mentioned it? Why hadn't he asked if everything had gone all right? Because it would have given her an opening to scream? Yes, Harry would allow no such opportunity. He was taking her for granted, had merely assumed she would comply with the wishes of his club acquaintance, but had plainly made no allowance for that personality. Bastard! Her thoughts were suddenly very bitter, and she wanted to hurt the man in some way, preferably mentally, for there was no doubt that he would return violence in kind; however, the possibility of severing his splendid cock teased her, and a smile wrinkled her mind. There was only her nail scissors or the razor blade for the job, and it was a messy operation and invariably fatal, or so she was given to understand from the Sunday newspaper accounts. There were no lessons learned in fatality, not by the person who died anyway.

'Harry,' the young woman said quietly. There was no reply, so she turned over towards him. 'Harry, are you asleep?' He was expected to reply in the affirmative! Jane didn't believe he was asleep, and wanted to talk and re-establish their relative positions in their new relationship, but the man, if he wasn't asleep, had no intention of talking. She plucked idly at the hair on his chest, when another thought danced into her head – shaving those into a heart while he slept, black being the appropriate colour. Her hand moved slowly over his stomach. 'Harry?' Still no response. Pushing the bedclothes back, Jane slid carefully down on Harry, and worked herself into a comfortable position. At one time Jane had had reservations about plating, which had somehow seemed perverse and wrong, but had accepted that it wasn't after Harry's argument – the man could make anything sound plausible – and recognised that her attitude had been governed by inhibitions and ignorance.

Feeling herself growing more urgent, she disengaged and slithered back up the man's torso with the agility of a snake; she liked the top position, that way his big fat cock really massaged her clitoris, but it was quite difficult unless Harry consciously participated. But he didn't, so parting her legs across him, she carefully sat on to his erection. He felt un-usually huge, every spare drop of blood must have engorged him, and her cunt had swollen too. Jane worked herself up and down from her hips, enjoying the method for its slow-ness without the male. Still she was unable to decide whether the man was awake or asleep. He disturbed convincingly as they approached orgasm, and muttered emphasis words equalling his physical commitment; he struck blindly, violently, without control, still not allowing himself to open into consciousness as his body arched up off the bed towards hers in a sexual spasm. He was asleep, Jane decided, but his muttering grew louder, more impassioned as he locked into orgasm; the harder he thrust up from the bed the harder Jane smashed him down again, delighting in so dominating him, in his loss also; his dissipated effort might have been from a visit by succuba. At last they were still, passions ebbed, his cock went slack inside her, something that didn't normally happen. After a while Jane moved herself from the man and tried to get him up again, only couldn't. Finally, she took the felt-tip pen from the pad by the phone and drew the most enormous erection stretching up his stomach from where his penis hung down. Jane kissed it affectionately, then lay on top of Harry and pulled the covers up over them, he didn't complain about her weight.

Daylight found them parted. Jane wasn't surprised, as one supposedly moved some three hundred or so times in sleep to prevent stiffness and blood clots. On waking, Jane reached out for Harry, then opened her eyes, the man was gone; his departure was only as far as the bathroom. She rose and stretched and stabbed on the electric radio and went to join Harry. The man was shaving. Jane placed her lips against his shoulder, then moved over and sat on the loo. Harry glanced at her through the mirror, but didn't speak.

'Did you order breakfast?' Jane flushed the loo, then ran the shower.

'You kidding? Maybe some lunch. And what was the fucking idea of drawing that prick on me? – I'll get spots.'

'You couldn't get yours up. What time is it?' She stepped into the shower, avoiding wetting her hair.

'Brushing on. Lots to do with little of the day left, baby.' He frequently imitated movie producers, but only with her, never in those clubs where people liked being seen. His face glistened a smooth blue when he mopped the water away. 'Why didn't you clean your bath out last night?'

'What?' Jane said from the shower, pretending not to have heard. The man was scrupulous in his ablutions and couldn't have used the bath, not even after her, unless it was scrubbed out. 'I wanted to take a bath, you hadn't rinsed it,' he said, raising his voice.

'For the hotel to clean.' She stepped from the shower.

'Slut.' The man watched her impudent curtsy, then noticed her pubic hairs. 'What on earth have you done?' He moved closer. 'Are you mad, baby?'

Feigning disappointment – 'Don't you like my pubic-heart, big boy?'

'Quite amusing' – gathering up his shaving tackle was more interesting. 'People will think you mad.'

'Possibly, but then I won't be showing it to people,' she said pointedly.

There was an awkward pause as they exchanged looks via the mirror, finally Harry quit the bathroom. Jane dried herself, and after cleaning her teeth with his brush that he had left behind, she carried it through to him. 'This yours, baby?' she mocked.

The man had almost completed dressing. Sartorial elegance left little to be desired. The man possessed both the style and manners to blend unobtrusively into any society, though Jane suspected his origins were very humble. Harry's age was difficult to guess, anything between thirty and fifty could have accommodated him, he was a chameleon, never one colour or a single personality, but changing constantly to suit the set he was mixing with. At best he was witty, urbane and thoroughly charming; Jane had never seen him at worst, but guessed he would be treacherous and violent. Smiling sweetly, Jane said. 'Did you sleep well, lover?' She promptly switched on the radio which he had silenced.

'I had a hideous night's sleep, partly your doing I suspect – shut that noise, baby, please.'

She obliged him. 'Succuba?'

'You're one and the same, though she's more gentle – and more conventional.'

Jane didn't rise to the bait. She was hungry and went to the phone and ordered coffee and jam rolls for breakfast, before proceeding with her morning toilet. Her pants and naked breasts seemed to embarrass Harry more than either herself or the waiter who fetched the tray. She poured coffee and took the jam rolls without dressing further. There was silence. Harry would tire first and speak of the previous evening.

At last the man said: 'What's the matter, baby?' He sipped coffee awkwardly.

'Matter, Harry? Should there be?' She continued her breakfast, deciding not to mention Gil, who could become a second string, like a secretarial course for an actress; that would be her wisest move, denying meeting the man, after all it wasn't unreasonable that he could have skipped out before her arrival. With such a second-string prospect she could consider objectively what Harry might have to offer, recognising now that that juncture was approaching with Harry where either she worked or they parted, and Jane doubted her departure would exactly delight him. She wouldn't object to working for Harry, if that was what he really wanted. What she didn't want to accept was that Harry had seen, decided, and steered her in his direction, then had taken her so much for granted not to even consider it necessary to say the words. Harry Bleedew and his infuriatingly assuming attitude was the sole bone of contention, he made her feel used. Jane smiled to herself at the irony of the situation, twelve hours ago she had been of a mind to do anything for the man, anything he might have asked her to do. But now because he hadn't in fact asked her she would offer nothing, not even a kind thought.

'You have jam round your mouth.' The man sipped more coffee as Jane's aspish tongue emerged and licked away the jam. Another pause and Harry said: 'How'd it go last night?' – he practised awkwardness.

'Go, Harry?' Her manner was bemused – then suddenly enlightened. 'Oh, well, what else could you expect? You were asleep, so naturally you weren't particularly good, lover.' She offered nothing else.

'What about Gilbert?' he enquired.

'Who?' Breakfast was more important to Jane.

'Wasn't there a guy here yesterday evening, an associate of mine?' He seemed anxious now.

'Associate? None that I saw, lover. What would he be doing here if you weren't?' – playing the classic ingénue.

The man gave her an oblique, suspicious look from across the bed. 'How did you get in? I gave the key to Gilbert?'

Calmly – 'I assumed it was you who left it in the door.' He didn't believe her, she sensed, and was unable to look up at him; the last of the jam was meticulously spread on the piece of roll. Jane suddenly looked at the man. 'Why should you give this Gilbert guy the key?' – the right mixture of hostility and bewilderment was employed.

Harry rose purposefully from the bed. 'Are you singularly unbright, or just being bloody obtuse?' He moved across the room and raised Jane's handbag and proceeded to search it in a casual manner, much as he might have had he been asked to fetch something from it.

Twisting herself slightly, Jane watched him in silence, fearing the man would find Gil's card and the sixty pounds. Relief spread imperceptibly through her when he closed the bag and put it down. 'What are you looking for? – maybe I can help you.'

'Aspirins – they're not important. Hurry up and finish, and get dressed, baby. The day's nearly gone.' He went and washed his hands, then returned to titivate himself at the wardrobe mirrors.

Jane didn't move, having decided to play out her dull-witted rôle. 'Why was that guy supposed to be here last night, Harry?' The man looked at her through the mirror, but didn't speak. 'You wanted me to fuck him, didn't you? You wanted me to work last night, and just then you were looking for the money' – her look was that of a betrayed child trying to withstand the sudden hurt of understanding.

Possibly Harry was a better actor. Head bowed in complete humility, he came slowly across to the bed, and reaching for her hands, he nodded apologetically – Jane might have applauded the performance had her hands been free. 'That was my intention, baby. The guy saw you with me one night. The simple solution, it seemed, to get me out of trouble.' The man was now showing restraint in the best tradition!

'Are you really in trouble, lover?' Harry nodded, too ashamed to speak. 'And would it help you if I worked like that?' – of course it would, you fucking bastard! Her angry thoughts outpaced her words.

'Every little helps, baby. But if you don't want to' – he shrugged apathetically.

'Do they pay very much?' she asked with apparent interest. 'I mean enough to help you?'

'Those sort of guys pay forty or fifty, depends how nice the girls are to them. Sometimes they want to give them the moon.'

'Oh I wouldn't want the moon, just the earth and sun and stars.' She laughed and placed her lips lightly against his. 'Would it make any difference to us, Harry? Will you think less of me, maybe not want me any more?' The man's assurances were almost credible, a lesser sceptic than Jane would have believed. The words were well-worn and sat easily on the man's tongue. Jane smiled to herself as he pushed her back on the bed and kissed her. 'I'll do it for you, Harry, if it'll help you. After all, screwing's screwing.'

The man didn't even flinch. 'I appreciate that, baby, I really do.' He slipped his hand into her pants and stroked her appreciatively. 'Hey, we've got to see Monty about placing you, before I get carried away here.'

Jane rose for her dress, wondering how many women Harry had sold the same way, and how many had believed his words. She might have believed unquestioningly at one time, might even have believed today but for Sir Gilbert. However, she would give Harry's proposition a try, if only for being too lazy to object too much or seek any other kind of work.

11

Monty's Place was a club on Berkeley Square, almost next door to Annabel's. It was the sort of place that everyone who ever aspired to anything desired to be a member of, but wasn't. Monty's place was a very expensive habit, and that was virtually the only bar operating there, as past schools and regiments meant little in themselves. Monty's Place was a new concept in club-life. Monty owned the entire block of six floors and basement through which his club spread, offering everything from gambling to discothèques to those private dining rooms of a bygone age. The empire was ruled by Monty from his sixth-floor suite.

Monty was a colourful sluglike creature whose age would have been as difficult to pin down as Harry's, his manner was flamboyant, though Jane very much doubted that his business instincts were, as they sat at one of the bars drinking very soft, dry white wine. Every time she looked at the man he reminded her more and more of a slug, and until she got used to the idea she had to resist smiling. Monty had taken an instant liking to her, he never stated as much, but she could tell from that look that was usually indicative of lust, desire, a need to possess; few understood that they could never truly possess her, and Monty the Slug certainly wouldn't, no matter how much he paid. There was just no way she could fancy that man, and no way she could imagine that she would want to fuck him. However, that wasn't what she was there for specifically, but to work as some kind of hostess.

The club proprietor stated his requirements, his club was exclusive and exceedingly tasteful, and his clientèle the only worthwhile consideration. He didn't want hostesses who looked like whores, but also had some reservations about Jane's almost angelic beauty. Jane did nothing to try and influence Monty, knowing there was no need, that he had no intention of allowing her to slide through his fingers. She assumed Harry realised as much for he didn't push or try a hard-sell.

With Harry remaining at the bar, Jane was given a regal tour, and wondered how many other would-be hostesses had received such attention from the boss. As they moved from floor to floor in the then deserted club, Monty explained the set-up, the only part open to members during the day was the ground-floor restaurant, bar and reading room, and at the high membership fees Monty didn't even mind members using the reading room primarily for reading!

A club during the day with sunlight filtering through shutters and creeping over wraps seemed strange. And difficult as it was to imagine the night-time effect, Jane just knew she would like working there, wandering around and taking her pick of perhaps the world's most wealthy men. The prospect was very exciting, suddenly it was like another doorway on the world opening.

The conducted tour ended in Monty's suite at the top of the building, somehow Jane figured it would. She openly admired his taste, which pleased him and his face puckered into a smile; the apartment was exquisite if a little effeminate. The maid was told to bring coffee, which Jane wanted instead of a drink.

'What are you doing about accommodation?' the slug enquired like a personnel officer.

'Harry's got that together,' she offered as though not really happy with the arrangement.

'Well, if you have any problems I'm sure one of the girls will be able to help you out.'

Jane decided to test the man – doubtless he was testing her in some way. 'Would you mind if I looked over your apartment?' she asked in a candid, almost childlike manner. The man hesitated, and Jane played that advantage: 'You think me terribly forward? – I'm sorry.'

'No, you're just very straight and open,' he apologised.

Warmed by her triumph, Jane wandered around his apartment commenting on paintings and furnishings. He left her to wander, and when Jane rejoined him in the reception room he was playing the piano. At first she had thought the music was a record, then immediately considered his playing a nervous affectation, though couldn't really imagine why he should be nervous – unless he believed she was his Princess. Pleased when she identified the music, the man enquired if she played. Jane regretted saying yes; her limited ability wasn't entirely lost, but lack of practice didn't recommend it. Monty was encouraging in the excuses he made for her.

Over coffee Jane became astounded by the man's apparent vulnerability, and clearly recognised that if her will couldn't achieve dominance, at least it would influence him if she so chose; he talked openly of his dreams and desires, and Jane's interpretation was that despite everything, his wealth and power, he was probably quite lonely. Harry was completely forgotten by the young woman until Monty mentioned him.

'What does Harry mean to you?'

'He's a friend,' Jane replied, 'one I'm fond of' – she lied easily. The slug seemed pleased, and Jane was puzzled. Perhaps her apparent loyalty pleased him and possibly he believed that loyalty was a thing that, if truly earned, was never readily lost, and believed he could gain her loyalty. Whatever his thinking, Jane knew her position was favourable and could be effortlessly advanced in a few subtle moves once she was installed.

Harry had grown impatient. When she left the club with him his pace down the Square was brisk; they cut through Curzon Street and down into Shepherd Market. Jane thought the Market was beautiful, and guessed she would enjoy living there, even though her stay at the flat there was only to be temporary. The sun danced on polished pieces outside small antique shops, and Jane imagined herself spending time milling around with all the other people, picking up objects to consider; sitting outside cafés sipping lemon tea; browsing over books or simply watching this little world go by from her window.

Stepping into the doorway set back off the pavement, Harry selected a key from his large bunch and opened Janet Orga's door. Jane wondered if all his keys opened such doors.

There was an increasing feeling of trepidation in Jane as she followed Harry up the close carpeted stairs. The young woman was curious to know what Janet Orga was like; doubtless a heavily committed prostitute, probably in love with Harry at one time, if not still. Jane knew it wouldn't be long before she made alternative arrangements if Janet Orga and her flat transpired to be anything like she imagined all prostitutes and their flats, old and over-used.

The apartment seemed to have a certain style, Jane thought, as Harry opened the door at the top of the stairs and admitted her. It didn't rate with Monty's apartment, of course, though surpassed all her own previous flats.

The professional lady emerged from the bedroom wearing a white nylon housecoat. She greeted Harry very coolly, and was introduced to Jane. The young woman was mildly surprised by Janet Orga, who wasn't quite as she believed regular prostitutes should be. Instead she had a strong earthy, motherly quality that Jane had always admired in women, and wasn't even old and bedraggled. Jane felt a little disappointed, wanting the woman to be a screwbag for whom she could feel nothing but loathing; that would have made rejecting this set-up easier, and alternative arrangements, probably with one of the girls at Monty's, that much more justifiable. When she offered her hand, Jane recognised a look of admiration in the other woman's eyes, though saw no reason for her to be at all envious as the frame which held her together was really very presentable; and Jane could consider it from a fair advantage, being able to see almost everything Janet had on offer. Wanting the contact with the hooker to be as brief as possible, Jane felt slight annoyance that the woman held her hand so long, and finally wrenched it away with an embarrassed laugh.

There was a silence; a glance from Harry; an offer from Janet.

'Coffee? – it's fresh.' She led Jane into the kitchen, where a poodle yapped from the corner, but fell silent when Janet snapped back.

Jane was curious to know what private business Harry had summoned the professional lady into one of the other rooms for; the bastard probably wanted to check her receipts and take his whack. She would cheat him at every turn, Jane decided, he certainly wouldn't receive the promised percentage of all donations squeezed from Monty's patrons; each week would find her with a new and more plausible reason for their apparent lack of generosity towards her. Jane wondered whether Janet cheated the man, that was if it was possible to cheat on the Harrys of the world in any real sense. Probably she cheated, but even so the young woman knew she wouldn't be able to trust or confide in her, for regardless of short-changing him herself, Janet would be his woman and almost certainly report all such indiscretions. The man was likely giving her such instructions at that moment.

Jane smiled sardonically to herself, unsure why, with her eyes open as they were, she was even going along with this set-up; lethargy she suspected, as it certainly wasn't the singular attraction of Harry any longer, and there were other alternatives. With the right manipulation she felt sure she could work herself into Monty's apartment; then there were the arrangements that could be made with the other hostesses at the club, and there was Sir Gilbert Munny also, yet still she was allowing herself to be pushed along this particular channel without resistance, as though it had been expressly designed for her twenty-two years.

Shrugging mentally, Jane moved over to the dog and crouched to stroke him. She liked dogs, all animals in fact, and offered affection which animals could sense instinctively.

'What's your name, baby?' Jane wasn't expecting a reply; only the mad, and sometimes the terribly lonely expected their pets to talk back. The dog had a nameplate on its collar, and on reading it Jane laughed, immediately feeling better disposed to this prostitute whose dog was called Harry. The thought suddenly struck Jane that Janet would probably harbour the same apprehensive feelings about her, would fear that her presence was to spy for Harry. Instantly her mind sought a means of dispelling those inevitable doubts the woman would have, then questioned why – mistrust was no foundation for friendship, when friendship would only make her eventual escape harder.

Janet returned; Harry had departed; Jane was annoyed.

'He said goodbye,' Janet informed her. 'He'll probably see you at the club tonight.'

'Oh great – didn't he leave me any bread?' She allowed anger to show. 'I'll have to buzz round and get my things together – this is all I have.'

'I can loan you cab fare, if you like.'

Shaking her head – 'It's the principle. Dumping me and splitting like that, the cocksucker – I wanted to get a new dress for work tonight.'

The two women regarded one another across the table,

and for a moment Jane almost believed the prostitute would offer her money for a new dress, but in a way was glad the offer wasn't forthcoming. She could afford the dress herself.

'What club are you going to, Monty's?'

'You know it?'

'I worked there for a short while – before this.'

Jane considered the woman thoughtfully, and was no longer quite so excited at the prospect of the club; perhaps all hostesses from Monty's Place finished up in similar situations, admitting anyone who cared to ring their doorbell. What was there to recommend that existence, just money? Perhaps it was a nymphomaniacal need combined with avarice, Jane mused, which caused women to arrive here. Somehow Jane didn't see that as her route, despite her present lethargy over the course of her future. While enjoying money as much as any girl, she preferred men spending it on her to either earning or amassing it. She enjoyed sex more than most and money would never be its sole motivation, there had to be some other attraction before Jane slipped her pants down and opened her legs. A man had to turn her on, and one with halitosis and body odour could never have got to fuck her with offers of money; however, it was really quite easy to find something attractive in the most repulsive of men if one tried.

'Didn't you like working at Monty's?' asked Jane.

The PL raised her shoulders. 'This is more profitable. Come on, I'll show you your room.'

Leading Jane out of the kitchen, Janet indicated workroom and bathroom, then took her upstairs to show her the spare bedroom. It was small and neat and acceptable as a temporary stopping point, Jane considered, but knew it wouldn't remain as tidy very long – being slovenly, servants were part of her design for living. The woman rapped on about her work routine and hours, offering advice against bringing men friends back, pointing out the obvious dangers – Jane had no intention of bringing men back and not simply because she didn't want to be busted as part of a brothel.

Leaving the PL to continue her business, Jane went to collect her things from her previous pad, which took the entire afternoon, after stopping off at St Laurent to buy a new outfit to start work in. She sorted her possessions into two lots, essentials and those essentials that she could manage without for a short time, and on such occasions she always questioned why she accumulated so much. Janet would probably have a fit if she took it all to her place, and anyway it would only have to be moved again shortly. Two suitcases were managed with, the other three were locked and left.

There was a man on Janet's doorstep, he was middle-aged and had a familiar doormat-look about him, Jane thought, but was in fact unknown to her. He was admitted by the entryphone; Jane smiled at him and had him carry her two cases up the stairs, managing the dress herself. The man probably hadn't bargained for porterage, and if he was figuring she was the hooker his hopes were shattered when Janet opened the top door. An embarrassing little scene ensued until Janet took control and whisked the man into her work-room, leaving Jane to carry the bags up to her own room.

Time seemed to evaporate, suddenly she might be late. After moving around the exhaust-filled West End and unpacking, she needed a shower, and the bathroom was through the work-room. Jane knocked lightly on the door, but got no reply. There was something of the voyeur in Jane and she was really turned on from watching others making love; however, she had never seen a professional conducting herself and so cautiously pushed open the door. To her surprise it wasn't the man who had carried up her cases now getting his off, and she wondered how many Janet fucked or sucked in a day. A man naked save for his socks, which were probably forgotten in his passion, flapping around on the woman like a sheet in the wind, was a comical sight, but Jane stemmed her inclination to laugh. Janet's eyes caught hers, questioning her presence. Indicating the bathroom,

Jane was given permission to pass.

'Don't mind her,' Janet said as the man craned his neck, 'it's only my maid.'

When she re-entered from the bathroom the work-room was deserted.

Jane expected an embarrassing scene when shortly Janet appeared in the doorway of her bedroom. She glanced at her through the mirror, and the older woman smiled apologetically. 'Sorry about that,' said Jane.' Time's getting away from me, I'm going to be late.'

'Sorry you had to see it.'

'Did he mind too much?'

'The client?' – mildly disgusted. 'He's the last consideration. A third party's a bonus of sorts.' Her brief laughter was as awkward as the silence it preceded. Then Janet said: 'You're very beautiful.'

'Yes.' The young woman felt ill at ease with such compliments from women whose age couldn't justify them. It was no different from a man telling another he was very handsome, and certainly no less obvious. Through the mirror Jane watched the woman's approach as far as the bed. Possibly she was a lesbian, but finally Jane dismissed the possibility, using her clients as an argument.

'Your dress-sense is very good. So many girls have no idea.'

The new outfit Jane had on was white crocheted silk, white silk pants and naked breasts quite visible through the stitching. 'You don't think it's all too much?' Jane hadn't considered that prospect before, her question was merely for the sake of interjecting the older woman's remarks.

'It's really very lovely.'

The door buzzer sounded and Jane felt a little relieved when the woman excused herself and went downstairs to answer it.

Turning back to the mirror, Jane considered the front she presented to the world. Was it in fact too much? Monty's was very respectable, and for her own sake it wouldn't be wise to appear risqué. Jane tilted the mirror; the attire was exquisite and her doubts receded. She considered the sweep of the gown to her breasts, and ran her hand over her naked throat; her single pearl on the white silk band would be the finishing touch, she decided. Possibly she might even encounter the delicious man who had given it to her.

There was no set brief for her at the club, apart from helping to keep the customers content in spending their money. She could move from floor to floor; introductions could be effected, the waiters, whose acquaintance would have to be made, were best at that; invitations could be accepted, arrangements made, provided discretion was exercised. The club's aura of respectability was such that members could bring their wives if they so chose. There were dozens of girls performing various functions, and all remained smart and fashionable young women, there were no childish costumes depicting animals.

Jane was an instant success. Any misgivings about her attire were immediately dispelled; Monty the Slug was enamoured, and whenever he disengaged himself from running his club he slithered around the young woman, complimenting her and effecting introductions to none but his very special patrons, joking that leaving her at the table would put fifty per cent on the bill.

Intoxicated over her success, Jane wanted the night to continue without end. So much attention was heaped upon her she hardly had time to absorb her ambience or those people who were part of it on her level. What of the other girls? She had barely made contact, a smile and a brief hello in the ladies' rooms were hardly friendships struck.

A brief appearance was made by Harry. He saw her and waved, and seemed a little put out when she only nodded back – Jane was in the company of at least one lord, possibly two. Harry would have to accept his station!

When Monty made his move Jane wasn't at all surprised, in fact she had expected it much sooner, only pressures of the club had delayed the man. They went to his apartment, but Jane still had no intention of letting him screw her; that would have placed her down on the level of all the other girls who worked at the club, doubtless Monty had been into each of those. From his effort in trying the ugly bastard would truly come to deserve her before she allowed him into her pants, if ever; then the very prospect of her would cause his pulse to jump and his cock to stiffen in anticipation. Skilfully Jane manoeuvred the conversation away from his slipping into her, to clothes; Monty the Slug offered more compliments, insisting that Jane wore single colour outfits every night, preferably in crocheted silk. Jane was prompt, yet discreet in pointing out the cost, when the man issued a company cheque to cover two such outfits – they might merely have been overalls.

Three nights' work at Monty's might have been her ideal holiday, even with putting down the man's increasingly amorous advances, it was all highly enjoyable. However, with Monty's persistent attention she wasn't really making much headway with the clientèle and so consolidating her position in that direction, which was after all why she was at the club. Also Harry was growing more and more impatient, she was surprised he hadn't made some comment before now, not that he had had much opportunity, but presumably he would before long. And before long the real confrontation would come about when she would be obliged to remove her pants for Monty; then she would either have to try and hold him or start making firm connections with the club's élite. The donations so far received were token and hardly worth even mentioning.

Tomorrow, Jane told herself, as she lay on her bed, she would give Monty a taste, mark his true intentions and proceed accordingly. She didn't know the man well enough yet to form a firm opinion, and her resistance could have been making him more irritated than determined, the result of which quite possibly could have been her placing her own immediate future in jeopardy.

Jane could hear someone moving around in the lower

224

part of the flat and guessed it was Janet disposing of yet another client. God alone knew how many were given some, Jane couldn't even speculate. It sounded like the shop was just being closed, later than usual, then perhaps she had had a special up. Jane glanced down at the poodle where it lay on the foot of her bed, just outside the circle of light. Strange how the dog had adopted her, she mused, though perhaps it wasn't so strange, after all how many dogs would have tolerated their owners had they the choice? Perhaps the other woman, Masca, had cared for the dog. Janet certainly didn't.

There was a gentle rap on the bedroom door. Jane sighed wearily as Janet cautiously pushed the door open and entered. Nice as the PL seemed in some respects, the young woman just couldn't take to her, and didn't really want to reach out and embrace the woman in friendship, anyway. Possibly because she was afraid to, afraid of what Janet represented, figuring she was very likely the end product of her own type of existence. It certainly wasn't lesbianism that turned Jane off; she had been into those scenes and had had a good time, even the old bull dykes could be a turn-on if you didn't let them get under your skin.

The woman came and sat on the bed. 'Tired?'

'A little.' Conversation wasn't easy. 'My neck and shoulders feel rather stiff, can't imagine why.'

That might have been an invitation. Needing no other opening, Janet rolled the young woman over and began massaging her neck and shoulders.

'I didn't mean for you to do that, Janet. You must be tired yourself.' Despite herself, Jane enjoyed the woman's strong fingers kneading her muscles, forcing the stiffness out.

'I quite enjoy doing it, I find it relaxing myself.' She worked on in silence for a while, her fingers claiming more and more of the young woman's back.

Silence was like a malignant growth, which Jane felt she had to sever right away before its hold was so vast that it completely enveloped her. 'Have you been busy?'

'Fairly. I don't know where they all come from – in spite of their boring sameness, no two faces are ever the same, or maybe I just forget them.' She continued massaging.

'You don't think very much of your clients, do you?' Jane intended her remark as an idle comment but was afraid it sounded reproving and the woman would bite on it. Only she didn't.

'No, not very much' – closing that path of conversation. Her hands moved down over the young woman's back to her bottom. Jane tensed instinctively. 'There's isn't an ounce of surplus fat on you.' Janet's tone was admiring.

'That's fine now, Janet, you don't have to do any more.' Jane was sure nervousness was edging into her voice, the prospect of not wanting to get heavy with Janet and put her down was the cause.

The would-be masseuse made no attempt to stop. 'It's all right, I don't mind doing it for you.' Her hands were working down the young woman's thighs now rippling and kneading the flesh. 'Roll over, Jane.'

Despite herself the young woman found herself obeying, anticipating what might easily happen from that point, but simply hoping that it wouldn't. Rolling over on to her back, she stared belligerently at the PL who eased open her dressing-gown slightly and started massaging the tops of her thighs. Jane was grateful that she still had her pants on, for although the only protection they afforded was psychological, without them the move there would have been all too easy, a comment on her pubic heart the obvious step.

To Jane's surprise the woman's hands made no inroad, but diligently rolled and kneaded the muscles along the tops of her thighs, as a result Jane began to feel mean over her hasty judgement. Perhaps her offer was nothing more than a genuine wish to give some comfort, and who was she to judge Janet or cast disdain anyway. Doubtless she would have entertained a straight homosexual relationship here had the lady come bearing the right gifts and had the circumstances been more favourable; however, all that had in fact happened was that Janet had been friendly and had tried at every opportunity to be helpful. And Jane's feeling of self-disapprobation increased the more she considered her shabby treatment of the woman.

As though sensing her disapproval, Janet stopped working. There was a hurt expression in her eyes, and she said in subdued tones: 'You don't want me to do this. I'll go.'

'No, please,' Jane said impulsively, and reached out to the woman, but still couldn't embrace her; disapprobation moved to self-contempt. 'Please don't go, Janet. I like you doing it, only you must be tired' – she couldn't offer anything else. 'Please stay.'

Jane regretted those words, they amounted to an invitation and she saw that look of expectation now enter the woman's eyes that had been present on their first meeting. All her misgivings returned as the woman resumed massaging her thighs; that was all she was doing, and Jane was so involved with reassuring herself that she hardly noticed the older woman's hands move along the inside of her thighs, but as they did she experienced prickles of excitement, and knew she was a little wet.

'What do you think of me?' Janet asked conversationally. 'Do you like me?'

'Of course I do.' Jane felt the reassurance was too quick to sound anything but false.

'In what way do you like me, Jane?'

'Don't know you terribly well. But, I don't know, you're pleasant, intelligent; you have a nice personality . . . ' Jane's thoughts were racing ahead, trying to anticipate the woman.

'Do you think I'm attractive still? – no, I suppose not, any looks I had are going, and fast.'

'They're not. You're still a very attractive woman.' It was the truth, but she knew also that she was apologising for her earlier unspoken judgements. 'Men must find you very attractive.'

'Do you find me attractive, Jane?' – almost beseeching.

Jane didn't reply. Suddenly she was conscious of the position the woman's hands had advanced to, the fingers of one gripping the inside of her leg, while the thumb of the other was laying on her lower abdomen with fingers running down her covered vagina, the pants material pushed into the lips slightly.

'You're wet,' Janet commented with a tremor of excitement in her voice. 'Did you come?' The young woman looked but made no reply. 'Have you ever been made love to by a woman, Jane?' Her fingers eased Jane's pants to one side and gently stroked the moist, pouting cunt.

With a nervous, embarrassed laugh, Jane reached down to remove her hands. 'Please don't do that,' she said.

There was resistance; Janet didn't want to remove her hands. The earlier hostility and intolerance returned to Jane's face, while Janet wore an almost desperate mask of betrayal.

'Can I plate you?' – she asked nicely.

Pausing momentarily, Jane considered the proposition. Plating wasn't any different for it being a woman's lips, and she did like being eaten. But finally she resisted.

'Please, Jane,' the older woman simpered, 'you said I was attractive, and you liked me. You said you wanted me to stay. Please let me plate you, please, you'll like it – I want you, Jane.'

In a moment of compassion Jane almost capitulated, but instead pulled the woman's hands away from herself and tried to sit up. A brief struggle ensued when Janet made a desperate attempt to go down to Jane and finished up kneeling on the floor at the side of the bed in an attitude of prayer, with Jane kneeling away from her on the bed, pulling her dressing-gown about herself.

'Please, Jane. Let me love you, please, I've waited so long . . . love you . . . let.' Her assertions of love were pitiful, desperate, as though the young woman was her last hope. She reached out, but Jane might have been a thousand miles away. 'Please, Jane.'

Possibly Jane had never been more cruel than at that

moment, she said with a forced calm: 'Would I have to pay you for that scene, Janet, or you pay me?' Her words cut through the woman, laying her open, and tears fountained from eyes so unused to crying. She tried to speak in reply, but couldn't, and shortly rose up and fled the room.

At the woman's departure Jane felt empty, and regretted the pain she had inflicted; then the reason for her acting that way lost its prominence in the queue of priorities to become almost non-existent. What right had she to inflict such pain on another woman, a terribly lonely woman who had merely reached out for friendship? Jane felt suddenly mean and despicable, wanted to go to the woman and apologise, offer her friendship and try to help her relieve the loneliness, only couldn't. She couldn't force herself to rise up off the bed and make that gesture, because she knew that it might help commit her to that existence. Tears began to blur her vision now, and she hoped never to arrive at such a position where it was necessary for herself to seek friendship on a hit or miss basis.

Without removing her dressing-gown, Jane pulled the bed quilt up over herself. She was feeling chilled and immediately knew why, prospects for the future; she hoped to God that she was never as committed or desperate as Janet, and reassured herself that she wouldn't be. But reassurance notwithstanding, it was still with her chest heaving and her eyes glazed with tears that Jane drifted into sleep.

Voices awakened her, they were heated and indistinct, and Jane wondered who they belonged to – Janet and a client? the second voice was male. It was daylight when everything was viewed with a new, clear perspective, and Jane remembered the shitty way she had reacted to Janet a few hours earlier. Thoughts instinctively projected towards the PL in apology; probably the woman hadn't taken exception to her treatment, but still Jane was uncertain how she would face her.

The poodle jumped up on to the foot of the bed, pleased to see her awake, and when Jane reached out it bounded nearer for stroking. 'My little pooch.' Jane sat up and ruffled the wool around the dog's ears. 'At least you're pleased to see me.'

She stopped playing with the dog and listened again as the sharp voices from downstairs pierced the floor. Perhaps Janet was having trouble with a client, perhaps she should go and offer her some support, that would at least seem to be some form of apology.

There was something familiar about the man's voice, Jane thought, only couldn't identify it at first as words were little more than sounds without shape. At last she recognised it was Harry Bleedew, but couldn't guess the reason for his presence downstairs. Her mind groped vaguely. Her own name was spoken and still it gave her no insight. There was a short silence, then noise on the stairs, and finally the man pushed open the bedroom door; it was immediately apparent to Jane that he hadn't come to wish her good morning. What had she done to anger him? Janet, who had followed the man up, had fallen silent, her argument lost. Jane stared at the man, and the violent scene she foresaw wasn't a clever premonition; she thought to slide under the bedclothes, but ostracising herself wasn't going to eradicate the problem that was angering Harry.

'You cunt,' the man said, 'you fucking cunt!' There was no longer tolerance in his voice, nor the gentleness Jane had once known, even the smart accent he normally employed was lost.

'Why?' she demanded, showing indignation.

'I s'pose you thought I wouldn't find you out, you liberty taking cunt!' Four paces found him at the bed. Jane cowered instinctively. The poodle barked from the bed in defence of its new mistress, but Harry wasn't put off. 'A friend of yours was anxious to contact you, he was very upset that you hadn't communicated with him.'

Light suddenly made everything clear. The Lord Peter had found out about Sir Gilbert Munny. 'I can explain,' she began.

'Bet your life you can, you cunt. So you hadn't seen him! – and like some fucking jumbo I believed you and went and paid the hotel bill.' Exploding, he lunged forward at Jane, but she managed to evade him. Then the poodle was off the bed and snapping gamely at the man's heels, and distracted him long enough for Jane to scramble out of bed. But the dog was easily disposed of. Harry's foot sent it yelping painfully across the room.

'You pig – you cruel pig.' Jane went for the man, but her slaps were ineffectual and she wished she had armed herself as his fists struck her first on the right cheekbone, then above the left breast, causing her to reel backwards in pain.

'I'm not the prick you seem to take me for. Let's see if your man'll be so interested in you by the time I'm finished – that dog won't even look at you . . .'

Arms flaying violently as the man advanced at her again, Jane questioned why Janet didn't help her, and she found the answer in an instant; the quality of friendship she had offered was being returned in kind. Her mind began clouding with fear . . . she wouldn't be able to go to Monty's tonight if she was bruised . . . 'Monty!' she called desperately, only wasn't even sure whether any sound was emitted. There was more pain in her face, from left side now; she could hear some screaming, possibly it was herself or Janet, and the noise mingled with the yapping, whining dog – her mind apologised to pooch for its suffering and moved quickly on to entreat for help. Help me, Gil. Please help me, Gil . . . there was no immediate answer. Something struck her in the stomach, and the pain was almost unbearable, she felt sick and faint, but strove to remain conscious . . . this was bitter and cruel, she had done nothing to deserve such treatment. She didn't owe the man anything, he didn't own her, he didn't have the right to make such demands; her protests increased, but grew more and more confused in her mind as pain began to dominate . . . Gil, Gil, her thoughts screamed a thousand times . . . where was he? Why don't you stop him, Monty? But Monty the Slug only smiled. More blows fell on her and she felt her body tearing apart, the pain and noise and confusion was all too much. Slowly sinking toward unconsciousness, her arms flayed desperately, trying to take hold of something real; then she was blind, a murky greyness swam before her eyes and she sank lower and lower. The base of her cranium struck something sharp and pain seared through her body, touching every nerve ending, that was the final spiteful blow.

12

The intermingled scent of gladioli and smell of antiseptic filled her nostrils and entered the vacuum of her mind. Existence then was running through a field of blue gladioli while simultaneously tripping through an operating theatre; they were going to amputate her legs to prevent her running through the field and trampling the beautiful, unique flowers. Jane offered arguments against losing her legs; couldn't they see that she was merely a spirit, a weightless body who floated through that sea of flowers without damaging a single bloom? However, they were brooking no argument, the surgeon had been engaged for the amputation and couldn't be released until he had completed his task. The young woman fled blindly. Yes! Now she remembered the blindness, that obviously explained why her sense of smell was so acute. The smell of the flowers jostled for prominence with the antiseptic in her nostrils; blooms brushed her naked thighs with the softness of lips, or were they the surgeon's fingers plucking at her flesh? The young woman had an innate loathing of anything remotely connected with hos-

pitals. Who had given them permission to take off her legs?
Someone had to, even to remove the legs of a corpse consent
had to be given. Who was responsible for her now that she
couldn't see? Why didn't the flowers save her? The surgeon
advanced, his breath was warm on her face; he had dark
truculent eyes, so familiar for their lack of compassion, she
could see them clearly, they were impressed on her inner
eye. Trapped, she appealed for help, but no one answered
her cries, no one cared it seemed. The eyes drew closer, their
owner was speaking, explaining that the amputation would
be made from the hip, while Jane's protests remained
unheard.

Finally her subconscious forced her through the only
channel of escape, then the eyes before her were no longer
black and truculent, but a powder-blue and smiling. A voice
confronted her: 'You're back in this world at last.'

A riot of colours about the room caused a turmoil which
momentarily swamped her vision, and it was some while
before Jane fully realised she could see, but on trying to
speak she found she couldn't. The man with the powder-blue
eyes leaned closer to her, saying things she didn't immediately understand; he was doing something to her face. What
was he doing to her face? What was wrong with her face? —
fragments of the preceding episode in her life hastened back;
the recollection of going blind a few moments ago; the pain.
What had caused that pain? Frantically she groped among
those blank chambers of her mind. What had happened to
her face? Was it a terrible mess? Someone had hit her, the
owner of those dark, murderous eyes. Raising her hand
towards her face was a great effort, and before it arrived
there the man, who she assumed was a doctor, stopped her.
When he spoke Jane knew the words but didn't understand
their meaning.

'Instinctive, even after three weeks.' He was addressing
someone else in the room. Jane attempted to turn and see
the third party. 'No, don't move, Jane,' the doctor said, 'I
won't be a moment.' He was removing a tube of some sort

from her face, and the worst possible combinations were conjured up by the young woman's confused mind. 'There,' the doctor offered finally, having removed something from her mouth. 'How do you feel now?'

Speech was still impossible, Jane found, and she had a thousand questions to ask. Her brain searched her mouth for her tongue, but it wasn't there, the cavity was dry and numb – having her tongue removed wasn't a possibility she had considered, and couldn't begin to assess which was the lesser of the two evils, blindness or dumbness; the current affliction, whatever, was always the worst.

The doctor said: 'Dehydration,' and nodded at the third party.

Jane saw his gesture, and realised that he knew she was mute. The third party was a nurse who raised Jane up slightly and allowed her to sip some water, which immediately freed her tongue and the nerves in her mouth. Suddenly speech was possible, only then she could think of nothing to question. Perhaps the time. 'What time is it?' The words were slurred slightly where the muscles of her tongue were slack.

The man smiled at the nurse, then at Jane as he checked her pulse. 'I fear you've missed any appointment you may have had, Jane.' He seemed satisfied with her pulse. His hands moved around the back of her neck and base of her cranium. 'Tender?'

'A little,' she replied. 'Am I in hospital?' The young woman was growing worried, the place seemed like a hospital, yet she always assumed hospitals had communal wards. She was isolated and wondered why.

'You took rather a nasty fall.' He sat on the bed and shone his flashlight in her eyes. Again he seemed quite pleased. 'You had us quite worried.'

'How long have I been asleep?'

'Little over three weeks – I think we can start her on light solids now, sister.'

'Three weeks' – it was like another blow. 'How ... ?'

'You were severely concussed, Jane.' The doctor's casual abstracted air illogically presumed the woman's knowledge. He started writing up her progress chart.

'You mean I've been here, unconscious all that time?' Jane found it hard to grasp.

'The head's too delicate to be batting furniture with.' Returning to the side of the bed, he pressed his fingers around her ears. 'Painful?' She shook her head. 'Good. Any headaches?'

'Not really. Sort of dull, muzziness.'

'Cobwebs of those three weeks. It'll clear soon.' With a needle he pricked various points on her arms, asking her whether it hurt. Ridiculous – naturally needle jabbing was painful! He tried the same with her feet, and afterwards as the sister pulled the blankets up over her, he said: 'I'm afraid we haven't kept your heart trimmed.'

Seeing him smile at the sister, Jane assumed it was a private joke, until remembering her pubic hairs; then she felt as though a thousand hot needles were stabbing her flesh. Her embarrassment didn't pass unnoticed.

'There doesn't seem to be anything wrong with your memory, Jane. It was rather elegant. I wouldn't be surprised if some of our nurses aren't copying you.' He scribbled more on the chart.

The flowers lining the room were puzzling her now. Was it possible that Harry had brought them? Possible, but she guessed improbable; then wondered what had happened at that flat after her concussion. Perhaps Harry had delivered her to the hospital or Janet had called the police. Jane was nothing more than curious, not really wanting to resume any association with them, not even with Monty. In future she would stay on her own, she would be much better off and didn't need bastards like Harry. Or maybe she would take up her friend Hilda's offer and go into the massage business with her; it was easy to screw guys there, that was all most of them went to a massage for anyway.

'Why am I in here on my own?' Jane asked.

Passing the chartboard to the sister, the doctor turned back to her. 'Partly because you were concussed, and in that state one's apt to talk.' He smiled at her apprehension. 'We only record the occasions, Jane. But also on your guardian's instruction.'

'My guardian's instruction?' she questioned vacantly.

'He decided that you should have a private ward.'

Her guardian? Jane was bewildered and wanted to question the identity of her benefactor, but feared all that might have gone before, and also the possibility of either appearing foolish or in a more serious state as the result of the blow. Her attention turned back to the flowers. There was something about gladioli that should have told her everything, but that lay just beyond her reach; the correct clues wouldn't arrange into an answer and the more she tried the more frustrated she became. Monty! she almost said his name out loud. Of course, his apartment had been filled with gladioli. She felt relieved, a little pleased also; as Monty had gone to all this trouble for her, he would have surely fixed Harry for hurting her. Her racing thoughts stopped at that point and questioned: Would Monty the Slug have gone to so much trouble for a chick who had frustrated him as she had by refusing to screw him?

'The flowers?' – she addressed the doctor. 'Where did they come from?' The information had become vital to her.

'From your guardian, I'd imagine' – his look questioned the sister.

'Yes, Sir Gilbert sent them – aren't they lovely? He's been most concerned.'

Gil, of course. The man's image passed like light through her mind. All the bastards had sprung to mind, and only the bastards, while she had forgotten dear, generous Gil. He was concerned, and probably felt responsible, possibly he was indirectly; he cared about her, cared for her, loved her even.

That prospect warmed her, rather like an uncertain investment suddenly seen to be paying off. She conjured the man's image, as though to consider the goods once more before

237

committing herself, but his impeccable form appeared face-less, and despite effort she was unable to furnish the man with features. At once she became agitated. 'I can't remember what he looks like.'

'That isn't so tragic, Jane. You'll remember as soon as you stop trying,' the doctor comforted.

'Won't be long before you see him anyway,' said the sister.

That was another prospect to fill her with consternation. What kind of hideous mess did she look? What was her face like now after the beating? Broken? Scarred? Fear took hold and tried to force up panic. Very tentatively her hands reached for her face, but the doctor grasped her wrists, preventing her, which immediately accentuated panic. Jane trembled, convinced now of the horrible result.

'No need,' the doctor said, 'you're still very beautiful.'

Unconvinced, her mind seized the fact that he hadn't said unmarked – there were scars, broken tissue, probably a broken nose, yes, she could feel her nostrils distended. How could she consciously face her benefactor? Panic swept over her, and she struggled to feel her face. 'I'm hideous, I know, I know!'

'That's silly.' He took her hands to her face. 'There. Sister, will you fetch a mirror? There isn't a mark on you, Jane. You're truly very beautiful.'

The mirror didn't lie, there was no trace of violence, she was merely white and raw-boned from her protracted sleep.

Jane felt strangely lightheaded on lowering the mirror, relief and her general debilitation being the cause. How many times after a party had she wished for three weeks' sleep? Now twenty-one days had left her with less strength than a newly born kitten, sitting was exhausting, and she certainly couldn't have made the bathroom for a wash. However, by the time her benefactor arrived, laden with yet more gifts, she had been washed and fed, her hair strenuously brushed, and she had been put into silk pyjamas which were complete strangers to her.

Still no image of Gil had returned, but she knew him

immediately he entered the ward. A nurse relieved him of his packages and he moved over to the bed, where Jane gazed up at him from sunken eyes. He was as he had been at the hotel, distinguished looking, and with the same diffident manner. He raised her hand in his, and for a moment the young woman believed he would kiss it, but he didn't, not even after the nurse departed. Jane was almost disappointed.

'How are you feeling now?' he asked quietly.

Jane tried a smile for him. 'Very weary, surprisingly enough.' Her eyes continued to measure him, and the man shortly looked away in the awkward silence; Jane sensed he had reams to say, which he seemed unable to bring himself to say.

'The doctor said I wasn't to tire you – I'll go if you wish.'

The same apologetic man who was anxious not to intrude on her or to tire her, while she wanted to embrace him in gratitude. Cautiously she raised his hand to her lips. 'Thank you.' She smiled again; her sincerest offering at that moment.

There were so many things to say, so many things to ask. What of yesterday? Yesterday gradually dissolved in its importance. Who gave a shit about yesterday. A shroud was thrown over her past, allowing it to die unmourned; then tomorrow was all important. The man brought her briefly up to date. Taken unconscious to hospital by a woman called Janet Orga, the hospital had contacted him, he told her, on finding his card in her bag; he hadn't pressed charges against Harry Bleedew, assuming she would want neither that nor the attendant publicity. The tomorrows were filled with too many details for Jane to absorb, and although the man hadn't included it – he wouldn't make such a despotic assumption – instinctively Jane knew their marriage was likely to be somewhat in the not too distant future; that was what she would work at, and figured she would have no difficulty at all in making it happen.

Sir Gilbert's physician called and examined her, and afterwards pronounced her undamaged, but wanted her to stay put another four days for observation while she regained her strength before her discharge.

Little short of Bond Street had arrived, dominated by St Laurent, and Jane selected clothes and accessories at her leisure as though it was her birthright. She saw the looks in the assistants' sad eyes, and recognised them for what they were, the looks of envy that ugly women had for the beautiful before learning to compromise, that young girls had for movie stars, the poor had for the rich – she had often been envied, it was nothing new to her, but Jane felt rather pleased. The young woman wanted for nothing. Her taste in clothes was good, and when advised by experts, it was exemplary. Everything from Vidal Sassoon hair to Gucci shoes was laid on, no detail had the man not accounted for.

On the fifth day of consciousness Jane was impatient to leave the Middlesex Hospital, and it seemed Gil would never arrive for her. Convalescence at St Moritz had been mentioned, though she had no particular wish to go there, and told the man so the moment he arrived. He seemed curiously relieved. Instead she would go to his house in the country.

Hospital porters were summoned to take her luggage, and Jane stepped out on the man's arm to the man's car to be driven to the man's house by the man's chauffeur. The Rolls-Royce whispered over the miles along the M4 once clear of Central London's traffic congestion, while the man whispered pleasantries to Jane, still in his hesitant manner.

Installed in Sir Gilbert's house at Marlow, Jane found that her new home was all she had imagined it should be; large and comfortable and tasteful, and she knew her life could easily be complete in such surroundings. Jane wanted to dance with happiness, for until then she had been wandering lost and now she had found herself.

At the house there was Helena, who at first Jane foolishly took little account of; mistaking her at once for Gilbert's housekeeper, then merely taking her for his sister-in-law. The woman's condescending manner towards her was infuriating. Obviously she didn't meet with Helena's approval, certainly not as a friend of dear Gilbert's, and Jane dreaded to think how the older woman would react on learning that they were to be married – Gil hadn't proposed as yet but he would. Henela was jealous, and Jane was shrewd enough to soon realise just how jealous and fucked-up she was, for without any doubt Helena expected at some time to fill her late sister's place officially. Once she had got her bearings, Jane instantly fathomed the whole situation. Gil didn't want the woman around, but was a nice guy who was loath to give offence and so couldn't ask her to leave, while the woman was a cunt and too wilfully insensitive to depart of her own volition. Her departure would be effected, Jane decided, just as soon as Gil made clear his intentions.

Jane then wondered just what the man's immediate intentions were; having put forward no proposition, they certainly weren't sexual, not at that point anyway; possibly at some time in the future they would lean that way, they were bound to, he would almost certainly want some return on his time and money.

Idly Jane mulled over the question of a sexual relationship with Gil, considering how long she could make him wait for her if she so chose. There was no reason why she should necessarily yield her jewel up to him the instant they were married, Gil would patiently await her; she imagined his patience being eternal, his understanding her every excuse for their not making love, his assurances in trying to dispel her every apparent anxiety. Jane knew for certain that she would break down in need of a screw long before Gil ever would, she was already getting very horny, as it was over four weeks since she had been fucked and that was as long as she could remember going.

No mention had been made of how long she was to stay, and each for their own reasons chose not to raise the question; however, Helena tried to make capital on the issue, but Jane refused to rise to her. Other inroads were constantly attempted by the sister-in-law, but Jane rode them well and with the ease of knowing it would be herself to finish the course, with the sister-in-law out on her arse; Helena set the rules, but Jane was proving more proficient at the game.

Shortly a state of war existed between the two women, a perfidious, insidious battle for survival, with every point counting and every knock representing a point. Helena was the less shrewd of the two and never missed her opportunity of striking whenever an expression of Jane's indicated her past – some of which were offered purposely – but Jane was never so foolish as to jump on her rival in the same way in front of Gil; then she was tolerant of the older woman's bitterness and always forgiving, and in so displaying her own generous nature she did nothing but endear herself a little more to the man.

If ever a moment was right for a proposal of marriage, Jane felt an evening of her third week at the house was it. They had the house to themselves as Helena had been invited out by an old flame; Gil and herself had a quiet dinner together and they talked, each allowing the other to know just a little more of themselves – the information Jane imparted being always slightly guarded – they laughed across the table and were happy together. The man was content. While Jane was more happy than she had ever been; she had masturbated several times but hadn't found much relief, had considered screwing the gardener, who was about eighty; the chauffeur, who was a cretin and never free of Gil, and even the dog when it had sniffed around her a couple of times. An Alsatian was supposed to be quite a turn-on she had heard.

'I love you, Jane' – the words were quiet and sincere.

Accepting the statement with a kind of grateful relief, Jane replied calmly: 'I know, Gil. You're very kind, very generous.' There was a table between them and four walls enclosing them, with light that enabled the man to look into her eyes and search her soul; that wasn't the position Jane wanted to be in then, she wanted darkness to enfold her in case of betraying herself with a look she would instantly regret. 'Gil . . . ' She began on a note of apparent hope that spanned a generation, and a dinner table. The young woman

242

G. F. Newman

rose and swept through the dining room and out into the garden, where the warm night air brushed her cheeks. She knew Gil would pursue her.

Slowly Jane moved across the lawn towards the river where it passed the bottom of the garden, scents from the flower-clustered borders drifted across to meet her nostrils. The man was silent on the grass behind her as he came to her side and fell into step.

After a while, he said: 'Was it wrong of me, Jane?'

Jane smiled faintly and shook her head, then slipped her arm through his before continuing along the neatly trimmed grass by the river. At times she found the man's hesitancy irritating, and this was one such time.

'I dream and hope,' the man continued, in a subdued voice, 'and although I suppose I have no right to, I include you in those hopes and dreams. Is it possible that at some time in the future . . . ?' He hesitated again. 'I'm much older than you, Jane, certainly old enough to be your father . . . Have I any hope at all of including you in my future? No, you don't have to answer. I'm embarrassing you and making a frightful fool of myself.'

His preamble sounded like a bad movie, Jane thought, growing bored, but then stopping, she turned to him and said: 'I'd like you to include me in your future, Gil, if it'll make you happy.'

'The prospect of having you here in my life on a permanent basis would make me very happy, Jane. Perhaps I sound very foolish, but I do love you.'

She placed her lips against the man's cheek in a display of affection. 'How would this permanent basis work? Would you have your lawyers draw up a contract?' There was a smile on her face.

'Don't mock me, Jane, please don't . . . '

'Oh Gil, you're insane. I wasn't.' Slipping her arm around his back, they continued to walk along the river bank. The young woman was growing irritated once more by the man's uncertainty, which was perhaps understandable, if not really acceptable; she wanted him to get on with his proposal of marriage so she could build the next story of her future and state the terms. She offered him another lead: 'I've been happy here, Gil, really happy.'

The man seemed elated in his own low key way. 'That pleases me, Jane . . . even encourages me.' His pause wasn't for effect. 'Dare I ask if you'd consider becoming my wife?'

The young woman stopped, and pulling her arm away, turned to him. 'Are you asking me, Gil?'

'Is it too ridiculous a proposition?'

'For me possibly. I couldn't hope to amount to the wife you'd need, or command the respect your wife should have. Helena's the proof.'

'Jane . . . you silly girl. I love you.'

'What about your son . . . ?' she began.

'Robert will adore you when he meets you. But forget Robert and Helena, and everyone else, they're unimportant compared to you. Please say you'll consider being my wife.'

They were the words she wanted to hear, her terms were agreed readily enough.

'Yes, Gil. I'll be your wife for as long as you wish; for as long as you're prepared to suffer my selfishness, and tolerate my awkwardness, and don't nag me about my past.'

'Jane, I love you.' He summoned the courage to kiss her, but didn't press the physical contact further. He was very happy.

A feeling of well-being enveloped Jane, not dissimilar to a feeling of satisfaction on concluding a good business deal. A number of small-print drawbacks existed, such as Helena of course, but they were minor and would cause no great difficulties.

Jane was still in bed, and unfucked, when Gil broke the news to his sister-in-law the following morning, but she imagined the scene between them; Gil's apology in the face of Helena's anguish and martyrdom. Afterwards Gil came up to her room and tentatively kissed her good morning, making a lunch arrangement with her before departing for the City.

There was no good morning wish from Helena when Jane finally arrived downstairs with her bathrobe loosely tied about herself. The young woman wasn't prepared to suffer for the sister-in-law's benefit, and took her coffee and honey roll to electric music in the morning room. Helena was busy making phone calls, and afterwards, said in passing: 'Please dress, child. I've some friends coming who'll have no wish to see you sprawled around like a fish-wife.'

Jane bit her lip thoughtfully, giving the woman no such satisfaction as a display of temper. 'If they're male, I'm sure they'd have fat erections which they would never get up for you.'

'You vile little gutter-snipe.'

Destroying the woman verbally would be easy, Jane guessed, but smiling in the face of adversity was easier and almost as rewarding, she even gave a mock curtsey. 'Aren't you going to congratulate me on my engagement to Gil?' Gil, however inadvertently, had inserted into Helena's side a knife which Jane felt no compunction about twisting.

'Do you really imagine that a disgusting person such as yourself could ever take the place of my sister in Gilbert's life?' Her words were malicious and biting. 'Why, Sarah was his life, the very air he breathed almost. How can you even presume to usurp her place?' – Helena was growing very agitated.

'Usurp sweet-FA,' the young woman managed calmly, 'I'm not even going to try. I know what I can give Gil – he's in love with me.'

'Love?' Helena retorted as though the proposition was too ridiculous. 'The poor man's infatuated, nothing more. You've flaunted yourself and you think captured your prize. But Robert will soon bring him back to his senses and convince him just how ridiculous he's being, you'll see. Robert cherishes his mother's memory; he certainly won't allow his father to degrade it in such a cheap manner.'

'You don't care anything for Gil.'

'Foolish child. You've been our guest for three weeks and

you believe that? We're as close as can be. I've dedicated myself to him these past three years.'

A sour smile appeared across Jane's lips. 'You're really one pathetic, fucked-up bitch, Helena. Why don't you let go? – he doesn't want you, and never did. Gil has only suffered you out of kindness. But I won't, lady, and you'd better believe it. When we're married you'll have to take your dildo and screw yourself elsewhere.' Wheeling away, Jane started out, the battle hers; however, the now deathly white sister-in-law wouldn't concede defeat. Helena pursued her, grabbing her arm. 'You stupid, stupid . . . when you're married? That'll never happen,' she screeched. 'Robert won't permit it. Gilbert won't want it, not when he realises just what an evil creature you are.'

'We'll see. May I have my arm back? – I have to dress and meet Gil for lunch?' There was a pause. Frustration got the better of Helena as she raised her hand as though to strike Jane. 'That really would be a mistake, you frigid bitch. I'd slap your fucking tits up round your face!'

With a shudder of fury Helena yielded. 'Get out of my sight, you, before I do something I might regret.'

Possibly Helena deserved pity, but Jane hadn't a spark of compassion, to her the woman was merely a scheming bitch who wasn't quite clever enough – or was she? Seeds of doubt about Robert not accepting her had now been sown, and the son took the form of a positive obstacle, whereas before he had simply been someone to meet at an unspecified time in the future.

Despite Gil's assurances, the unknown quantity which Robert represented continued to worry Jane; however, anxiety proved without foundation, for when the son came down from Cambridge for the wedding he was completely enamoured, and Jane recognised in his eyes that look seen often in men's eyes. Suddenly the prospects were more exciting. Robert was a younger version of his father, but possessed qualities of beauty he could only have taken from his mother, and Jane was turned on by him so much that she wished then that Gil was his son. In spite of Robert's obvious delight at his father's new found happiness, Jane foresaw great possibilities with him; he would be capable of loving her if she permitted it, and she certainly would permit that.

The wedding was a quiet affair with just a few close friends of Gil's, and Helena's of course, but it made several national newspapers, with photographs; that was excitement for Jane, especially the extra interest she suddenly generated for becoming Lady Munny.

Soon afterwards her existence settled back into rustic quietude; Robert returned to university – he would be back home shortly for the vacation, which seemed a lifetime away to Jane, who even began to miss Helena now. She could easily have been spiteful to the servants had she wished, only they offered little sport. Her life with Sir Gilbert Munny very shortly became a cosseted, well-ordered bore, which she had never imagined any luxurious existence could be. They shared the same bedroom, though not the same bed. He had fucked her twice to date, if it could be called fucking. His efforts were that pathetic. She managed to get him erect, but the first occasion when she went down on him he was so embarrassed by the move that he lost his hard-on immediately; then finally getting into her, he came so quickly that as horny as she was she didn't orgasm herself. He never attempted to invade the privacy of her bed, there was little point; nor ventured near her unless invited, and her need notwithstanding, he was invited less and less. The twenty-eight years separating them also separated their libidoes, and he seemed perfectly content to simply possess her, to have her exquisite doll-like presence around him; therefore, like that considerate father he was leaning more and more towards, he never pushed or made marital demands. Jane grew steadily more weary of their existence, having given up trying to arouse the man sexually.

'Robert's coming down the week after next,' Gil announced one morning as he was dressing for the City. Jane, who was sitting in bed taking coffee and scanning the fashion pages, was delighted at the prospect. The man smiled through the mirror. 'You like Robert, don't you?'

Guilt pricked her fleetingly. 'What a strange observation, Gil. He's your son right to his fingernails. How could I help but like him?' She returned his smile.

The man came and sat on her bed and kissed her lightly on the forehead. 'I'm glad. He thinks you are perfectly enchanting – then I always knew my son to be very discerning. I'm pleased you'll be friends, he needs friends.' Gil paused awkwardly. 'He was always so very fond of his mother, her death hurt him terribly.' He became silent and pensive.

Jane reached out and took his hand gently in hers; that was the style she had seen in the movies. 'Do you still miss Sarah terribly, Gil?'

He looked at her through suddenly vacant eyes. 'It's awfully hard to exist with someone for so long without missing her – the hurt diminishes with time, the pain's less acute, but there's always a certain emptiness, a piece of oneself lost, no matter how fulfilling a new love is.' He kissed her hands. 'I couldn't be more happy or fulfilled than now – the loss is simply those few tiny brain cells I'm sure die on such occasions.'

'That how Robert misses his mother?'

'Perhaps to a greater degree. I was never close enough to him to tell how much he really missed her. The young get over their hurts quicker.' The subject was closed at that point, and Gil rose, straightening his waistcoat. 'I'm glad Robert's coming down, he'll be company for you. Can't be much fun for you at times here on your own.'

Wondering if the man had read her thoughts, Jane said: 'Sometimes it gets a little lonely.'

'You need someone your own age around the place.'

'Silly,' she offered prudently. 'Anyway, I can always go up to town and meet you or some friends.' She felt the man was drawing her, only couldn't guess the reason; perhaps he wanted her to admit that she felt she was being buried alive in expensive, respectable, sedate Marlow, and was desperately in need of a good screw.

'How would you travel up? Train? Taxi? – not much freedom.' He shook his head as if to dismiss the matter, then from the dressing-table drawer he collected a small, neatly wrapped box which he gave to her. 'A present – small token of my appreciation.'

Appreciation; Jane thought about the word briefly, how revealing it was; not love or passion or even affection, they dealt with emotions which embarrassed her husband. Appreciation was the right expression for him. She considered the box, which would almost certainly be jewellery, then displayed the prescribed amount of excitement. 'Do I open it now? Please?' She would add whatever it was to her growing collection – one day she might even be known for her collection of jewellery. Following his rules when receiving presents seemed to please the man, so Jane did so.

'Not yet, my pet. First you must dress.'

Definitely jewellery! After showering, she dressed purposefully in blue denims, then joined her husband downstairs. 'Now?' Permission was given, and as Jane ploughed through the masses of tissue paper she began wondering if there was anything at all inside. Finally the small flat key she found might have been a joke, only jokes weren't Gil's style. 'What does it open?'

'Your present in the garage.'

An Aston Martin Volante. That was the kind of sports car every man dreamed of owning, and which Jane always hoped her boyfriends would drive; it was cherry-red and like an erect, reaching phallus that could never lose its bloom. The young woman was unable to contain her excitement, she wheeled about and threw her arms around the man, kissing him. 'Gil, darling, it's wonderful, wonderful. Is it really and truly mine?'

'Provided you promise to be careful and not drive too fast.' Slightly embarrassed, the man freed himself from her embrace. 'I couldn't bear to see you broken and hurt. Please be very careful.'

Jane regarded him thoughtfully, touched by his concern. 'I'll be careful, Gil – promise.'

Jane was careful to be careful in her husband's company; then she drove at reasonable speeds, didn't squeal away from traffic lights, race other cars, screech on and off roads, or brake violently in the drive, knocking up the gravel. However, in no time at all Jane tired of her new toy, wearied of driving around, racing about with no real place to go. In spite of the car's value and power and beauty she quickly appreciated that it was no more than a commodity for getting from one place to another, with no inherent quality of fulfilment, and was puzzled at the ease with which she had been deluded by it. To relieve the boredom Jane picked up two young men on different occasions to have them fuck her in the car; the interior of the car was quite accommodating with its reclining seats, only the first guy couldn't get an erection to order and with the second, although he got it up okay, Jane was apprehensive of him, thinking he might be dosed. Finally she gave up the practice on the road, deciding quite definitely that the prize wasn't worth the candle.

If little else the car offered a certain freedom, not that she was a prisoner, but if the chauffeur drove her, then that meant he knew, and he was Gil's man. Jane could drive up to London and return in time for dinner with ease if she chose, and the appeal to visit a few ghosts of her past grew more and more. Finally she chose.

Monty the Slug was delighted when the young woman swished into his club, causing the lunchtime patrons to stir. He gave her lunch in his apartment and Jane found the man's pandering quite reassuring; she knew he would still delight in taking her pants down on his circular bed, but knew him to be too much of a coward to even contemplate forcing that position now. And she found he turned her on even less than he did before.

To her surprise Harry Bleedew arrived at the club as she was on the point of leaving. Jane was disappointed that the man wasn't ex persona grata there on account of beating her

up, also she was frustrated at not being able to instantly pay
the bastard back in some particular nasty way. But she still
fancied him like mad, just seeing him there was enough to
make her forget the past and want to go down on him
straight away. Harry invited her to his place for a drink, and
she accepted and drove him across Oxford Street to his
apartment in Portman Square. They didn't get as far as the
drink, but Jane didn't really care; Harry was as horny for
her as she was for him, and when she reached into his fly and
took hold of his enormous cock it was enough to make her
forget everything past. Harry was the only guy Jane ever
swallowed, all the rest she spat out. Piece by piece their
clothes came off on the white long-hair carpet in the main
area of the apartment, and three times Harry screwed her.
Three orgasms he achieved, while Jane lost count of the
number she had; she always was capable of multi-orgasms,
but with Harry she just couldn't stop coming. He left her
weak and trembling and content when he finally climbed off
the floor and went to wash his hands.

'Wouldn't you like to come back with me, baby?' Harry
said in his movie producer accent when they were dressed
and businesslike once more.

The young woman looked askance – she had had all she
wanted from him for the present. 'And have you sell my car
and all my jewellery, baby?' she sneered. 'You know what
you are?'

He smiled blandly. 'You were rather silly with old Gilbert,
trying to keep him a secret. We could really have striped
him – probably still could.'

'You'd stripe a fucking church dormouse if you got the
opportunity.'

Harry had taken umbrage, but he shrugged, trying not to
give her the satisfaction. 'Well, if and when you fancy me
going into you again you know where to find me. But of
course I won't buy you back, baby.'

'Buy me back?' Her brain grappled with the meaning.
'Why should you? And who'd be selling me anyway?'

Satisfaction showed in the man's smile, he had won an important battle. 'Baby, your old Harry's an opportunist – you didn't imagine I'd let you go to such a wealthy guy without asking the market price? Old Gilbert couldn't pay me fast enough.'

The information shattered the young woman, causing her, paradoxically, to feel used, prostituted; like a commodity her husband might have rated no higher than the car he had bought for her, and Jane wondered if she had a trade-in value.

After leaving Harry's apartment, and driving out of town towards the M4, Jane seethed, feeling hurt for the first time in a very long while. And at first not even questioning whether it could be true, whether Gil could be that shallow; then questions immediately jumped into her head: Did she love Gil? Did it matter anyway? What if he had paid Harry? Wasn't she just using her husband? But finally: wasn't there a fairly important principle at stake? – there was, she concluded. However, by the time she reached the motorway emotions had receded and she decided that the proposition wasn't true, but was in fact Harry's spite; then she immediately began feeling better and the speed the car picked up helped release all her frustrations.

But it was true after all, the distress that contorted Gil's face when she confronted him said so. Jane almost wished he would lie and deny the transaction, if only to save accepting those unpleasant connotations which the truth represented, but he was too ridiculously honest. 'How much did you pay for me, Gil?' Her words were angry and she didn't really want an answer. 'Did you haggle? Were there other bidders? What am I, Gil? What commodity do you equate me with – a sack of potatoes? a cow? whore . . . ?' Momentum was increasing her incensed feeling, and she wondered if she wasn't in fact overplaying her hand for the sake of an abstract principle which, at base, she didn't care anything for anyway. Perhaps she ought to give the poor sod a chance to explain, possibly his reasons were justifiable.

'Jane, please,' he began apologetically. 'Listen to me.'

'Will you put me back on the market if I don't?'

The man nodded feebly. 'I deserve that. Giving him money in those circumstance was contemptible, but it was the only way I could see . . . '

'The only way you saw to own me. But he didn't own me, I wasn't his to sell!' As her anger continued rising Jane only just managed to prevent all those minor frustrations and irritations of their relationship flooding out.

'I didn't give him money in order to own you, but simply to keep him away from you. I saw no other means to keep him from plaguing you, short of going to the police.' He paused. Jane was silent now, finding the benefit of doubt as easy as doubting. 'If I've offended you, Jane, then I'm sorry, that was the very last thing I could've wished for. All I wanted was for you to be spared any further suffering.'

Regret began to push to the surface, prickling Jane's skin, and she sought fragments of justification for her attitude. 'Why the secrecy? Why couldn't you have told me?'

'Fear, I suppose. I was afraid of this very argument, afraid that you might have felt beholden to me, might even have married me as a result.'

The tears Jane summoned up looked so good that she turned away on to the pillow. The man came swiftly to her side and sat on the bed, and hesitantly put his hands on her shoulders.

'I've been an awful fool,' he said, 'and this shows me as being an even greater fool, certainly a very clumsy fool – everything I did was for you, for your good. And if I had thought for one moment that your affection and constancy could have been bought, I'd have spent every penny I possessed.' There was a long silence, which the man ended with one last apology. 'I'm sorry – sorry.'

He rose off the bed. Jane turned from the pillow. 'Gil.' Tears glistened in her eyes as she stretched out her hands. The man came back to her and she kissed him.

Inviting her husband into her bed was her apology. She

would invite him after every scene where possibly she was in the wrong, and there were bound to be other such scenes unless life shortly bristled with excitement, and for her part it was by far the easiest way of apologising, boring as it was. Jane considered why the man was so inadequate in bed, possibly it was because of her, that he was scared of her as a father might be of his daughter, or an older man of a young woman's mockery; however, none of the possibilities really accounted for the donkeylike fashion he employed to fuck her. One, two, three, light off, mount and hurry through the motions to the climax as though the first one to arrive earned a prize. He made no allowance for enjoyment, then perhaps he didn't find the act enjoyable or couldn't concede that it should be – an act necessary in begetting children. Before marrying a man there was quite a lot one should know about him beside his bank balance, and now Jane was only just beginning to appreciate that they were still strangers. He certainly didn't know about her oral contraceptives or would realise just how futile his carnal efforts were, but then possibly his sole design wasn't a child, they hadn't discussed the matter, and certainly hadn't discussed their sexual requirements. There was a lot about the male-female relationship Jane didn't understand, and wouldn't presume to – for her sex had always been instinctive and invariably spontaneous, performed with guys or chicks who reacted and enacted with her. But now there was a need to understand within the act and continually give to it, when basically she was herself a taker, and the need to reach out and span the gap where the man fell so short of her requirements made the whole process niggling. Every sexual encounter before had at least been fun, but with Sir Gilbert Munny even that aspect was lost. The sexual limitations of her marriage bed were added to the boredom and general lassitude experienced in her marriage, and the total was discontentment. Knowing herself as she did, Jane knew her discontent would shortly erode even the official existence of her marriage.

13

The prospect of Robert's imminent arrival down from Cambridge did a lot to cheer Jane, but his actual arrival proved something of an anticlimax; he was a stranger too, she suddenly realised, much younger than the stranger she was living with, that was all, and the hope she had irrationally invested in him wasn't immediately fulfilled. However, with their ages being compatible, possibly they would soon become friends and get something going together, Jane truly hoped so.

When Jane considered her stepson she found him so much like his father in so many ways that she wondered if he had inherited the man's sexual ineptitude along with his diffident charm, but wasn't at all sure if sexual ineptitude was hereditary. Finally she dismissed the possibility, after all Robert was of a different generation, her own in fact, and each generation progressed at least two steps further than the previous. Fleetingly Jane questioned if contemplating the

255

young man's sexual competence wasn't rather presumptuous, but then remembering his looks on their very first meeting, she decided that it wasn't.

Conversation over their first breakfast together wasn't easy, all three seemed aware of the strain, and the son made the generation gap between husband and wife all that more marked as he addressed first one, then the other, somehow comments never generally seemed pertinent.

After a while Gil's remarks took on a different aspect entirely, and he no longer spoke as though to wife and son, but rather as though addressing son and daughter, Jane noted. She felt positively relieved when he finally departed for his office.

Returning from dutifully seeing her husband to his car, Jane found Robert had left the breakfast room, and she grew a little alarmed – perhaps he didn't like her after all! The young man had moved through into the sitting-room and was sprawled along the couch. 'Thought you'd run away from me,' Jane said, joining him.

'Why would I do that?'

'Maybe you don't approve of me.'

'Nonsense.'

There was a brief pause. 'Would you like more coffee?'

'I'll get it.' He started to rise, but Jane placed her hand on his shoulder. 'It's okay.' She asked the maid who was clearing the breakfast room to fetch more coffee. 'We've about covered all the small talk' – sitting opposite him.

'Yes – how about the weather? Did you see that enormous streak of lightning the night before last? – quite unbelievable.'

'Quite unbelievable!' responded Jane, recognising the game immediately. 'I wouldn't have believed it had I not seen it with my own eyes.'

'I saw it with my own eyes, too – then it rained.'

'But we were expecting it.'

'What else could we expect after that streak of lightning?'

'Like a streak of bacon.'

256

'Rained pigs and horses.' Robert smiled, only the smile wouldn't contain his mirth, so he laughed, and Jane joined in. They were laughing loudly, as much through the release of nervous tension as mirth, when the maid fetched the coffee. Robert tried to drink some coffee, but couldn't immediately. Their laughter began to abate, then Jane said: 'There were rain spots as big as elephants' feet.'

The coffee began to cool. Each found a more sober note until their eyes met, when they simply hooted like schoolchildren again. At last the laughter faded.

'No more weather conversations, I promise, not even if it snows.'

'I'm not expecting snow,' Jane said. There was a short silence. 'Conversation was a bit awkward at breakfast.'

Robert agreed, but didn't go into the cause. After a while, he said: 'You're the last possible image one could have for a stepmother. Stepmothers should really be middle-aged nasties.'

'Disappointed, Robert?'

'Not with my father's choice for a wife, more disconcerted – as a stepmother you're obliged to take your stepchildren to the wood and leave them there. But instead of fearing you as tradition dictates, I'm delighted. I think it's fantastic.'

Immediately assuming it was another game, Jane rejoindered: 'Ah, but if you're naughty I've got the traditional cupboard upstairs to lock you in, and it has a small hole in the door to poke food through to fatten you for the witches.'

'Not the witches! I promise I'll be good.' The young man smiled and shook his head. 'I find it hard to grasp that father could've met and married someone as original as you – I almost feared he might marry Helena.'

That was a compliment that Jane liked, but she remained prudent; she didn't want to make a move towards Robert that would draw a reaction like that from his father when she tried to plate him. 'Why?' she said simply.

'Share indexes, finance, that's his life, and you represent

a move totally out of character – one thing father isn't is inconsistent.'

'You don't approve.'

'Are you kidding? End all the taboos, break down the barriers. I'm surprised, but I approve.'

'It's as well, you risked being locked in the cupboard.'

'There, you see. Father would think us both mad for this conversation, it isn't consistent with profit-and-loss-sanity' – this pedantically.

'That's not very kind' – still prudent. 'You talk as though Gil's got one foot in the grave.'

'I didn't mean to be unkind, but he's not exactly a whirlpool, is he? Do you find life a hurly-burly of excitement now?' Robert said casually.

Instantly the young woman wanted to reach out to Robert in the only way she knew, seeking his sympathy for her dull existence in the process, but she remained cautious and looked askance instead, offering no immediate reply, and considering if this could possibly be some get-up for testing her; however, in that event she doubted that Gil would have had any part, but it could just conceivably have been a devoted son's move; certainly such a shitty trick wouldn't have been beyond Aunt Helena. Jane said: 'I can purchase whatever excitement is needed.'

'Can you? – the meaningful excitement?' They held each other's look, and the young man shrugged finally. 'I'm sticking to my surprise at the old man's inconsistency, doesn't do my ego any good when I continually yield. You realise that you shattered Helena?'

'You don't like your aunt?'

He gave a wry smile. 'About as much as she likes you – I had to suffer her letters about how you destroyed the beautiful and sensitive understanding she and my father had.'

'Did they?' – Jane harboured a curious, inexplicable feeling about the young man's relation to Helena, something warned her to be wary.

'Helena's a malicious bitch. Even my mother thought so.

258

How did you get her to quit?'

'I guess she realised she'd lost when we married. She just left.'

'I'm sure my father's grateful for that at least.' He rose and set his coffee cup down decisively. 'Care for a walk?'

She accepted, and they walked slowly through the grounds. She was sure he was better than Gil at skimming pebbles across the surface of the river, but the young man's knowledge of the shrubbery wasn't as comprehensive as his father's, despite his boyhood spent in the gardens. While they walked, Robert spoke of his mother, and when he hesitated, Jane prompted him; she was curious, for at times the presence of the first Lady Munny was very strong around the house, and at such times Jane felt especially like a daughter or a guest. Robert was chatty and over friendly here, all of which could have been caused through nervousness; he almost seemed to be trying too hard with his talk of his childhood at that house, of the games in the gardens and parties on the river. Why was he trying so hard? Jane questioned, as she exchanged skimp, guarded information about her own childhood, careful not to put out too much of herself lest she created an opening that made her vulnerable. In spite of the young man's friendliness, probably because of it, she was a little suspicious of him; Helena floated around in the back of her mind, along with some design of betrayal and subsequent destruction. Jane tried pushing her doubts aside, and brushed on to new topics.

The gardens were vast, and Jane hadn't quite realised how vast. Robert led her right along the river bank and back through in a circle, touching parts of the grounds the young woman never knew existed. Their tour ended behind the house near the converted stables, where Jane's sports car was erect and reaching on the gravel parking area. The young man stopped to admire it.

'This is the chariot of sin Helena often mentioned.' He trailed his fingers along the bodywork. 'Your choice?' he asked, strangely.

'Gil's entirely.' She was puzzled at his attitude. 'Why? – something wrong?'

'Another inconsistency.' Robert shrugged. 'Mother died in an Aston Martin. Still, I shouldn't let that worry you.'

Don't let that worry you! His words rattled around inside her head; what was it, some kind of joke? Feeling desperately insecure at that moment, Jane wanted to draw into herself, away from the young man and wait for him to fill in either his own or Helena's colours with bolder strokes.

'How about giving me a ride?'

Vacantly Jane agreed, now wondering about Gil's choice of car. But Robert surely wouldn't have invented such a thing that could so easily be checked if he was simply testing her for Helena. The argument afforded some crumbs of comfort to her greedy thoughts.

Sliding in behind the controls, she glanced once at her stepson, then accelerated away down the drive. She decided to try and rattle him, but he didn't object to speed or even swallow hard when she hit some of the bends like a mechanical speed-freak.

'What speed have you reached?' he asked calmly, and when Jane smiled wryly, added: 'Better not let the old man know.'

The whole time he seemed to be intentionally classing her along with himself and apart from Gil, the young woman thought. She considered whether she ought to just take a chance and reach out for him, offering to take him as a lover rather than fuck around awaiting the result of the cat and mouse game he might or might not be playing with her. 'Would you like to drive, Robert?'

'If you trust me.'

'With my life.'

'It might well come to that,' he said, and they changed positions.

He enjoyed driving the car. Jane recognised in him that enjoyment she had first found in the car; he drove fast and dangerously, but not particularly well, then finally at a reasonably safe speed. Watching him more than either the roar or the car dials, Jane felt growing inside her an urge that was as demanding as the tickle in the throat of a child in a hushed church, she wanted to reach out to where his legs cut across the edge of the seat and touch his penis to see if it would stiffen with excitement. The more she tried to put down the thoughts the harder they seemed to resist. Occasionally Robert turned towards her and grinned through their silences; then suddenly when he looked round he didn't grin, and Jane felt panic snatch at her throat; betraying herself was that easy, the young man had realised it all, could read her thoughts. 'Do you think it will rain?' Jane asked quickly, trying to cover her embarrassment.

The young man laughed. 'I've been expecting it?'

'Yes.' There was a long silence. Jane stabbed at the radio, allowing the jangle to smother her thoughts. 'Do you have a girlfriend, Robert?'

'Stepmothers shouldn't ask those sort of questions – have you chopped the wood? Swept the chimney? Fetched the shopping? They're stepmother questions.' He grinned. 'Yes, I have. Several in fact.'

'Do you sleep with them?' The question surprised her, and she went on quickly: 'Another non-stepmother-type question. Sorry, did it embarrass you?'

'Not really – it was a little unexpected. I make love to them whenever the opportunity arises. University offers a number of opportunities.' His manner was almost blasé now. He changed gear into a bend. 'There's a pub along the road, right on the river. Shall we stop?'

They stopped and Robert fetched drinks to the garden bench where Jane sat.

'Your sex life wasn't idle curiosity – I thought perhaps you might get some of your friends down. We could have a party.'

'I considered bringing someone, but decided you might have thought it an imposition.'

'Someone special?' Jane asked as she sipped her drink.

'Not really, the only one available.'

Suddenly she wondered if he masturbated as an alternative, probably he would deny it anyway. 'So, inadvertently I've frustrated your sex life.'

'Better that, stepmother, than bread and water in the cupboard.'

'We could still have a party if you'd invite some friends.'

'What about father?'

The question was non-specific, but there was a slightly deprecating look on his face, Jane noticed. 'Is he adverse to parties? – the question's never been raised.'

'He might feel a little out of things if they're all our age.'

'Oh well,' she persisted regardless, 'we'll invite some of his friends too, and have a proper party. I'll speak to Gil about it this evening. But afterwards some of your friends could stop-over for a while as house guests if you wished.' It was a plea on her part, Jane realised a little ruefully, and hoped that it wasn't too obvious or reckless.

On the way home, Robert said: 'You're really very lonely in this existence, Jane, aren't you?'

The young woman tensed, finding herself poised on a precipice of indecision. She sighed heavily, trying to give herself time for clear thought, not knowing whether to immediately weep and confess her increasing need for the lost recklessness of yesterday, or to emphatically refute the suggestion. 'At times it gets lonely with Gil away in town where every other visible sign of life is. But I'm not complaining' – being seen not to complain was important.

'Unless marriage achieves all the excitement, all the intensity that a beautiful woman can find in life then it shouldn't exist.'

Jane closed her eyes in case he read the truth there too soon. She thought about his words, considering if he wasn't stating his own case and that for her freedom and right to take a lover. Glancing apprehensively across at the young man, she now noticed the bulge in his trousers; the erection might have spoken reams. Jane wanted to smile.

Robert made an all-out assault on her, and at first Jane wasn't sure whether he was trying to keep her cheerful for his father's sake, hers, or his own. While Gil remained absorbed with his business affairs, there wasn't a moment left for Jane to wilt or grow bored; the son worked harder than any official entertainments guide, and on a personal level and at things which Jane would have suspected had a strictly sexual motive to them had they been proposed by anyone else.

One morning he suggested they go swimming a few miles up river at his childhood haunt. The lack of a costume almost deterred Jane, while Robert ventured that they could swim nude – his embarrassment indicated his intention, and he apologised, lacking the nerve to continue forward with a straight proposition. Finally Jane decided to chance bra and pants rather than going to buy a costume, but their plans were almost ruined by Aunt Helena's impromptu arrival.

'Oh, Christ!' exclaimed Robert on seeing the woman's car sweep up the drive. 'I wondered how long it would be before she came visiting me.'

'Go out through the kitchen, get into the car,' Jane said commandingly. 'I'll pretend you're not here. Take the towels.' She directed the young man hastily towards the kitchen, pleased that she might cheat Helena out of doting on her nephew.

'Jane, my dear,' Helena said expansively as the maid showed her in. The greeting was almost pleasant, probably for believing Robert was somewhere within earshot.

'Helena' – Jane was cool. 'You should've phoned to say you were coming. I'm just going out.'

'It was Robert I called to see.' Malice edged in as she announced the purpose of her visit, and she made no effort to hide it.

'Robert? He isn't here, Helena.'

'But he was coming down early this week?' – there was surprise on the older woman's face. 'He must have arrived – where is he?' she demanded.

At any moment Jane expected the woman to pounce on her and accuse her of hiding the young man to keep him from her. 'He's gone to stay with some friends from university before coming on here,' she offered evenly.

A self-satisfied smile spread across Helena's face. 'Your doing, no doubt – he's never before refused to come down during the holidays.'

Accepting the indictment, Jane shrugged, and the Aunt departed in small triumph. From the window she watched the woman climb back into her car and drive away, not questioning at that point the ease with which she had accepted that Robert wasn't down.

Moving out through the kitchen to the garage, Jane put the housekeeper wise as to Robert's professed non-arrival – Helena's rule was still bitterly remembered and she had no friends among the servants.

Robert wasn't visible in the car as Jane drove down the drive; he remained crouched while the car swung away along the road and travelled a little distance from the house, in case Helena was still around.

Rising up into the seat finally, Robert said: 'Thanks. One thing I didn't want today was her pent-up bile.'

'She seemed put out – I think she believed me.'

'Hope you're right,' Robert said thoughtfully.

Jane glanced at him and smiled cheerfully, more relaxed now for having almost decided that he wasn't on Helena's side and set on betraying her; however, fearing betrayal as she did, the doubts weren't easy to eradicate completely. 'You'll have to spend the night in the garage, hiding from the Aunt.'

He laughed. 'I'd have to spend my life in the garage.'

Had dear Helena believed a little too readily? Jane pushed the doubt to the back of her mind.

The tributary of the Thames had remained as isolated as it had been in Robert's childhood, and they each selected their bush to change behind separately. The thought of creeping around and peeping on the young man jumped into

Jane's head, she was curious about his moments of aloneness, curious to know if the prospect of herself naked with only a bush separating them did anything for him, the fact of being his stepmother notwithstanding; also if the prospect did excite him, whether he physically stimulated that excitement, suppressed it or quickly released it. But she continued to undress without going to peep on him. The thought that Robert might be peeping on her where she stood naked behind the bush intrigued her, and without checking whether he was, she stroked herself delicately with her hands for his benefit, then stretched her pants between her legs and ran them down the lips of her vagina in a sawing motion as she sometimes did with a stocking. Then Jane had an increasing awareness of a soft yearning she had for the young man, and didn't even question the moral aspect of satisfying it; infidelity was merely a necessity when a husband was less than adequate, and even in consideration of the event it was doubtful whether she would have judged the prospect of sex with the son of that husband particularly immoral. Pondering his reaction to her simply wandering around to him naked, she was amused, but finally pulled into the peach tinted pants she had fetched to swim in; the moment wasn't right, Robert's need wouldn't yet be sufficiently acute to make his reaction so reckless. Her breasts disappeared into the matching bra, as the young man called to her, wanting to know if she was ready. Emerging from her bush, Jane saw him dive into the water. 'Cold?' she shouted when he surfaced.

'Beautiful. Come on in.' He trod water and stared intently at her, his eyes gazing as though mesmerised; he would probably have drowned or died from exposure had Jane not lowered herself into the water! The spell broken, Robert swam towards her.

'It's freezing,' said Jane.

They swam together, flaying, splashing, sunlight glinting on the water as it broke; their bodies occasionally touching, offered sudden warmth, comfort, promise. Jane splashed him, then retreated, but she was pursued and splashed back; water erupted into a fury of tiny white pendants as their arms flayed, and they shrieked through the turmoil. Finally Jane called for a truce, and the ensuing stillness had a strange, unreal quality about it as they trod water. Through the stillness Jane found the young man staring intently at her again, and for a moment she believed he was going to pull her to himself and kiss her, just as it happened in the movies, and she was disappointed when he didn't; then, she allowed embarrassment to enter between them and the moment was lost. Her arm struck the water without warning, and as a sheet of water splashed over him, Jane shrieked and struck away for the bank. Robert pursued her. Being the stronger swimmer he passed her and pushed her under as he did so.

Recovering herself, Jane trod water and watched the young man climb out on to the bank and turn smiling. He was quite beautiful, she thought, his body lithe and wiry, smooth and hairless; his slightly indented chest glistening as surplus water ran off him. The young woman hadn't realised just how attractive he was till then, and she felt very horny and wanted to fuck him more than anything. She swam to the bank as Robert reached up a towel and began drying himself.

Her intention wasn't to pull him back into the water, but it seemed Robert assumed that it was, and shook his head with a smile when asked for help. Jane attempted to get out on her own but couldn't first try. 'Please help me, Robert darling' – then the young man couldn't not help her.

Just as soon as Robert hoisted her from the water, Jane realised her bra and pants were pointless, for sopping wet they were suddenly completely transparent. The young man was unable to take his eyes off her, and his reaction was without control. Standing unmoving, Jane watched his struggle, which without any doubt he was losing. An involuntary quake started across his lithe frame, and at that moment Jane was more curious to know how he would break. Her eyes ran over his torso to the lump that was forcing out his swimming trunks; her thoughts went out telling him to embrace her, but he just stood there awkwardly trying to conceal the source of his embarrassment with his towel. She could tell how much he wanted to fuck her, but he was scared to take the initiative, and would remain on that ledge of indecision forever.

There was only a slight hesitation between her decision and the beginning of her move, and Jane wasn't sure if Robert's move was made because of that hesitation or because of her move, but he fled behind his bush, mumbling an apology, while Jane instantly groped for some insight to her miscalculation of this personality. She wanted to fuck him, he wanted to fuck her, and here they had the opportunity. He was simply scared, she decided, desperate for her but desperately afraid of her.

Surprise was what struck Jane first on rounding the bush after Robert. She found him there with his shorts down on his thighs, his cock clasped feverishly in his hand, jerking in a frenzy. Immediately overcoming her surprise, Jane experienced compassion for the young man for having forced him to this, and she moved quickly to him. 'Don't, Robert, don't' – her words were urgent.

The young man had a good hard-on yet responded to her touch; he turned on her in alarm, anguish clouding his eyes, mumbling her name through his tormented apologies over the uncontrollable need he felt.

Jane soothed him. 'Here, let me have it, don't waste yourself.' They sank to the grass together, Jane's free hand pushing her pants down and kicking them off, while Robert with trembling inept hands struggled with her bra. Jane completely removed his swimming shorts and knelt forward to him, her hands enfolded his cold hard balls and her lips slid over the head of his penis. She ate more of him, while his words became more articulate.

'Oh Jane, my darling. I've wanted you – oh God, I wanted to have it with you so much. You can't believe how much. I'm sorry, sorry' – his tortured, guilt-seared apologies were incessant. When her mouth became disengaged, Jane offered a stimulating verbal, and the young man needed no prompting to go down to her; there his tongue apologised even harder, and despite its general lack of control, Jane really became turned on, and felt she might achieve all the orgasms her husband had deprived her of. She cried out as she grew more horny – 'Fuck me! Fuck me now, Robert, put it up now! I want you to jam your big prick up me as far as it will go!' The effect of her verbal on Robert was astonishing, he obliged her and she sighed gratefully; his cock thrusting inside her was pretty nice, the young woman decided, and her vagina contracted and clung to it as though it was never going to let go. Robert worked frantically, floundering occasionally, and Jane guessed he wasn't going to last long, but she didn't really mind for he had potential, and she knew he would get better. Jane became acutely aware of the wetting inside her to the fullness of her first orgasm, and that was good enough. 'Christ! – come! Come with me, right up to me.' Robert was very obliging.

Tears filled Robert's eyes when he was spent and still at last. Jane didn't know whether they were tears of happiness, sadness, shame, confusion or guilt, but suspected that he was feeling very guilty as he lay on top her behind the bush, his cock receded and still, but hanging in there by the skin. Retrospect was worthless now of course, the act was done, he had stepped over the threshold and no sense of guilt or shame would make them unfucked.

Jane eased her shoulder where a twig hiding in the grass was digging into her, and Robert, thinking she wanted to get up, rolled off her, mumbling. The words were missed but Jane knew he was still offered an apology. They both lay on their backs staring up at the open sky. Jane's thoughts posed questions. Would it rain? What if someone was watching? Was that scene satisfying? How long would he cry for? Then: Has he stopped crying? Come to terms with his conscience?

'What's the matter?' asked Jane, glancing round at him.

There was no reply. Robert continued staring up at the sky. Jane saw a tear well out of his eyes and trickle down into his hairline. She reached over and brushed her hand along his peach-smooth chest and still he didn't stir. Her hand moved down and clasped his genitals, there she found a response; finally the young man had come to terms with himself over fucking his father's wife.

Jane and Robert spent a lot of time together, almost every free moment. Their looks, their smiles, their laughter, their sighs were all for each other, and but for Jane herself, they might have been well-intentioned lovers. Sometimes Gil was with them, but mostly he wasn't; when he was he seemed delighted by their obvious friendship, and when he wasn't he hoped they had fun. Sometimes Jane wondered if he suspected that she was fucking his son and the fact that he was really quite good had brought about the change in her; however, at base she didn't particularly care if he did, Gil was a sexual bore, a provider of material comfort, that was all. Robert experienced a few bad moments about deceiving his father and Jane helped him to find justification with her self-justifications. Gil was generous enough to want this development, she told him, for all that he cared about was her happiness, and his son's happiness. Jane didn't accept that this was happiness as she would design it herself, but even the self-gratification that it was something in an otherwise boring situation.

Even Helena no longer represented any real threat, having yielded, it seemed, she accepted their friendship, and quite philosophically too. She had her moments with Robert, only wasn't able to make any impression on him, or none that Jane noticed.

There was an international money conference being held in Switzerland, and Gil, as a very important financier, was invited to attend. Paradoxically Jane felt let down when the man announced his intention of going alone, even though his departure would mean three uninterrupted days and three nights with Robert – possibly her deflated feeling was on account of the fact that Robert was growing more and more intense, and a trifle boring as a result. She offered to fly with her husband, but he turned her down, assuring her the trip would be very dull, and thanking her.

If slightly irritated, Jane stayed behind with her untroubled conscience. Robert had an equally untroubled conscience, as he had recived strict instructions from his father to keep the young woman company and prevent her growing bored; that might have meant slipping his hand up her skirt and feeling her moist cunt through her silk pants just as soon as his father had gone, only he no longer appreciated that that didn't really turn her on any more. Jane had started that game, touching Robert in Gil's presence, making him get an erection under the table, then it had been amusing, even a little exciting.

Night-time with a lover in an illicit affair was quite nice, and being fucked time and again was always worthwhile, Jane found; however, there were points against her spending a whole night in bed with Robert as that move gave him impractical ideas of making it permanent, and he talked of approaching his father to ask him if he would divorce Jane so that he could marry her himself.

For herself Jane wanted no part of such a design, she had recently grown very accustomed to her comfortable life and wasn't about to join any breadline with a student; Robert as an entity just didn't have enough going for him to recommend such a drastic course; now had it been Harry, she might have given the proposition serious consideration. The young man accepted her argument, not easily at first, but easier it seemed for the distraction he found in fucking her.

On the second day of Gil's absence the entire household staff were off for the afternoon. Jane, to relieve the boredom, let Robert fuck her in various contrived, sometimes awkward, sometimes amusing positions about the top part of the house. Afterwards they took a leisurely bath in the main bathroom, and there in the soft scented bath water they fondled playfully with one another. He stood and Jane knelt to suck him, her fingers massaging his arse and controlling her rhythm. Afterwards they swapped positions. Jane stood with her legs apart in the wide bath and Robert crouched into her. Jane's long, well manicured fingernails bit into his scalp, and she held his head against herself while he ate her pussy.

Neither of them heard the sound of the car, nor of movement in the lower part of the house – no one would ever be heard moving on those thick carpets. Anyway the most natural thing for anyone to do on entering a seemingly deserted house, unless for a felonious reason, was to call out and announce his or her presence; in that event Jane and Robert simultaneously naked and wet beneath bathrobes may have been suspicious, but suspicion would have been the only thing that could have existed. But what doubt when they were discovered, Robert plating his stepmother in the bath?

Helena shrieked horribly on pushing into the bathroom – having first peeped into the bedroom. 'Knock, you fucking bitch!' Jane screamed at her.

Robert jumped up in great alarm, almost slipping over as he grabbed for the towels.

After her initial shock, Helena shuddered involuntarily as disgust and alarm locked her in a vice-like grip – doubtless she equated oral-genital contact with child-bayoneting, or something similar. Jane didn't ask, but returned the verbal tirade she finally got from the older woman. Of course in his aunt's eyes Robert was the innocent party led vilely astray by Jane, but nevertheless he wouldn't escape retribution. This was all Helena had prayed for; the betrayal; the vilest kind of infidelity; the situation was shells for her biggest cannon, and now she could shoot down their farcical marriage, regardless of who might be hurt. She answered Jane's scathing counter by intimating that her intrusion was heaven-directed to end these satanic proceedings that were going on behind her brother-in-law's back. Poor Gilbert would finally realise who truly loved him.

Helena departed, almost smiling.

That strange inexplicable feeling Jane had had about the relationship between Robert and his aunt flooded back, and thoughts of betrayal crowded her mind again, perhaps this was the pay-off; then the thought crossed Jane's mind that Robert had set her up and given his aunt the ammunition in order to precipitate this situation, so that he might eventually be able to propose marriage to her. But finally she dismissed that as being impractical, for various reasons, one being that Robert was now fleeing with her to avoid the inevitable confrontation on Gil's return – though probably that would have been necessary for effect in either event!

They were driving away in the Aston Martin, but as Jane gazed vacantly through the windscreen and along the bonnet the super phallic symbol most definitely at that moment seemed as though it had wilted somewhat.

The existence she had there in the sedate world of Marlow and the affairs of Sir Gilbert Munny were ended, another threshold crossed, for better or for worse, and there was no going back. Jane glanced round at her two cases which had been hastily packed, there were certain things she just couldn't, wouldn't quit without, but the rest of her stuff she would send for, and guessed Gil wouldn't sue for its return, not even for the return of her jewellery which she had with her also. Despite everything she didn't think he would prove spiteful or vindictive; in fact she could probably have stayed on in the marriage and brazened out dear Helena's faithful recounting; and in all probability Gil would have understood her need and forgiven her, only that would surely have proved even more intolerable. The curious thing was that although not really loving the man she knew she couldn't bear to see him hurt and suffering. He would suffer of course, but she wouldn't have to see it. Anyway she needed this break as much as she had needed Robert's hard cock when she had, both were inevitable.

Jane looked across at Robert who drove in silence, his face etched with anxiety, his eyes wearing a vacant, abstracted glaze, doubtless he was pondering where their relationship was going. Jane didn't imagine they would be going very far together, a matter of weeks, days, even hours and they would split. Robert would start getting guilt hang-ups, and the tedium for her in the relationship would suddenly escalate; he wasn't strong enough, nor interested enough, nor that good a lover to hold her anyway, and with extraneous pressures such as Gil's presence fucking him up, she guessed she would jump at the first excuse to split out. Probably she would look Harry up, or maybe Monty the Slug; Jane had no fears that she might be without prospects, or openings in town, she had the money and the style currently to get in anywhere, and fuck anyone. Turning her head, she allowed her eyes to fall into the harmless middle-distance.

They arrived in London, but the city wouldn't swallow them, it seemed, despite their throwing themselves headlong into that abyss of noise and light, that confusion of transient bodies; they remained on the surface like two insoluble, indigestible entities, and Jane knew why. At first she resisted the prospect. And with an incredible pace they proceeded from stopping-point to stopping-point, seeking the distractions that might spare purposeful thought, trying to ignore that whole emotional field just immediately behind them, not wanting to engage it in any conscious way.

Neither guilt nor conscience-stricken thoughts hammered at Jane, but rather the indecision over the choice before her; there was a choice before her still, and there always would be, simply because of what she was, she guessed. Walking a dividing line between two almost equally unreal worlds, that belonging to Gil, and that offered there in London, Jane knew she might as well have been walking kerbstones with the choice between stepping into the road or on to the pavement.

The young man at her side began to whine, he didn't want to do this and that didn't appeal; he was scared, a mouse, one of life's punters. Yes, that was what he was, a fucking punter! Jane had known all along of course, but was suddenly very weary of him. At best he had, she supposed, served a useful purpose in as much as he had helped her out of the situation she had been thoroughly bored in but too comfortable to quit. The next corner, or the next club, and she would ditch him. Goodbye Robert. Hello whatever.

London was wide open to a girl with a serviceable cunt, and Jane was amenable.

Epilogue
The Punter

Eighteen Lovely Ladies. The legend danced in neon-lit perspex on almost every street and alleyway of Soho. He had always thought strip-clubs would provide an amusing distraction, but had in fact rightly kept a slightly deprecatory sense of proportion about the whole business. And along with prostitutes it was perhaps the single biggest type of business in Soho – perhaps restaurants clocked up more establishments, eating was more sensual at times, he found. The man moved through and stood at the back of the last row of seats of the mock-up theatre which was about the size of a cupboard; the whole place smelt of stale sweat and semen trapped in unlaundered underpants. This place, like all the others, was a cheat of course, there were no eighteen ladies, but one sagging-titted, shagged-out pig with lipstick who had varicose veins and who scratched among the sprout-blue stubble of shaven pubes as though she had crabs. He had known from the start that it was a cheat, all the strip-

275

clubs and clip-joints were, he was probably born knowing what a cheat it all was; in fact the strip-club establishments in toto had only eighteen women between them, and none very lovely. From the window of his flat overlooking Old Compton Street he had seen the strippers hurrying from dive to dive, clutching their vanity cases and stuffing hot dogs in their mouths where there was no time to stop and eat. However, despite himself, the man didn't stop going to the low-life establishments outside his door, it was compulsive almost, the same with his visiting the brasses. In pockets of clearness he often appreciated that there was more value in pulling himself off, only from the word go masturbation had been taboo. While dipping into the wet apex of a woman's legs, and getting an orgasm was in line with man's basic instincts, notwithstanding the fact that you had to pay or that they didn't care.

'Margot – Young Model – 3rd Floor', the sign was painted on a perspex box and lit-up right by a door on the pavement, at the end of Old Compton Street. It caught the man's eye constantly, and quite often he stopped in there to see either her or her companion Diana, who was in the same building; the unsuspecting might have thought they were two more brasses in the block, but in fact Collette and René were names both women used also for a change around – punters continually like the prospect of 'New Model' and the Trade Description Act never operated in that area. Young Model! – even the sign was looking rather tatty now, and that was looking a good deal fresher than the brass herself. The man almost laughed out loud in the street, prostitution was the profession of eternal youth; the Young Models rarely changed their signs, and yet the punters never stopped falling for their shallow tricks.

Turning away, the man suddenly broke his step when he saw the woman along the pavement staring at him. He had seen the woman before, and had probably been tapped-up by her, but hadn't been with her. He saw her from his window as she plodded the street in the early hours. The woman was in her mid-forties, broken and sagging like she was falling apart, with dirty, split blonde hair. No professional lady with a place to hang her sign would be on the streets at that time of night, he realised, and felt a tinge of compassion for the ageing prostitute. A smell wafted across from her as he moved past, it was the smell of decay, of vomit, of death itself, and he shivered and quickened his pace. He would have to have been very pissed to have entertained her in any way. Perhaps once, a lifetime ago, that old prostitute had been beautiful and desirable. Perhaps, he thought with a slight sense of relief that she was behind him.

Another legend loomed before him as he walked back down the street, an advertisement for a movie. Movie houses were quite good places for picking up women, particularly late-night movies, he might even find a freebee there.

The cinema wasn't very full. And when the movie started to drag he found himself counting heads. Those present were mostly women, it seemed – that was doubtful in fact, only he was prick-dominated and apt to notice women – brasses the majority of them, he guessed. It had been raining earlier, and some with the price preferred late-movies to either bashing in the wet or the continuous crash of the pin-tables along in the neon arcades where they operated from – not that a war movie with six-track stereo was likely to afford them quieter relief!

His eyes strayed from the burning carnage in celluloid to the PL's on offer, wondering how many were going to score. Most of them probably; there were more punters than brasses; a thigh pressed, a breast squeezed, cunt felt, and anything from a one to a ten spot might be earned with or without the rubber. A half-look was enough, night eyes were sharp, and even his curious gaze when it settled momentarily on the woman across the gangway was taken as a proposition. The old tom raised five fingers; the man might have sneered at her presumption, only didn't, but didn't approach her either. She looked at him with sad, appealing eyes which shortly hardened in animosity when still there was no response. The brass turned, glanced back, and finally turned away to look for a more hopeful prospect; another occasion she might have dropped two fingers and haggled; then on another occasion he might have accepted. The five pounds wasn't what he objected to; he wanted a scene, but nothing so mundane as that broken-down old tom. Quite what it was he was after he didn't know, but something apparently worthwhile might present itself and he would go for it in an instant, and would perhaps finish up with little more than a dose!

Scratching his cock as though in anticipation, he rose out of his seat, no longer interested which of the movie stars won the war. Outside the night was quite mild, and although the rain had stopped the roads were still wet where there was insufficient traffic at this hour to disperse the water. Turning away from the cinema, he moved off idly down the Street towards his apartment which was conveniently positioned on the corner of Dean and Old Compton Street, especially as he was a guy who got more than his share of erections.

There was some kind of action going on in a doorway which was set back off the pavement, and the man immediately shortened his step to make quite certain what was going on. Then once past he turned and retraced his footsteps, there not three feet from the street a spade brass was getting her living. She was spiked against the wall, her trousers and panties down on her thighs; her client, who was probably a stranded out-of-town punter, was giving it to her like he believed that was the experience. Crossing the road opposite them, the man stopped and watched; they didn't notice his presence, or anyone else for that matter; not that there were many people about then. If that had been himself desperately screwing that brass in the doorway it would have been his ill-luck to be busted by the fuzz, he thought, as he continued watching.

Governed suddenly by the out-of-towner's orgasm they rocked together and shook, probably a bucket of ice-cold water was the only thing that would have parted them then – like dogs. Their sex was easily equated with dogs, he mused, as the scene drew to its conclusion. Spent; they quickly parted; the black bitch hoisting her panties and trousers; the dog allowing his shrinking cock to slide into his fly, trailing semen. They emerged from the doorway, and without speaking further, the SB turned right, while the out-of-towner turned left, and moved down to the greaser's hot dog barrow, on the corner of Frith Street, and joined two other out-of-towners who he seemed to know. He hitched his strides as though having laid the woman to waste and began his recount of the fuck for those lesser men who were obliged to feed off his experiences.

With a slight feeling of disgust for sex at that level and fleetingly drawing a comparison to himself, he turned away in the direction the brass had taken, yet despite himself he noticed he had a hard-on. Along the Street he saw the spade stopping at a car window across the road, negotiating with the driver.

On the corner of Dean Street there were two spade brasses, one quite young and one about thirty-five, and a young white brass who was incredibly beautiful; they were in conversation, discussing market trends probably. The two spades were vaguely familiar but he hadn't seen the white girl before, he would definitely have remembered if he had. The man's look on passing was enough to establish contact, though none of them were rushing forward to make him a proposition. He turned back and stood looking at them. The younger Negress, who was the prettiest also, seemed amused and started to smile – he missed what she said in her pidgin-language, but the other two women were amused now. Uncertain whether it was mirth or malice they were offering, the man stepped back to them, his eyes surveying them like a buyer at a cattle market.

Unlike most brasses, especially those who ever ventured on to the streets, these three had quite a bit to recommend them. Fixing the younger Negress with a look, he said:

'Fancy going for a drink?'

The pretty SB raised her shoulders. 'I wid me fwiends.' Her friends silently appraised him.

'What are they, chaperons, or something?'

'S'right honey,' the older SB said, her manner somewhat weary. Maybe she had been out all night.

Briefly he considered the situation, there was some kind of daisy chain to be had here if he handled it the right way, and he had always been looking for that kind of scene. Nodding thoughtfully – 'All right.'

'All of us?' the young SB said.

'Why not.'

'Twenty-five each?' the old SB said hopefully.

Twenty pounds apiece was shortly agreed.

'Where's your place?' asked the white brass.

He nodded across the road. 'Just up there.'

They hadn't realised just how close, when he led them up to his apartment. They were wary at first, their eyes searching around the flat, as though expecting hidden movie cameras to be turning, or men with bulls' pizzles to spring out; relaxing, finally reassured, they offered compliments about the apartment – it wasn't fantastic like they suggested, but compared to the slums he imagined they lived in, it was probably quite nice.

They inspected things, appraised things; watching all three at once would be difficult, and he was a million to lose one or two trinkets that would fit discreetly into handbag or pocket. Without exception they drank scotch and asked for their money up front; payment in advance was quite usual and he paid each of them. The three brasses exchanged glances, they were going to work now; each knew what the other was holding, though they didn't generally work naked in sight of each other.

'Do you want to take a shower?' he said to no one in particular, but included all three.

'You think we are dirty den, honey?' the older SB returned.

'Quite probably' – evenly.

'Wot you want den, man?'

'What did you think, a wank?' Experimentally he slid the younger SB's skirt up over her narrow hips, revealing her yellow panties; she offered no resistance and so he slipped his hand down inside her panties and felt her. She was quite dry and he wondered when she had last had an orgasm. He inserted a finger – he had to start somewhere! – and turning back to the others, said: 'Get undressed.' Neither of them moved. 'C'mon – these off!' He yanked violently at the flimsy garment, splitting the seams and ripping it clear away from her.

'Hey, man!'

'I'll buy you new ones. Come on then, let's see what you're holding' – with the authority of a punter who had overpaid. 'I'll give an extra ten to whoever can fork herself off first – the bedroom's through there.' The brasses moved into the bedroom where they stripped. The women looked at one another a little apprehensively, then almost cautiously began pushing their fingers into themselves, before a chain reaction took place; soon one noticed another speeding up slightly, so followed suit.

Amused delight was the feeling which ran through the man as he watched the three women; amused by the power of money and what it could get women to do, even for the relatively small amounts he was able to put on offer; delighted with the scene he had bought, and his erection which seemed to be getting bigger and bigger. The two SBs and the white brass made an interesting tableau on the large bed where they were forking off, earnestly trying for that ten pounds extra. They were each almost as different as black was from white, but then with only a single thought; how to beat the punter and stripe him. He hoped the pretty SB would be the first to achieve orgasm – he would fuck whoever arrived first – but accepted that it would probably be the older one, or even the beautiful white girl. He stepped out of his clothes, his penis hard and reaching. Suddenly he was like a racing punter watching the field as it ran nearer and nearer the post, urging his horse on to win, while anxiously watching the other runners. His eyes kept returning to the pretty SB, but it looked to be a close run race between the older SB and the white brass. Then without warning the young black girl cried out, and moving over to her, the man immediately supplanted her fingers with his own. She was suddenly wet. He knelt forward, shunning the prospect of plating her at this stage, and thrust his cock into her. High and involved as she now was, her vagina clung to his penis; while generally cold with punters, like most of the prostitutes, her cunt might otherwise have been a bucket. All three PLs would be committed now, with a head waiting to burst into flower at the point of insertion. He would definitely get value for money.

The brasses were very skilful, he shortly realised that. Sex was their thing, and soon they were dictating, dominating completely. They might have had some secret unspoken language, for he found himself being passed forwards and backwards between them as though with some special design. Two orgasms had been achieved by the man when finally he arrived at the thighs of the older SB who was definitely the best fuck of the three, her experience could be measured. The other two worked on him with their mouths, giving him tiny bites on his shoulders and arms, his buttocks and his thighs; slowly they destroyed him, causing metabolism to increase through urgency to frenzy. Very soon the scene took on ambivalent nightmare quality; he was running through two birch-lines it seemed and the further he progressed the deeper the birches cut into his flesh, but he wouldn't stop and didn't really want to. He was caught up and being drawn further and further forward by the older SB, while the other two professional ladies were now drawing blood with their teeth; the pain becoming sharper and more delicious, as he was becoming more delirious.

Then he noticed how weak he was growing, he was close to exhaustion, yet conversely he was still hitting the older

SB, in and out, in and out, as if caught up on some machine. He didn't believe he could orgasm a third time, but desperately wanted to so that he could finally drift away into unconsciousness, that seemed the only way. He wanted to rest and recuperate, only the sharp, stinging pain from those teeth wouldn't let him fade; in and out, in and out, he continued as though on some perpetual-motion machine with no greater purpose other than to give them orgasms. Then without warning an involuntary tremor ran through his body, and he rocked and shook with the greatest, most debilitating orgasm he had ever experienced, his entire stomach and intestines felt as though they were being wrenched out with the exquisite pain, but at the moment he didn't care, he didn't want to stop, he wouldn't stop, he knew the search had been worthwhile.

The man snapped from his reverie.

The three brasses at the corner stood looking at him a little bemused, as though believing he was demented. Seeing their expressions hardening, the man felt a sense of panic rising; he knew he couldn't just stand there and hope they would read his mind. He had to make some proposition. 'Are you girls in business,' he said quickly. The women looked at one another and laughed, but only about four notes between them.

'Fuck off,' the young white girl said in a tone that brooked no argument. 'Before we call Old Bill.'

The man started to back away.

'We'll have you nicked for soliciting,' the older SB said, and the three women hooted with laughter.

The punter withered visibly then turned and hurried away down the Street with the PL's laughter echoing in his ears. He hurried past the entrance to his apartment block, and straight on down Dean Street. He had no immediate direction, but would continue punting.

THEY'LL GIVE THEIR ALL FOR
A PIECE OF
PARADISE...

California Dreamers

Norman Bogner

Rodeo Drive is Los Angeles' priciest square mile, where the
well-heeled hedonists of fantasy city spend their millions. To this
Mecca of merchandising are drawn the beautiful, the bizarre, the
all-consumingly ambitious:

BOBBY the idealistic architect who longed to build churches – and
instead created citadels for the worship of wealth...

CLAIRE the jilted small-town beauty who followed him West – to
success in a business where only the most ruthless survive...

HILLARY too young, too voluptuous, too rich – she snatched any
thrills she could get, and paid the price...

GIOVANNI ex-movie actor and society restaurant owner – who had
laid-back LA at his feet until he found he cared for someone...

Where money talks – and walks, and makes love – they'll sell
body and soul to buy a dream of paradise...

GENERAL FICTION   0 7221 1760 4   £1.79

Only sinners are sacred in

KING
of
HEAVEN

the sexplosive novel of small-town life,
from the bestselling author of
FIRE ISLAND

Burt Hirschfeld

Since the Gault family drove out the Injuns generations ago,
they have ruled King of Heaven, the county seat of Tokeneke
on the Alabama/Florida border, with a rod of iron. Alcohol,
dancing and illicit sex are banned . . . but everyone (including
the Gault family) knows how to get hold of them, in this small,
steamy Southern town, where folk are publicly devoted to the
Lord, but privately enslaved by the passionate desires of their
bodies. Then suddenly the uneasy quiet of King of Heaven is
shattered, when a terrifying rapist is at large, and revelation
upon revelation explode . . .

In the compelling tradition of the bestselling *Peyton Place*,
KING OF HEAVEN tells the whole truth of the passions and
power struggles sizzling beneath America's Bible Belt.

GENERAL FICTION   0 7221 4820 8   £1.95

IT STARTED AS A GAME ...

'"I'll take care of Mr High and Mighty ..."
... she was quite looking forward to her
confrontation with the overbearing Marco ...'

... A VERY ENJOYABLE GAME ...

'She had never felt this way before; never felt
herself melting, being absorbed, being concen-
trated; all feeling and no thought.'

... THAT SOMEHOW GOT OUT OF
HAND ...

'"Stop it! Stop it at once! I'm not playing games at
all! And ... I like to be asked first" ...'

BUT WOULD THE GAME EVER END AND
LOVE BEGIN?

Read

LOVE PLAY

ROSEMARY ROGERS

bestselling author of
THE CROWD PLEASERS
and **SWEET SAVAGE LOVE**

ROMANCE   0 7221 7436 5   £1.75

THE VEGAS LEGACY

OVID DEMARIS

Bestselling author of THE LAST MAFIOSO

Ruthless multi-billionaire Rufus Boutwell made his fortune in the wild days of the Nevada gold rush. He bought up land and politicians, then promoted gambling and prostitution for his own profit – while trumpeting the virtues of personal freedom. Now, as head of Nevada Consolidated Mines, he is about to launch the mightiest political coup of his long career which will make or break him forever. . . .

From the barren sands of the Nevada desert to the razzamatazz of a Vegas-style Republican convention, THE VEGAS LEGACY is a whirlwind-paced saga of greed, drugs, sex, ambition and corruption . . . in the blockbusting tradition of Harold Robbins and Mario Puzo.

GENERAL FICTION   0 7221 30163   £2.50

A SELECTION OF BESTSELLERS FROM SPHERE

FICTION

SMART WOMEN	Judy Blume	£2.25	☐
INHERITORS OF THE STORM	Victor Sondheim	£2.95	☐
HEADLINES	Bernard Weinraub	£2.75	☐
TRINITY'S CHILD	William Prochnau	£2.50	☐
THE SINISTER TWILIGHT	J. S. Forrester	£1.95	☐

FILM & TV TIE-INS

WATER	Gordon McGill	£1.75	☐
THE RADISH DAY JUBILEE	Sheilah B. Bruce	£1.50	☐
THE RIVER	Steven Bauer	£1.95	☐
THE DUNE STORYBOOK	Joan D. Vinge	£2.50	☐
ONCE UPON A TIME IN AMERICA	Lee Hays	£1.75	☐

NON-FICTION

THE *WOMAN* BOOK OF LOVE AND SEX	Deidre Sanders	£1.95	☐
PRINCESS GRACE	Steven Englund	£2.50	☐
MARGARET RUTHERFORD – A BLITHE SPIRIT	Dawn Langley Simmons	£1.95	☐
BARRY FANTONI'S CHINESE HOROSCOPES	Barry Fantoni	£1.75	☐
THE STEP-PARENT'S HANDBOOK	Elizabeth Hodder	£2.95	☐

All Sphere books are available at your local bookshop or newsagent, or can be ordered direct from the publisher. Just tick the titles you want and fill in the form below.

Name_____

Address_____

_____

Write to Sphere Books, Cash Sales Department, P.O. Box 11, Falmouth, Cornwall TR10 9EN

Please enclose cheque or postal order to the value of the cover price plus:

UK: 55p for the first book, 22p for the second book and 14p per copy for each additional book ordered to a maximum charge of £1.75.

OVERSEAS: £1.00 for the first book and 25p per copy for each additional book.

BFPO & EIRE: 55p for the first book, 22p for the second book plus 14p per copy for the next 7 books, thereafter 8p per book.

Sphere Books reserve the right to show new retail prices on covers which may differ from those previously advertised in the text or elsewhere, and to increase postal rates in accordance with the PO.